DIVORCE
IS MURDER

DIVORCE
IS MURDER

A TOBY WONG NOVEL
A VANCOUVER ISLAND MYSTERY

ELKA RAY

SEVENTH
STREET
BOOKS®

Published 2019 by Seventh Street Books®

Cover images © iStock
Cover design by Jennifer Do
Cover design © Start Science Fiction

Inquiries should be addressed to
Start Science Fiction
101 Hudson Street, 37th Floor, Suite 3705
Jersey City, New Jersey 07302
Phone: 212-431-5455
www.seventhstreetbooks.com

10 9 8 7 6 5 4 3 2 1

ISBN: 978-1-63388- 542-4(paperback)
ISBN: 978-1-63388-543-1 (ebook)

Printed in the United States of America

For Eloise—fierce wielder of the spatula

CONTENTS

1   Chapter One: Blast from the Past

6   Chapter Two: Misgivings

11   Chapter Three: Fifty, Fifty

17   Chapter Four: BFF

23   Chapter Five: In the Cards

32   Chapter Six: Bad News

37   Chapter Seven: Unreal

42   Chapter Eight: Dead Flowers

55   Chapter Nine: On the Case

63   Chapter Ten: The Brother's Grim

69   Chapter Eleven: Prime Suspect

76   Chapter Twelve: Mystery Package

83   Chapter Thirteen: Paranormal Energy

95   Chapter Fourteen: Dearly Departed

105   Chapter Fifteen: Person of Interest

112   Chapter Sixteen: Motel Sex

120   Chapter Seventeen: Moths

124   Chapter Eighteen: Oh Brother

128   Chapter Nineteen: Name Game

138   Chapter Twenty: Dirty Laundry

147   Chapter Twenty-One: Hate Mail

153   Chapter Twenty-Two: The Other Woman

163   Chapter Twenty-Three: The Great Escape

177   Chapter Twenty-Four: Shattered

182   Chapter Twenty-Five: In Recovery

185   Chapter Twenty-Six: Catfight

190   Chapter Twenty-Seven: Full Circle

200   Chapter Twenty-Eight: Seeing the Future

CHAPTER ONE:

BLAST FROM THE PAST

The firm's secretary, Pamela Powell, doesn't knock to seek permission to enter, but merely to announce her presence. It's one of many things that annoys me about her, some others being her liberal use of Charlie body spray, her constant gum-smacking, and her insistence on calling me "the new girl" when discussing me with clients.

"Come in," I say, but the door's already swung open. Pamela totters across the room. Her heavily powdered cheeks are flushed.

In her sixties, Pamela has worked here since Mel Greene and Philippa Olliartee founded the firm in 1981, back when it was the only all-woman law office in Western Canada. Pamela still dresses like Dolly Parton in *9 to 5*, her wardrobe comprised of tight satiny shirts, pencil skirts that necessitate Geisha-sized steps, and—despite her bunions—towering heels. She now pats her bleached bouffant and pushes her *Tootsie* glasses up her nose. "You've got a new client," she says, as though she can't quite believe it's possible and has teetered in here to share the good news. She purses her frosted lips. "A man," she adds, with a leer.

I nod. Having only moved back to the island two months ago, I don't have a ton of business yet. But it hasn't been *that* slow. What response does Pamela want? "Okay," I say. "Can you send him in, please?"

"Will do," she says. "But can I just keep him out there for a couple more minutes? Pretty please?"

Seeing my confused expression, she bats her spidery eyelashes and smiles. Behind glass, the clumps of mascara are magnified into tarantula legs. Either she's winking, or there's a clump in her eye. "My oh my! Just wait till you see him," she says.

Another knock. Another come in. Whoever it is—the client who's got Pamela all aflutter—actually waits until I've invited him to enter before stepping, slowly, into my office.

He pauses. I catch my breath.

Holy crap. No wonder Pamela looked feverish. After all these years he's still godlike. In fact, he looks even better than I remember.

"Toby?"

"Josh?" I stand.

He steps forward and shakes my hand, his tanned face cracking into that familiar smile: perfect teeth and clear aqua eyes beneath golden brows. His hand feels warm and huge. He's bigger than I recall, but then, he would be, given that he's now a grown man instead of a boy. Well over six feet tall, dressed in faded jeans, a cream cotton sweater, and flip-flops. Even his toes are tanned.

He returns my once-over and laughs. "You're still little," he says.

I sit down, feeling shaky and a bit silly. Yes, I'm still little—five foot one, and ninety-three pounds, not much bigger than I was that summer. That summer. I recall my first sight of him, on a big yellow bus en route to summer camp, and the first time we spoke, in the woods, the day I got lost.

There I was, a scrawny fourteen-year-old in a pink hoodie, clutching a compass like it was a lucky charm, feeling sick with worry. Everywhere I looked there were trees. And ferns. And moss. There was no sign of a trail. Where the hell was I?

I spun around, the compass's needle wiggling like the chin of a Bollywood dancer, jauntily, this way and that way. It meant nothing to me. I shook the thing. Which way was I meant to go?

Instead of paying attention during orienteering class, I'd been lost in a fantasy about me and Josh, the most beautiful boy at camp, the most unobtainable. Now look where my daydreaming had got me: lost in the woods with the shadows lengthening, the greens turning grey, the temperature dropping. Soon, my face would grace a million milk cartons and MISSING posters. I'd be the cautionary tale told to generations of campers to come: *she should have listened.*

Branches swayed. Grasses rustled. Even ordinary sounds seemed ominous. Vancouver Island has bears—and cougars—just waiting for dark. The cougars rarely attacked adults but stalked smaller prey. My size. Something crackled. What was that? The swish of swaying bushes set me spinning. I could feel my heart crackling in my chest like pop rocks.

I froze, too scared to cry out or to run. Whatever it was, it was big and getting closer.

A flash of yellow, a glimmer of red. And there he was: Josh Barton—even more beautiful up close, like Adonis in my Grade Eight textbook. He barely seemed real, like there ought to be golden rays shining out of his curly blond head.

I stood, open-mouthed, as he pushed his way free of the brush. That laugh as he gazed down on me, one golden eyebrow lifting in pleased surprise. "Hey, Toby? What are you doing out here?"

Oh my God. He knew my name. My throat was so dry it was hard to talk, my cheeks baboon-butt red, my knees shaking. "We're um meant to be orienteering and I uh got lost." I held up my compass as proof. But of what? My stupidity?

Luckily, he laughed again. "You look so shocked," he said. "Don't worry. Our group's orienteering too, and I think I know where I'm going. We're close to camp, you know."

Looking into his eyes I felt weak with relief and embarrassment. A minute ago I was lost. Dead meat. And now the cutest boy in camp was here, talking to me—a total no one. "That's great," I said, wishing I didn't sound so lame. If only I were cool and witty, the kind of girl who always knew what to say. Pretty. Sexy. Blonde. His type of girl. Not scrawny and flat-chested. Not Asian. I attempted a smile. "I guess this is my lucky day," I said. "After all."

He smiled back. "And mine." He stepped closer and brushed a

twig from my hair, his hand falling against my cheek. I froze and our eyes locked. His Adam's apple bobbed. "Toby?"

"Yeah?"

"Do you want to, like, go out somewhere?"

Given that we were at camp and had no places to go, this made no sense. But I knew what he meant. He cupped my chin and pulled me closer. I held my breath. Was this really happening? Could this golden boy actually like me?

Our eyes closed and our lips touched. All the chatter in my head switched off, replaced by a clear single note. Like a bell. My first kiss.

So that's how they were meant to feel.

"Toby?"

I blink. For one bizarre moment I confuse the past with the present and think I just kissed him—right here and now—in my closet-sized office. Immediately, I flush. I bet I look as feverish as Pamela had. I lean back and take a deep breath, reach for my pen. It feels cool and solid. I click it. What's the matter with me? Instead of paying attention, I've been daydreaming about that stupid camp. Has he been talking to me?

However long I was spaced out, Josh doesn't seem to have noticed. He's got that same pleasant smile on his face, like this is a perfectly normal encounter. "So you're a lawyer now," he says. "I didn't realize it was you. A friend recommended the firm, and Mel Greene recommended you."

I nod. "I just moved back, from Toronto," I say. Because of my mom, who has—had—cancer, except I don't tell him this. I grip the pen. I can't seem to remember my normal, professional script, the way I put new clients at ease. It's just too strange to see Josh Barton sitting in my office, after what? More than nineteen years. "And you?" I manage.

"I was living in L.A.," he says. "But I missed the island. I moved back to Victoria last year, after I sold my company. Me and Tonya."

My stomach drops. Tonya? No, it can't be the same Tonya. But from the way he said her name, I know it is. I look at my fingers, bare of rings, and feel a wave of heat, followed by a chill. My hand feels sweaty around my pen.

Josh runs a hand through his blond curls. "Remember Tonya?"

I find myself nodding. How could I not remember Tonya?

He must know I hate her, must recall what she did to me. Except he doesn't seem to. His voice is unchanged, his expression still pleasant.

"We ended up getting married," he says. "A year and a half ago. In L.A." He goes on to tell me how they met again in a Hollywood club where she was working as a hostess while waiting for her dancing/acting career to take off. Meanwhile he was building up his own IT firm, which he recently sold. I can barely listen.

Josh Barton married Tonya Cabrilatto, a girl whose vicious bullying left me—and no doubt countless others—scarred. And he married her! What does that say about the guy? I could never in a million years have predicted this.

He clasps his hands, his voice lower now, signaling difficult emotions. We're getting to the reason why he's here. He bites the inside of his cheek. I need to start paying attention.

He leans forward and fixes me with that blue-laser gaze, the one that makes me melt, just like it did way back when. He swallows hard, his gaze so sorrowful I have to stop myself from reaching out to him. But can I *really* feel sorry for him? What kind of guy marries a bully like Tonya? It's taken me years to get over that last night at camp. I've been claustrophobic ever since. I've had counseling, for crap sakes!

I force my attention back to the present, unwilling to revisit that awful night. Out in the lobby, Pamela Powell is on the phone, laughing about something. There's a dentist's office next door and, listening closely, I can hear the whine of the drill. My shoebox office feels stuffy. Josh tugs at the neck of his sweater, like he's hot, or just uncomfortable. "Toby?" he asks. "I made a big mistake, marrying Tonya. Can you help me?"

CHAPTER TWO:

MISGIVINGS

Beneath her denim bucket hat, Quinn looks incredulous. "Let me get this straight," she says. "Josh Barton has hired you to be his divorce lawyer?"

I nod. Since Josh stepped into my office two days ago, I've been dying to tell Quinn. With no clients this afternoon, I left the office at 5:00 p.m., sharp. We're now sitting side-by-side on a log on Willows Beach, eating an early dinner of fish and chips wrapped in newspaper. While the ink is undoubtedly bad for us, I'm glad the takeaway shop hasn't changed to wax paper yet. The greasy news-paper reminds me of my childhood. Quinn's mom often fed us fish and chips when she had to work late.

A headline on my chip-wrapper catches my eye: **Mannequin Stolen from Langford Sex Shop.** Some grad prank. In Victoria, this counts as front-page news. I consider pointing it out to Quinn but don't. Having never lived elsewhere, she might take it the wrong way and think I'm mocking our hometown as dull. She'd be right too, although I guess that's part of its charm.

Quinn reaches for a napkin. "Josh Barton. She shakes her head. "So who'd he marry?"

I take a deep breath. "You won't believe it."

My best friend frowns. "So it's someone we know?" She selects another French fry. From the thoughtful way she's chewing, I know she's casting various girls we know as possible Mrs. Bartons.

I peer out toward Mount Baker, its snow-tipped peak barely visible. If I didn't know it was there, I might not see it. It's late August and the days are already getting shorter. A cool breeze is blowing in off the water. I inhale the scents of seaweed and salt along with the greasy smell of our dinner. Normally, I'd make Quinn guess, but pregnancy has left her short-tempered—not surprising, given that her belly's the size of Gibraltar. And there's no way she'd guess this one, anyway. "He married Tonya Cabrillato," I say. Just saying her name leaves a foul taste in my mouth.

Quinn spins so fast her long blonde hair goes flying. "What? That bitch? From Camp Wikwakee?" Her mouth hangs open.

I nod, gratified. At least Quinn understands why I hate Tonya.

"Wow." Quinn chews on her knuckle, trying to take this in. "Unreal." She squints at me. "How long have they been married? Do they have kids? Have you met Tonya yet?"

Back when I first met Quinn, in kindergarten, she used to bombard the other kids with questions during Show and Tell. She hasn't changed. "No, eighteen months, and no," I say. "She's hired Marilee Rothwell, aka the Rottweiler, at Sutridge, Rothwell, and Beaufort."

Quinn shifts her position on the log. "I can't believe he married *her*! So what's Josh like?" she asks. "Did he look the same?"

I fill her in on Josh's appearance, doing my best to downplay how amazing he looks. Quinn can obviously read between the lines because she leans back and laughs. "I don't believe it! You're still into him!" She peels some batter off a chunk of cod and eats it.

"I am not!" I say, doing my best to cover the truth. "Do you really think I could be into someone capable of marrying Tonya?" I grab another fry only to change my mind. I was full ages ago.

Quinn tilts her chin, considering. "Well, maybe she's changed. You haven't met her in what, almost twenty years?"

Seeing my face she shrugs. "It's possible," she says. "People can change."

Can they? I curl my lip even higher. "Oh come on," I say. "We're talking about Tonya here. You don't really believe that!"

Instead of answering, Quinn pushes herself off the log. She clutches her belly. "I need to walk," she says. "My butt's killing me."

I scrunch the remains of our dinner into a ball of newspaper and lob it into the closest trash can. That done, we head for the hard-packed sand near the water's edge. Out past Cattle Point I can see a few sailboats heading toward Oak Bay Marina.

Despite being eight months pregnant, Quinn walks faster than me. Her legs are about twice as long as mine, and still slim in her jean shorts. I'm practically running to keep up. Quinn glances my way. "So will you take him on?" she asks.

I know she's talking about Josh. "Sure, why not?" I stop walking and bend to retrieve a piece of beach glass, then hold it to the light. Blue green, the same color as Josh's eyes. I stick it in my pocket.

Quinn stops to wait for me. She crosses her arms and frowns. "Because he's a jerk," she says. "Remember him and Tonya? Why would you want to deal with anyone from that stupid camp ever again? I'm just glad I haven't run into them!"

I shrug. That's not surprising, really. While Victoria seems tiny, after Toronto, it's hardly a village. Plus Quinn spends most of her time up at the university or on a boat, observing killer whales.

She's still glaring.

"Josh was fourteen!" I say, leaping to his defense. "We were just kids!"

"Right." This one word conveys her disapproval. "I just . . ." She hesitates. "After everything that happened at that shitty camp, wouldn't it be better to just . . ." She shrugs. "Stay away from those creeps."

"Josh wasn't a creep," I say, and Quinn rolls her eyes.

"Whatever," she says.

"You're the one who said Tonya might have changed," I point out. "So you're willing to believe she's evolved but Josh's still a jerk?"

She gives me a tight-lipped smile. "No. You're right. They're probably both still jerks."

For some minutes we walk in silence. While I don't want to think about camp, it's hard not to. Seeing Josh has stirred everything up. And then there's the shock of learning who he married. Is Quinn right? Should I refuse to represent Josh? But that seems crazy given how quiet it's been at work. I'm in no position to turn clients away.

Although I'm gazing out to sea, I'm not seeing it. Instead, I'm seeing my teenaged self, sitting curled up in the dark, hugging my knees, terrified. The memory makes me shiver.

"Toby?" My best friend jabs me in the ribs. "You're not listening!"

I nod a little too vigorously. "Um, yes I am!" I say.

Quinn looks suspicious. She shades her eyes against the sun. "So you won't get, like, emotionally involved with this guy?"

I stop walking. "What?" I ask. "Of course not! I haven't even seen him in over nineteen years! And I'm his lawyer! I can't believe you'd even think that! He's a client!"

"Okay." She holds up both palms. "Sorry." But she doesn't look sorry.

Further up the beach some kids are playing Frisbee. We watch as the wind catches the disc only to drop it in the ocean. The kid who threw it is forced to wade out and get it. He emerges, legs red from the cold, and flicks a jellyfish at one of his playmates.

When we hit the rocks, we turn back. Instead of walking on the beach we head up to the sidewalk. For some minutes we walk in silence. Then Quinn asks whether Josh and Tonya's divorce is amicable.

While I shouldn't divulge details, it's tempting. Sometimes, I discuss my wilder clients with Quinn, without mentioning names, of course. When I lived in Toronto, it wasn't an issue. But in this case, she knows both parties. I hesitate.

She turns to look at me and laughs. "I guess that's a no."

The esplanade is lined with parked cars. Some people are sitting in their cars, and others are lying on their hoods or seated in lawn chairs on the sidewalk. Music is playing. I catch a whiff of grease from the Willows Kiosk, and the smell of fresh-cut grass. I don't want to talk about Josh and Tonya anymore. "Do you want an ice cream?" I ask Quinn.

"Sure," she says. "But how bad is it?" When I don't answer, she looks smug. "Oh come on, Toby. I can practically read your mind. One look at your face and I know Josh and Tonya will set the bar for messy divorces to a new high. What's the deal?" We join the lineup outside the kiosk, behind two small kids clutching handfuls of change.

I grit my teeth. I know Quinn. She is not going to drop this.

"Allegations of adultery, mental cruelty, and deceit," I say. Plus, from what I gleaned about Josh's tech company, a shitload of money. But I don't mention that.

We are near the front of the line, the kids in front of us exchanging their coins for a paper tray heaped with fries. We wait as they pump a crime scene of ketchup onto the pile. "One chocolate twist and one vanilla," I tell the large, bearded guy in the window when it's our turn. We get the same thing every time.

I've been handed my cone and am turning to go when I spy a stack of today's newspapers sitting on the shelf, next to boxes of candies. I freeze. Above the fold lies a photo of a woman with long, bleached blonde hair. Tonya.

For a moment I think I'm imagining it, that it's someone who just looks like her—perhaps some minor celebrity. Someone pouty, blonde, and big-breasted. I pick some coins out of my purse and slide them toward the bearded guy, who's already helping the next person. "I'll take a *Times Colonist*, too," I say, and grab the top paper off the stack. He grunts. I tuck the newspaper under my arm.

Quinn has found a bench. I join her. My ice cream has already started to melt. I slap the paper onto the bench between us and take a seat.

Quinn's eyebrows ricochet. "Is that—?" She bends forward to read it. She removes her bucket hat and lays a hand on her belly. "Oh my God," she says. "It is her."

Although the paper is facing the wrong way I can still read the big black headline: **Aspiring Actress Goes Missing.**

CHAPTER THREE

FIFTY, FIFTY

Given Tonya's disappearance, I thought Josh would cancel his appointment today. Instead, he called to ask if we could make it earlier, which is why I'm in Starbucks at 8:15 a.m. on a gloomy Thursday, seated in a low armchair near the window. Rain is streaking the glass. On the sidewalk, people are walking fast beneath their umbrellas.

Maybe on account of this appointment, I dressed more carefully than usual this morning in fitted black pants, black high-heeled boots, and a blue, sleeveless mock turtleneck. Unfortunately I left my jacket in the car. While my top is cute, I'm freezing.

The woman at the next table looks up, her enraptured expression alerting me to Josh's approach. Sure enough, when I turn, he's striding my way. I withdraw my notebook and pen from my bag and lay them neatly on the table.

"Hey Toby!" He pecks me on the cheek. "No, don't get up! Am I late?" He checks his expensive diving watch.

"No, I was early," I say, surprised to see him looking so upbeat. Given that newspaper report I expected him to be anxious. It claimed the police feared foul play, which made *me* anxious, and I hate Tonya. And yet Josh looks as relaxed as he did in my office three days back, like he just stepped out of a yachting magazine.

"I'll just grab a coffee," he says. "D'you want anything else?"

I say no, then watch him as he waits in line. He's in jeans again today, paired with a white t-shirt and a blue blazer, everything casual but expensive-looking.

He sets his black coffee onto our table and smiles down at me. "You look cold," he says.

Given that every bit of my exposed skin is covered in goose

bumps there's no point denying it. "Yeah, a little," I say, and wrap my hands around my coffee cup.

"Here, take my jacket."

I start to protest but he drapes it over me. Still warm from his body, the blazer is enormous. I slip it on, my hands so far up inside the sleeves that holding a pen is impossible. "Let me roll those for you," says Josh and, before I know it, I'm holding out my arms like a toddler. "Perfect," he says, when the sleeves are rolled. He leans back and grins down at me.

So much for looking mature and professional. "Thanks," I say, fully aware that his jacket emphasizes my waif-like frame—he's six-two and I can still shop in the kids' department. Not that I'm eager to take it off—it smells too good, a male citrusy scent.

Josh takes a seat across from me. "Thanks for meeting me early," he says. "I'm still on the board of my old company and have a long videoconference later today."

I nod but feel confused. I figured he wanted to see me as soon as possible because of Tonya's disappearance. Instead, he's behaving like nothing's happened. "I read the news," I say. "About Tonya going missing."

Josh leans back, his face suddenly cautious. He scratches his chin. "You can't believe everything you read in the papers."

I wait. Is he saying that Tonya's not missing? But the story quoted the police, who asked the public for assistance in tracing her movements on Monday night. "Do you know where she is?" I ask.

Josh shakes his head. For an instant, his eyes flash with frustration, quickly hidden. He rips open a pack of sugar and stirs some into his coffee. "I have no clue. The cops questioned me yesterday. But I don't think there's any real reason to worry."

"So why are the police worried?"

Josh sighs. "She was seen down at the Oak Bay Marina late Monday night. Some passerby thought she might have been drunk." He goes to take a sip of coffee, then reconsiders. "That's where I keep my boat, the *Great Escape*."

I nod. All of this was in the *Times Colonist* article.

"She didn't show up for an audition the next morning. And someone found her dog wandering around at the marina."

"Her dog?" I ask, aghast. Would Tonya really abandon her dog? But this is Tonya we're talking about. To her, a dog is probably just a fashion accessory, something to update with the seasons.

Josh shrugs. "I guess one of her friends freaked out, said it was out of character."

"But it's not?"

Josh studies his hands. I note he's not wearing a wedding band. "She's an actress," he says, and I can hear the bitterness in his voice. "Who even knows her real character?"

I bite my lip. How could Josh not have known Tonya's true nature? Yes, I haven't seen her in years, but someone's basic character doesn't change. I recall the hateful rumors she spread about me, the way she'd watched to see my reaction, turned on by my shock and humiliation. She took pleasure in hurting people. It brought light to her eyes. That need to cause pain can't have changed.

I study Josh, now staring out the window. "So where'd you think she went?" I ask.

He sighs. "She's probably just off partying. She's always complaining how *boring* the island is. She wants to move back to L.A. More nightlife and her career." This last word is accompanied by a gesture of ironic quotation marks.

I make a note. "Did she party a lot?" It'd be good for his case if we could prove she had problems with substance abuse.

Josh shrugs. "Yeah, a fair bit. I didn't notice it so much in L.A., 'cause that's what everyone does, but here . . ." He toys with his coffee cup. "Well, I'm usually up by 5:00 a.m. running fishing tours." He gives me a sad smile. "Tonya hated going out on the water."

My latte has long since gone cold but I sip it anyway. "So no chance of reconciliation?" I've had plenty of clients claim to detest each other only to ditch their divorce proceedings and reconcile, or even remarry after the split was finalized.

Josh shakes his head. "It's gone way beyond that. We want totally different lives." He frowns. "What do they call it? Irreconcilable differences?"

"How about her allegations of . . ." I pretend to check my notes. "Mmm, mental cruelty and adultery?"

"Total crap," says Josh. His cheeks have reddened, which makes the color of his eyes even more striking.

"So she's lying?"

"Yes." He's not looking at me.

Something about his posture feels off, but I decide not to push it. We can come back to this point later, after I've had time to think about it. Or am I being too suspicious? "How about her?" I ask. "Has she done anything that could influence the settlement in your favor?"

Josh rubs his eyes. "I don't know," he says. "We've barely talked since moving back here. I moved out, oh, four, five months ago. And even before that she was out all the time . . ."

"With other men?" Is that where she's gone now? Off with some lover?

He shrugs. "Possibly. I mean, I saw guys dropping her off but she said they were gay." He smiles ironically. "Come to think of it she has a lot of good-looking gay friends."

"Do you recall any names?"

"She talked a lot about a French hairdresser named Florian Moreau," says Josh. "But he's gone back to Paris. I remember him because when he left, he sold Tonya his dog. It's one of those big puffy standard poodles. A purebred."

I nod. Poor thing, abandoned by two owners. Where is it now? But I'm getting distracted.

I ask him to spell Moreau, but suspect Tonya was telling the truth. A pedigree standard poodle sounds like the type of dog a gay French hairdresser would choose. *Stereotype much?* says a small voice in my head. I, of all people, should know better.

I recross my legs. "Okay. Who initiated the divorce?"

"I did."

"Why?"

The café is crowded, other patrons eyeing our near-empty coffee cups and trying to gauge when our seats will be free. Josh is staring out the window, frowning. "I don't want to keep living like this," he says. "We can't agree on anything. Where to live, what stuff to buy, when to have kids. I'd like a family but she's still obsessed with being an actress."

"To work out a settlement I need to understand your finances," I say. "In terms of total assets, what kind of sums are we talking about?"

Josh's mouth tightens. "About twenty-four, twenty-five million."

Dollars? I try to not to show my surprise. I figured he was rich, but not that rich. "Did either of you bring money into the marriage?"

"Yeah," he says. "When we got married I was worth maybe six mil."

"And Tonya?"

He shakes his head.

"Typically, the assets accrued during your marriage would be split equally," I say, doing the math in my head. Tonya's looking at around nine million dollars, plus possible alimony, for eighteen months of marriage. "I guess there wasn't a prenuptial agreement?" I say hopefully.

Josh gives a wry laugh.

I'm describing the information I'll need—a list of his assets, any insight into Tonya's accusations of adultery and mental cruelty, any behavior of hers that might point to deception—when he lays a hand on my arm. At his touch, I freeze. He looks into my eyes and I sit, mesmerized. I swallow hard. Josh and I stare at each other.

Starbucks, its chit-chatting patrons, and the rainy street outside all fade away. I'm taken back nineteen years, to a boy and a girl in the woods. I feel lost, scared and hopeful. I'm so tempted to tilt forward and kiss him.

"Give her what she wants," says Josh. The spell breaks. I'm back in Starbucks. The windows are fogged up. For a moment, I've no clue what he's talking about.

"W—what do you mean?" I stammer. An instrumental version of Nirvana's "About a Girl" is playing on the sound system. I wonder what Kurt Cobain would make of his songs turned to Muzak.

Josh shakes his head. His eyes look cold and determined. "Tonya," he says. "We'll split things fifty-fifty and I'll pay maintenance. Whatever."

"Are you sure?" I say. "I mean you were only married for eighteen months. If her accusations are unwarranted you might be able to get a better deal . . ."

He cuts me off. "It doesn't matter," he says. There are faint lines around his eyes, which, if anything, make him even more attractive. He places his hand on mine. "I just want this over with, Toby."

With his hand on mine, it's hard to think. I ought to pull my hand away, pull myself together. Instead, for way too long, I just sit there, enjoying the buzz his touch gives me. When he squeezes my hand, I take a deep breath. "Josh, I can file your divorce application," I say. "But obviously, the papers can't be served until we find Tonya."

Josh's nostrils flare. He withdraws his hand and makes a fist. Abandoned on the table between us, my hand looks tiny and pale. "Don't worry. She'll show up," says Josh.

I want to believe him.

CHAPTER FOUR:

BFF

I'm standing in the checkout line at Safeway when some women behind me start to bitch about how long it's taking. I turn to look at them and do a double take. No way. It can't be. And yet it is—the taller of the pair is Chantelle Orker, who was Tonya's BFF at camp, a girl not quite as nasty as Tonya, but not for want of trying. I blink, trying to take this in. Another familiar face from that awful camp. Why are they all popping up now, like poisonous toadstools, when I haven't seen them in going on two decades? Yet isn't it always that way, like the second you notice some excruciating new trend—like mullet dresses—you're bound to see them everywhere?

I spin around, hoping to God she hasn't seen me.

"Like, could this line be any slower?" moans Chantelle.

Her shrill voice takes me back to the age of fourteen, my short, scrawny frame clad in an oversized sweatshirt and a saggy-bummed tankini, which, according to the label, was made to fit ten-year-olds. I was standing on a rock overlooking Lake Philobee—otherwise known as Full-of-Pee—shivering.

"I'm not jumping into that!" I said. "Look at the water! It's mustard-colored!"

"That's the result of tannin. It's totally natural!" said our group's counsellor, Thelma, as though this were reason to celebrate.

"So's dysentery," I said, but Thelma ignored me. Beside me, Quinn shifted from foot to foot in an effort to keep warm. While this passed for summer in Western Canada, in most of the world we'd have been wearing jackets instead of swimsuits.

"Last one in is a rotten egg!" trilled Thelma. I shook my head in disgust. This might work on toddlers, but did she really expect it to motivate five teenaged girls?

Yet strangely, it did. Chantelle Orker went first, which wasn't surprising. She'd do anything to show off to Tonya and was constantly trying to prove how tough she was.

"Who-hoo!" she yelled, when she popped up, spluttering. "That was awesome!"

Liar liar panties on fire.

Louise Dobson went next, although it was more a forlorn shuffle-off-the-plank than a jump. What a sorry-assed suck-up! If Thelma told her to drink from Lake Full-of-Pee she'd claim it tasted like apple juice.

"I'm going," said Quinn, and jumped. The traitor!

That left me and Tonya on the rock. Tonya gave me a sneering once-over. "Nice swimsuit," she hissed. "I had the same one when I was six. But I think you forgot your water-wings."

I pretended to sniff. "I think you forgot your deodorant."

Her icy eyes narrowed. Faced with Tonya's dead-eyed sneer, being in that piss-yellow lake didn't seem so bad. The rock felt too small. Maybe she had the same thought because she ripped off her fleece top.

My stomach fell.

She was wearing a bikini in a hideous but effective shade of neon green, her breasts like dayglow melons. There was no way I could disrobe with those twin orbs glowing beside me. The contrast between them and my teensy nubs would be too stark, my humiliation too apparent. If she was the Rockies, I was Manitoba. Eyes fixed on the murky depths of Lake Philobee, I stood frozen.

"Come on! The boys are watching!" squealed Chantelle.

I followed her gaze. She was right. Just when it couldn't get worse. All the boys were watching us: obese Danny G and the jocks, Brock and Brent, tall skinny Luke, and smart serious Sam. And the Barton brothers, Josh and Mike, both too handsome to be real. My eyes snagged on Josh: red shorts and no shirt, a body straight off a sporting trophy. Thelma, meanwhile, was already swimming back to shore, freestyle.

Moving so fast I didn't see it coming, Tonya pulled down my

swim bottoms and jumped, leaving me on full display. Skinny, bone white, nearly hairless.

Shock and humiliation took my breath away. I couldn't move, couldn't think. I couldn't save myself, as frozen as an ice sculpture.

The sound of laughter snapped me out of my trance. "I told you she's eight years old!" cried Tonya. Another shriek of mean laughter. "Helloooo, puberty?"

I collapsed into the lake.

"Clean up in aisle three," says a loud metallic voice. "We need a cleanup in aisle three, please."

Without thinking, I glance down, relieved to see fitted black pants and a crisp cotton shirt instead of slack spandex. I exhale. Why, after all those years, can that memory still make my cheeks burn? It shouldn't matter. And compared to what Tonya did later, that morning in the lake was nothing. And yet . . . I feel nauseous just thinking about it.

Glancing back, I see Chantelle watching me through narrowed eyes. Oh no. She's recognized me. "Huh. I don't believe it!" Beneath bleached floppy bangs, she makes a sour face. "Toby Parsons?"

I swallow hard. Parsons is my dad's surname. I had it legally changed to my mom's maiden name when I turned nineteen. Since he left us, I didn't want to be saddled with his name. "It's Toby Wong now," I say. "But yes, it's me." I fight the urge to drop my shopping basket and run. "How's it going, Chantelle?"

She looks me up and down. "You look the same."

I know this isn't a compliment but pretend to smile. "Thanks." Nobody could say the same for her. Back at camp, she was tall but thin, with straggly brown hair and bad highlights. She's now five-ten and solid, with thick, muscly limbs and no waist, like a former weight-lifter gone to seed, her hair flat in front and shaved in back. Her neck has gotten thick. Unchanged are her calculating blue eyes and square chin, plus her horsy teeth, now framed by too bright lipstick. She's also the same odd orangey color I remember so well— both she and Tonya were addicted to fake tanner.

"Toby Wong?" she says. Her eyebrows—much too dark for her fried blonde hair—knit together. She's obviously trying to figure out where she's heard that name before. Then she gets it. Her scarlet lips fall open. "Are you a lawyer?"

"I am."

"Oh." She wrinkles her big nose like I smell. "Did Josh actually hire you?"

"He did." I wonder how she knew. Have she and Josh stayed in touch? Or is she still friends with Tonya?

Chantelle snorts. "I don't believe it!"

The line moves slowly. I shuffle forward. I'm only buying tampons, a Caramilk bar, and a box of Cheerios, but the express line looked even crazier than this one.

"Why'd he hire *you*?" asks Chantelle. The woman who's standing between us, an older lady reading the *National Enquirer*, peers over her bifocals with a curious look on her face.

"I don't know," I admit, then can't help adding: "Why do you care?"

"Tonya's my best friend," says Chantelle in a wounded voice, like it's totally obvious. Or maybe it is—they were thick as thieves back at camp, after all.

The woman between us folds up her tabloid. I guess we're more entertaining.

"D'you know where Tonya's gone?" I ask Chantelle, and her mouth tightens. She studies the candy display, some rows of worried Ws etched into her forehead. Is she anxious for her friend? I think of Josh's nonchalance this morning, his assertion that Tonya's fine, just off partying someplace. As her best friend, wouldn't Chantelle know? Is there more to the story?

Chantelle flicks her bangs out of her eyes. "Why don't you ask Josh?" she says, her voice rising in pitch. "Ask him why Tonya would feel the need to get away, why she'd had it up to here"—she chops at her throat—"with this place." She tosses her head, causing her dangly earrings to jangle. "Ask him about all those nights he left his wife alone and went fishing with Alana Mapplebee." The word "fishing" is accompanied by the same gesture of ironic quotation marks I saw Josh use earlier today, no doubt a mannerism adopted from Tonya. "If she went back to L.A., who could blame her?" says Chantelle.

I keep quiet. I shouldn't be discussing any of this with Chantelle Orker—or anyone else. Josh is my client. Was he lying when he claimed he'd been faithful? When I don't respond to Chantelle, she bares her teeth at me. She looks like an enraged palomino mule that might charge: all teeth, mane, and muscles.

I face forward and dig my iPhone out of my purse. I try to read the news but can't concentrate, too aware of Chantelle's hostile presence behind me. I put the phone away.

As well as being alarmingly old and slow, the man in front of me seems to be stocking up for Armageddon. There are so many cans in his cart it's a wonder it hasn't buckled. Behind me, Chantelle continues to rant. I'm still trying to figure out where I've heard the name Alana Mapplebee.

Finally, it's my turn at the till. I hand over my basket. The cashier has trouble reading the barcode on the tampons and has to call for a price check. When I look back, Chantelle is still glaring at me. The old lady with the *National Enquirer* is giving me a dirty look too. Some people just hate lawyers. I've grabbed my bag and am turning to go when Chantelle calls out: "Toby! You think you know Josh. He's so handsome and charming, so successful." She wags an orange finger my way. "But you have no idea! None! That's how sociopaths operate." Her voice is a hiss. "They suck you in and suck you dry!"

Supermarkets are always cold, and yet again, I left my jacket in the car. But it's not the temperature in here that makes me shiver. It's the bitterness in Chantelle's small eyes. If Tonya's best friend hates Josh that much, imagine how Tonya must feel. As a kid, she was a bad enemy to have. In this divorce, there's no way she'll fight fair. Am I really up to opposing Tonya?

It's almost dark as I walk to my car, the parking lot still full of vehicles but with few people about. High overhead, the lights shine dull orange. The wind is up. A white plastic bag swept up from behind a parked van swoops into my path. I jump, then feel ridiculous. It's just a bag! But meeting Chantelle has left me shaky. As I unlock my car I think of Quinn's advice not to take Josh on as a client. Was she right? Or is it high time I faced all of this?

I'm about to pull out of my parking slot when a blue truck cuts me off, forcing me to slam on the brakes. My seatbelt digs into my neck. I catch a glimpse of Chantelle at the truck's wheel, that snarl still on her face.

My heart pounds. For a moment, I just stay where I am, composing myself. My hands feel sweaty on the wheel.

If seeing Chantelle has affected me this badly, how will I feel when I meet Tonya? I hate that her bullying left such deep marks. I'm better than this, stronger than this, smarter than this. I know all of this. So why can't I feel it?

CHAPTER FIVE:

IN THE CARDS

My mom's door, which is usually open, is locked. After ringing the bell, I survey her brightly spotted lawn. No doubt to her neighbors' chagrin, my mother thinks dandelions look "cheerful." I push the bell again, unable to suppress a ripple of worry. Why isn't she answering? Then I hear her yelling for me to hold my horses, she's coming.

Seeing me, my mom smiles. "Toby!" she exclaims, as though my arrival is a huge surprise instead of something we confirmed yesterday. "I was just out back, cutting parsley for the potatoes." She steps forward and hugs me. I'm still wearing my lawyering clothes: black heels, a black pantsuit, and a pink cotton blouse. I remove my jacket.

"I thought we could eat on the deck," says my mom, as I follow her into the small kitchen. "It's so rare that it's warm enough." Most evenings, even in the summer, a cold wind whips in from the ocean, which lies about two blocks away. But tonight, the air is still enough to feel humid.

While my mom mixes the salad dressing I surreptitiously watch her. Before my dad left, my mother worked part-time as an accountant and dressed in pastel sweaters and ballet flats. She was the ultimate Asian tiger mother, driving me to endless tennis, violin, and French lessons, all of which stopped when my orthodontist dad took up with a shapely red-haired dental hygienist. The way some traumatized people find God, my mom found New Age mumbo jumbo. Yoga and astrology were her entry drugs, followed by reiki, color therapy, and aura repair. Her closet filled with gypsy skirts and our house could have passed for a crystal shop. All the energy

she'd put into being the perfect wife went into chanting and balancing her chakras. Worst of all, she began dabbling in the occult—
tarot, numerology, palmistry. She even had a real crystal ball. It was
mortifying.

Thankfully, she ditched the worst of the gypsy garb years ago,
but to my never-ending embarrassment, has spent the past nineteen
years earning her living as a fortune teller. Even after all this time,
I have trouble telling people. I look around her cramped kitchen.
"Can I help?" I ask.

"You can whip the cream for dessert," says my mom. "There's a
box in the fridge." She hands me the electric mixer. "Don't overdo it
this time." I nod. I make great butter.

My mom's hair, which fell out from all the chemo, is growing
back in again. It used to be pure black but is now the color of a thun-
dercloud. Both the color and the short style suit her. "I like your
hair this way," I say, as I pull the cream from the fridge. I can't stop
myself from asking how she's feeling.

"I feel good!" She opens the lid of a big pot and the smell of
steaming corn pours out. I look around the kitchen, every detail
familiar, from the checked curtains to the open-mouthed ceramic
frog that holds the scouring pads. As I whip the cream, I wonder
how many hours of my childhood were spent staring at that stupid
frog while washing my mom's mismatched dishes.

Before my mom got sick I used to feel trapped in this house, as
though time never moved. But since my mom's illness, that feeling of
being stuck in the past has been replaced by something scarier still—
the fear that my mom, her home, and our future together could
vanish as fast as her hair had fallen out.

I set the whipped cream back into the fridge and the doorbell
rings. "I'll get it," I say, glad of the distraction. "It must be Quinnie."
Since I moved back to Victoria, Friday night dinners at my mom's
have become a ritual for the three of us, as Quinn's husband, Bruce,
who's a cop, works the late shift.

"Hey," says Quinn, when I pull back the screen door. "Can you believe how hot it is?" Despite her light summer dress, she looks red-cheeked and flustered. I take the bowl of blueberries she's holding and lead her into the kitchen.

"Perfect timing," says my mother. She stands on tiptoes to peck Quinn on the cheek. "I hope you're both hungry."

My mom has made grilled snapper, baked potatoes, green beans, steamed corn, and a tomato salad. "Ivy, it all looks amazing," says Quinn.

Armed with plates, cutlery, and bowls, we follow my mother onto the back porch. High overhead, a floatplane putters by. I inhale the familiar summer smells: freshly cut grass, petunias, gas from the neighbor's barbecue. It's a perfect evening, the tsk-tsk-tsk of the sprinkler taking me back to my childhood. I imagine Quinn and me in our underwear, running through the sprinkler.

My mom lights some candles and takes a seat. Quinn maneuvers her belly under the table. I offer to fetch her an extra pillow and she thanks me.

Quinn and my mom chat about pregnancy, the aches and pains, the indignity of it all. Since it's a topic I know nothing about, I stay quiet and count the weeks since I moved back to the island. I know my mom feels guilty about my return, like I gave up some perfect life just because she got cancer. I think about Josh and how weird it is to see him again after all these years. And then Chantelle Orker. But Victoria is pretty small. Sooner or later, I'll run into loads of people I knew from school or camp or gymnastics classes. I couldn't wait to get away from most of them and haven't kept in touch with anyone besides Quinn.

Thoughts of people I haven't missed lead to thoughts of Tonya, and how much I dread meeting her. Seeing Chantelle was bad enough. I know it's childish but I can't help but hope that Tonya stays missing—or moves back to L.A., pronto.

Staring at my half-finished dinner, I am back at Camp Wik-wakee, the boys and girls on the old dock late at night, sitting cross-legged in a squashed circle. Overhead, the stars were bright but we didn't notice them, all eyes fixed on an empty vodka bottle, which Josh had set to spinning on the dock between us.

I blinked. The more times the bottle spun, the dizzier I felt. Each time it came my way I prayed it would stop. Stop! Stop! Pretty please with sugar on top! When it passed me I willed it to slide on. Go! Go! Go! My eyes hurt from staring at it.

It went slower and slower until it was almost pointing my way. My heart leapt. Yesssss! And then it rolled on, a little to the left, the wooden boards of the dock just warped enough to prevent it from settling. I held my breath. Please let it be me.

"Whoa! Nice one!" I heard various male voices making comments. All of them sounded jealous.

I looked up at Josh only to wish I hadn't. He wasn't looking at me but at Tonya—the mouth of the bottle aimed right at her crotch, which was showcased in a pair of pink shorts so tight it's a wonder she hadn't lost her labia to gangrene.

She smiled, first at Josh and then at me, a pointed, victorious sneer, punctuated by a mean giggle. Josh's face, meanwhile, was inscrutable, or maybe I was just telling myself he didn't look pleased. All the other guys looked like they'd kill to take his place.

Tonya reached for Josh's hand and led him down the dock, into the dark, her ass glowing like a nightlight in her microscopic pink shorts. Josh's brother, Mike, kicked out at the empty bottle, sending it skidding across the dock. "This game is stupid," he said, radiating jealousy like black smoke off a burning tire. The look-alike jocks, Brett and Brock, nodded in sullen unison. I guessed they were also hoping to wind up with Tonya. Pretty soon all the guys were checking their watches. Cries of "Get a room!" started up.

Disappointment filled my belly. I bit my lip, bit down my self-pity. I told myself it was only for a few minutes. But I knew it wasn't. Josh was gone, led away—and astray—by the camp's queen bee. Faced with what she could give him, our kiss in the woods meant nothing to Josh. Nor did our subsequent walks and shy hand-holding, our whispered conversations, the time he held me behind the boathouse . . . I hung my head. I'd never felt such betrayal. Was this love? Every breath hurt.

"I'm outta here," muttered Mike, already staggering to his feet. I wanted to run away too, to be anywhere but sitting here, pretending to be okay. Was my agony visible?

Way off in the dark, I could see Josh and Tonya, a single silhouette against the inky lake. My eyes went blurry. I'd never stood a chance. Why was I stupid enough to get my hopes up?

I rub my eyes. "Toby?" says my mom.

She obviously just asked me something. "I, ah, sorry . . ." I say.

She lowers her fork. "I asked if you've met anyone yet," she says, brightly.

I try not to groan out loud. She asks this question every week. "This is Victoria, Mom," I say. "All of the guys are either in university or in Depends. They don't call this the town of the newly wed or nearly dead for nothing." As soon as I say it, I wish I hadn't. I shouldn't be joking about death with my mother. I swig some wine, as if to dislodge the foot that's stuck in my mouth.

"Well, it's not like you met an army of eligible men in Toronto either," says Quinn matter-of-factly.

"Geez, thanks Quinn."

My best friend laughs. I down the rest of my wine and reach for the bottle.

"I'm glad you didn't marry young like me," says my mother. "But you're in your mid-thirties, sweetie."

Thirty-three-and-a-half is early thirties. But I don't bother correcting her. "I know, Mom," I say, more defensively than I planned. "Don't make it sound like I'm not interested in having a relationship."

"If you're so interested why haven't you been on a date in what, three years?" asks Quinn. I glare at her. How dare she gang up on me with my mother?

"I've been busy."

"Not as busy as Quinn," says my mom. She laughs and pats Quinn's massive belly.

After we've eaten the blueberries and cream and cleared the table, I volunteer to do the dishes. Given that my mom cooked and Quinn's heavily pregnant, there's no way to avoid this chore. My mom's dishwasher broke about a decade ago, and since she lives alone, it never seemed worth getting a new one.

I'm elbow-deep in sudsy water when I hear Quinn ask my mom if she could do a reading for her. It's mind-boggling how Quinn, who's a scientist and the most down-to-earth person I know, could have any time for my mom's delusions of clairvoyance. And yet not only does she love getting her cards read, but she's perfectly happy to tell everyone about these sessions. Some of her colleagues—also scientists—are my mother's clients. This just goes to show that even smart, rational people aren't immune to New Age bullshit.

I'm scrubbing the last pan when Quinn pops her head into the kitchen. She looks flushed and excited. "I had the best reading ever," she says. "My destiny was The Sun, which signals love, great news, and fulfillment. And my final result was The World, which relates to accomplishment and a wonderful change . . ."

She goes on like this for some minutes. I grit my teeth. Love? Big changes? Is my mother kidding? Of course Quinn's life will be full of love and new experiences; she's about to have her first baby!

"You should do it," says Quinn, as I carefully balance the final pan on the dish rack.

Rather than admit to not listening, I make a noncommittal noise, which Quinn clearly takes for a yes. "Ivy!" she yells at my mom, who's still in the living room. "Toby wants to do a reading!"

"Really?" asks my mom, her voice surprised and delighted. She steps into the kitchen. "You want me to look at your cards, sweetie?"

She looks so excited I don't have the heart to say no. I grab a tea towel and dry my hands.

"Do you want tea or coffee?" asks my mother. She turns to Quinn. "Can you drink coffee, honey?"

"Decaf," says Quinn. "If you have any."

"I'll have that too," I say. I wonder if there's any way I can get out of having my cards read. Maybe Quinn and my mom will forget about it. Or should I say I need to leave early to catch up on work? But it's Friday night . . . I blame Quinn for getting my mom's hopes up.

"Are you ready?" asks my mom, after the coffee is brewed. She pours milk into a small jug. I realize she's talking about my reading.

"Do you want privacy? Should I, like, wait in the other room?" asks Quinn. She stands in the doorway, filling most of it. It's obvious she wants to listen in.

"I've got nothing to hide," I say. This is the truth. While I'm privy to various clients' indiscretions, my life is an open book. More like a pamphlet, really.

Quinn smiles.

"Have a seat," says my mom. "I'll get the cards."

In most ways, my mother is easy-going. Too easy-going, I'd say. She lets people—like my dad, for example—take advantage of her. But there are a few things—all weird and totally irrational—about which she's anal, such as the rule that no one can touch her tarot cards unless invited.

As a kid I found these cards spellbinding. I loved the old-fashioned pictures, which, although in color, have a creepy, dimly lit quality. I loved the characters: a naked woman pouring water beneath The Star; The Devil stretching his wings; Justice looking glum with her sword and scales. Although I was strictly forbidden from touching the cards, I often did, always being careful to leave them just as I'd found them. Sometimes, I got away with it.

Quinn is already sitting at the kitchen table. I sit next to her. My mother hands me the deck and tells me to shuffle. I keep dropping cards. Everything related to the paranormal makes me uneasy. I hate how credulous people are, how eager they are to be tricked. And I hate that little twinge of curiosity I feel when my mom flips my first card. There's a thoughtful look on her face. "This card shows your present position."

I nod grimly, the lopsided cap of The Fool instantly recognizable to me.

"Hmmm," she continues. "The Fool. It suggests the start of an adventure, maybe one you haven't thought through properly. You need to pay attention to the details and not get fooled by things that look better than they are."

I nod, as does Quinn, who's sitting on my mom's other side, fascinated.

I try not to take the negative comments personally. If I believed, without a doubt, that clairvoyance is bogus, playing along with this reading shouldn't matter. But, while I'm pretty sure my mother lacks the gift, I suspect some people have dangerous talents. We aren't meant to know the future or talk to the dead. Some secrets should stay secret.

My mom reaches for another card. She shuts her eyes, as though listening to inaudible music. I heap sugar into my decaf. What if my mother's ham-fisted attempts get the spirits riled up? What if they take it out on me? She turns the card. "Goal or destiny. Hmmm, The Tower." She and Quinn exchange a look. Quinn stares at the card as though it were a poison pen letter. My mom stares at me. I feel as though *I'm* the one who was recently diagnosed with cancer.

"This card signals a big change," says my mother. "There's deception and disruption. You doubt yourself. You face adversity, even ruin."

The picture shows two people surrounded by massive hailstones falling head-first out of a tall tower that's been struck by a fireball. Could it get any worse? "So it's bad?" I ask. I was trying to be funny but my mom doesn't get it.

"Well," she says carefully. "It signifies that things will get shaken up, but that's not always a bad thing." She takes a sip of coffee. "It depends on the other cards." These turn out to include The Hanged Man, The Moon, Death, *and* The Devil.

"Wow, I've never seen cards that shitty!" says Quinn excitedly. She has the same look on her face that she gets when discussing killer whale sex, her current academic obsession.

My mom eyes me suspiciously. "Are you sure things are okay at work?" she asks. "Has anything strange happened lately? No new, troublesome clients? Or are there issues with your new apartment?"

I grit my teeth. Quinn is giving me a pointed look. Like me, I'm sure she's thinking of my one and only new client. Josh. The one with the missing estranged wife, whom the police think is in trouble. And I haven't even told Quinn about meeting Chantelle last night. I ignore her and shake my head vigorously. "Everything's fine, Mom."

My mom collects the cards, as though the sight of them laid out like that is giving her the heebie-jeebies. She shuffles. "Well, you'd better watch your back." She slips them back into their lacquered box. "Because somebody's out to get you."

Although the kitchen is hot, I suppress a shiver. I recall Chantelle's warning as I was leaving Safeway. While I neither like nor trust her, perhaps she was being sincere. Now my mom's reading seems to back her up. Except that's absurd. Coincidence, and nothing more. I feel mad at Chantelle for having brought up bad adolescent memories, and mad at Quinn and my mom for having suckered me into this stupid reading.

But most of all, I'm annoyed with myself. Why did I agree to get my cards read? Now my mom will worry, and so will I, because what if—just this once—she's actually onto something?

CHAPTER SIX

BAD NEWS

It's Labor Day Monday, that last gasp of fun before the nation's kids trudge back to school. A poignant reminder that summer is officially over. I'm pulling up in front of Quinn's bungalow when I see a FOR SALE sign planted in the middle of her neighbors' front lawn. Above the words *"I make dreams come true—for all your real estate needs, call Alana Mapplebee"* is a picture of a smiling blonde. I recall Chantelle Orker's sneering claim that Josh and Alana Mapplebee had "gone fishing." Was she Tonya's competition?

Instead of walking up Quinn's driveway, I make a detour to check out Alana. She and Tonya could be sisters, both with big, bleached blonde hair and ample cleavage, Alana's peeking out of a bright red suit jacket. I take an instant dislike to her, but maybe I'm just jealous. If I read Chantelle's innuendo correctly, Josh clearly has a type—my physical opposite.

"Toby?" I turn to see Quinn's husband Bruce, standing on their front porch, squinting at me. "What are you doing over there?"

"Oh, hey Bruce." I ascend his front steps and he bends—really far down—to kiss me. At over two hundred fifty pounds, Bruce resembles a giant, wooly teddy bear, his stocky body covered with dark fuzz and his eyes like two shiny black buttons under thick lashes. He's part Samoan and part Italian. Given that Quinn's parents are so successful and she's an academic, I know many people were surprised when she married a cop instead of some hotshot professional type. But Bruce's regular-guy demeanor is part of his appeal. He's warm and funny, as well as kind. The type of guy who performs silly dances to make small cranky kids laugh and will happily rescue a cat from a tree. If I had to call 911, I'd want Bruce to show up.

Now dressed in cargo shorts, a tank top, and a red apron, Bruce takes my bottle of wine and holds the screen door for me. "Thanks for this," he says, scanning the label. "Ooh, French. It looks fancy. Let's go and have some." His smile, like the rest of him, is massive. "Or did you want red?"

"Anything alcoholic," I say.

He shoots me a look. "Work trouble?"

"Nah, not really," I say.

I follow Bruce into their back yard, which consists of some patchy lawn and a couple of ragged apple trees. Quinn and her brother Dan are standing near a smoking gas barbecue. "Hey stranger," says Dan, when he spots me. It's been a few years since we last met, but Dan looks exactly the same—like a slightly older, sloppier male version of Quinn. They even have the same long blond hair, plus the same killer arm muscles and off-kilter sense of humor. I've known Dan since I was five and he was nine, back when he impressed me by singing the Transformers' theme song backward. He could also stick spaghetti up one nostril and have it come out of the other—equally impressive, but not in a good way. Dan gives me a hug and I congratulate him on his recent success. His first documentary film—about a group of First Nations kids who reenact Harry Potter scenes—was a big hit at the Toronto Film Festival.

I tell him I loved his movie and he looks pleased and embarrassed. Quinn told me he's been struggling with his next project and is freaking out that he's a "one-trick pony." I figure it's better to change the subject.

Bruce has just opened the wine I brought when Quinn's parents show up. Seeing me, Alistair waves. He's pushing Jackie, who's in a wheelchair on account of her recent accident. I wave back. Ali is the father I wish I'd had. Come to think of it, I'd like Quinn's mom as my mother too, although I feel disloyal to Ivy after thinking this.

After Alistair has helped Jackie into a lawn chair, I go over and hug her. I ask when she can ditch the giant cyborg-ski-boot contraption encasing her left foot and she grimaces. "About another month, if I'm lucky." One of the hardest-working and most physically active women I know, she's had to take time off work. The enforced inactivity is driving her crazy. "I haven't watched so much bad daytime TV since I was breastfeeding," sighs Jackie.

Two weeks back, Jackie was jogging along Beach Drive when a Dalmatian-collie cross bolted in front of her to escape an amorous Pomeranian. She tripped over its leash and broke two metatarsals in her left foot, and fractured her right collarbone *and* her left thumb, which means she can't write, type, or negotiate crutches.

Alistair hands Jackie a glass of wine she can barely hold. "To coming home," he says, clinking his glass against mine. "We're so glad you're back, Toby."

"It's good to be here," I say, and for the moment, it's true. I offer a toast to friends and family, and to Jackie's speedy recovery. Quinn mooches a sip of Bruce's wine. They feel like family.

The burgers are almost done when I ask Jackie and Alistair if they know Alana Mapplebee. They seem to know everyone in Victoria, Jackie a partner in the island's biggest criminal law practice, and Ali a vascular surgeon and part-time professor at UVic.

There's a weird pause, and it occurs to me that I've said something inappropriate. "The real estate agent?" asks Jackie. She sticks her bobbed hair behind one ear.

Quinn looks at Dan, who takes a swig of wine. "I dated her briefly a couple of years back," he says. "Why? What about her?"

"Her name came up at work," I say. Quinn gives me a questioning look. I ignore her and take a seat beside her mother, who's wearing a green calf-length skirt and a white cotton sweater. Looking at Jackie, I know exactly how Quinn will look in her late fifties: still blonde, trim, and beautiful.

When I decided to move back here, it was Jackie who recommended me to my new bosses, Mel Greene and Philippa Olliartee, former teachers of Jackie's at law school. Now, Jackie studies me. "How's the new job?" she enquires.

"Fine. I mean good."

Jackie looks thoughtful. "You're not bored out of your tree?"

I hesitate. I don't want word that I'm not loving this job to get back to Mel and Philippa. "It is slower than Toronto," I say, slowly. "But I'm just settling in."

"Right," says Jackie. We chat about work and local lawyers I've met or have yet to meet. She recounts a recent case in which her client—an elderly widow—had allowed her grandson to grow "herbs" in her backyard only to be arrested for marijuana farming.

"Who's ready for a burger?" calls Bruce.

The smell of grilling meat makes my stomach rumble.

I offer to fetch Jackie a plate but she declines, saying she'll get something later. Since I'm starving, I excuse myself and head for the barbecue. I'm loading up on condiments when Quinn sidles up to me. She's wearing a long yellow sundress with a ruched top that makes her breasts look enormous. "So why were you asking about Alana?"

I smack the bottom of a ketchup bottle until a huge glob pops out. "It's to do with a case," I say nonchalantly. I'm not going to discuss Josh's divorce with Quinn any more.

My best friend gives me a knowing look, then bites into her pickle. "Not Josh Barton, by any chance?"

"What?" asks Bruce. Still armed with metal tongs, he has walked up behind us. Something about his face causes both Quinn and me to pause. Bruce lowers his tongs. "How do you know Josh Barton?"

"We went to summer camp together," I say, confused by the intense look on Bruce's face. "And I'm handling his divorce from Tonya."

Bruce looks even more serious. "You know her too?" he asks.

"Same camp. But it's not like I *know* her. I mean, I haven't seen her in eons." I pick a carrot stick off my plate and chomp it in half. "I read about her being missing in the papers. Has she turned up yet?"

Bruce frowns. "No. Not yet." He checks his watch—like he expects news any minute. "We're still looking."

His clipped tone makes me uneasy. Why did Josh seem so blasé about Tonya's disappearance when the police are clearly concerned about her? I recall Chantelle's implication that Tonya had caught him cheating on her and skipped town. Have the cops spoken with Chantelle yet? "I met a friend of Tonya's last Thursday in Safeway," I say. "Chantelle Orker?" Bruce makes no response. I don't think I've ever seen him unsmiling for this length of time, ever. "Anyway," I continue. "Chantelle suggested Tonya had gone back to L.A. because of her marital difficulties."

Quinn waves her fork: "What? You met Chantelle Orker? When? What was she like? Last time I saw her she was podium dancing in some nightclub in, like, 2006. Is she still that weird orange color?"

Bruce just stands there, staring at us. The look on his face is making me uneasy. Ignoring Quinn's machine-gun questioning, I turn back to her husband. "Bruce?" I ask. "What's going on? D'you *really* think something has happened to Tonya?"

Now Bruce looks confused. He looks from me to Quinn. "It's been all over the news," he says.

Quinn and I both shake our heads. I spent the morning at my mom's doing yard work. Quinn stopped listening to the news in her first trimester, when a story about a school shooting left her sobbing hysterically. Suicide bombers. Police shootings. It's tempting to just stick your head in the sand.

"Oh," says Bruce. He rubs one giant hand and then the other on his red apron. "I guess you don't know. Based on some new evidence we've sent out divers. They're searching the Oak Bay Marina."

Quinn and I exchange horrified looks. Police divers. In the marina where Josh's boat is moored. We all know what that means.

Quinn touches her throat. "Does Josh know?" she asks, quietly.

CHAPTER SEVEN:

UNREAL

I mean to drive home but don't. It's not such a big detour and it's a beautiful afternoon to putter along Beach Drive, watching the classic cars driven by old codgers, the bikers in their neon spandex and pointy Star Trek helmets, the dog-walkers stopping to let their charges sniff each other's butts. There's Glenlyon School, like a miniature version of Hogwarts, with the sea deep blue behind it. And there's the walking path full of old folks dressed, despite the heat, in Burberry raincoats, and the oh-so-Canadian sculpture of iron wolves chasing a moose, then the wooden swing, the turnoff to Oak Bay Marina. I turn like someone in a dream. What am I doing here? I have no good reason to be looking for Josh Barton.

I park out on Turkey Head and sit in my car, the ocean shimmering to the horizon. Josh is my client, nothing more, and if his wife is dead, he's not even that. A widower doesn't need a divorce. I should go home. But I still don't believe Tonya's dead. How could she be? They say only the good die young.

With the sun shining through the windows, the car is hot. I shut my eyes. I can't stop thinking about Tonya, whom I still blame for some of the worst memories of my life—and yes, I know it wasn't *that* bad, that compared to ninety-nine-point-nine percent of humanity my existence is blessed and always has been. Every day, people endure real tragedy. I wasn't raped, maimed, or enslaved. My trauma was minor, ordinary, just part of growing up. And yet that night and its aftermath marked the end of my childhood and dented my faith—in others but, worst of all, in myself. I resent her for that.

Out on Beach Drive, a bus honks. I open my eyes. Why am I sitting here thinking about that stupid girl? What a waste of time. It all happened so long ago. I sigh. The truth is, coming back to the island has brought some bad memories back. I thought I was over this stuff.

I get out of the car and stretch. The breeze feels good. I realize I'm thirsty. I'll go down to the marina and grab a drink. Maybe an ice cream, if they've got the kind I like. Nothing to do with Tonya. Or Josh. I lock the car and shove the keys into my purse.

I descend the steps behind the coffee shop, where it's shady. Josh Barton is sitting alone at an outdoor table. He's got his head in his hands.

"Josh?" I ask it like I'm surprised to find him here, except I'm not, if I'm honest with myself. I was looking for him, and for the divers, except now that I'm here I don't want to see them, black and menacing in their wet suits. I don't want to see . . . her. I feel like a rubbernecker at the scene of a car crash. I'm not like this. What am I doing here?

I avert my gaze from the water and the docks and the boats, all lined up, shining white in the late afternoon sun. It's easier to look at Josh, anyway. "Josh?" I ask again.

When he looks around, his face is blank. He's in shock, I guess. Or maybe he's just tired. Have the police been hassling him? Upon recognizing me he smiles, some life coming back into his drawn face. "Toby. You heard about the divers?" I know he doesn't smoke but his voice has that rasp.

I nod, unsure how to respond. "Have they . . . found anything?"

His eyes skid toward the water, then away. "No." This single word catches in his throat. He motions toward a chair. "Please, join me."

I take a seat. "D'you know why the cops think she could be . . . here?" I ask. Bruce had refused to say anything. Even Quinn couldn't get a word out of him.

Josh shakes his head. "No. I heard it on the news." There's a can of lemonade on the table and he takes a swig. It's the kind of gourmet stuff they sell here, with an Italian name in swirly font. He upends the can, then crushes it. "But they're wrong," he says. "She's not dead. She can't be."

I'm not sure what to say. Does he have good reason to believe that? Or does he just hope not?

"She's vanished before," he says. "In L.A., when we fought." He stares out at the water but I doubt he's seeing it. "She went off partying. Drugs. Drinking. But she always came back." He rubs his eyes, his gaze finding mine. His expression is so open, so hurt and bewildered, that I can't look away.

"Did you guys have a fight?"

His face shuts down again.

For some minutes we sit in silence, him staring into the marina, me staring into space. I'm thinking of making an excuse to leave when he springs to his feet.

Without thinking, I look where he's staring and see the round head of a seal. Except it's a diver, his head shiny and black in a neoprene cap, the first diver soon joined by two others. The police boat motors into view, the driver speaking into a radio. The divers bob and vanish, then bob up again. My chest feels heavy with foreboding. They are dragging something.

I look away. I don't want to see this.

"Josh?" Should he really be watching this? It's bound to be traumatic. I stand and lay a hand on his elbow. He doesn't respond. I try again. "Josh, let's not stay here . . ."

He makes no answer.

I'm standing there, unsure what to do, when he exhales. He starts to laugh. It's so unexpected I take a step back. Has he lost it?

I glance over his shoulder just in time to see the guys in the boat pull her up—pale floppy limbs and clotted blonde hair, a flash of hot pink and black lingerie. Feeling ill, I grab the deck's railing. I shouldn't have looked. "What the—" I clap a hand over my mouth in horror. From the corner of my eye I just saw her head fall off.

Josh continues to laugh. "Did you see that underwear?" he giggles. "Fuchsia leopard print!" His wide shoulders shake. "Crotchless panties." He's snickering like a twelve-year-old in a PG movie.

I stand open-mouthed, unable to grasp why he's behaving like this. The woman he married has just been pulled dead from the bay! He might not love her anymore, but he once did. Is his laughter the result of shock? I want to shake him.

I'm stunned when he grabs me and picks me up, my wedges lifting off the ground. He hugs me and twirls me around. "It's not her!" he exclaims, his voice giddy with relief. "It's just a doll! I read about it in the papers last week. It went missing from a sex shop in Langford! Some stupid grad prank!"

When he sets me down, his cheeks are flushed. "I knew it wasn't her!" He smiles out at the dive boat in the bay, which is now motoring toward the dock. "I'm sure she'll show up soon. Maybe she's at a spa. Or a music festival?"

He sounds so certain I'm convinced: Tonya is off having fun, too selfish to care that people might worry. Like him, I feel relieved.

Josh grins at me. He motions above us. "Shall we go upstairs for a drink to celebrate?"

I hesitate, then say sure. Above the café lies a fancy restaurant that makes great cocktails. The view is even better up there.

"Great," says Josh, as he leads me up the wide steps. He's still smiling with relief. "I told you Tonya's fine." He glances back at the bay, which shines sapphire in the setting sun. On the beach behind it, three kids with nets are paddling in the shallows. Two kayakers have appeared from around the rocky point, droplets flashing off their paddles. It's a perfect end to the day, now that we know Tonya's not rotting in the water's depths. Josh opens the heavy door for me.

"I kept telling the cops she was fine," he continues. "In L.A. she once left for a whole week, just took off to some resort in Cancun."

The rosy sunshine pouring in through the restaurant's massive windows is blinding. I count the days in my head: it's coming up on a week since Tonya was reported missing.

As the smiling hostess leads us to our seats, Josh continues to list times Tonya went AWOL. "I told the police all of this," he says.

"She's irresponsible! But they wouldn't listen!" Sliding onto a bar-stool, his earlier relief has turned to frustration. "That dive op today, what a waste of tax payers' money!"

I nod, eyeing the cocktail menu gratefully. "Well, at least they solved one crime."

CHAPTER EIGHT:

DEAD FLOWERS

I'm naked and fresh out of the shower when Josh calls, at 7:19 a.m. on a chilly Wednesday morning. If it were almost anyone else, I wouldn't pick up. But the sight of his name on my caller display makes my heart speed up. Plus I'm curious—and anxious. Has Tonya turned up yet?

"Hello?" I say, a towel clutched to my chest and my hair dripping onto my one and only Persian carpet. Josh is talking so fast I can't get a word in edgewise. He is obviously very upset. "I just can't believe it," he says. "I was so sure she was fine! And now the cops want to talk to me again, and I've already told them everything I know. I just . . . who would do that to her? It makes no sense. Things like this don't happen here! This is Canada! That's part of the reason we left L.A. It's crazy . . ."

Because I've only just woken up, and need coffee, it takes a moment for his words to sink in. "Josh," I say. "Slow down. What happened?"

I can hear him swallow. "Tonya's dead. Her body was found yesterday, in the marina. The police just left. They think she was murdered. They want to see me again, at nine." His voice shakes. "I need your help."

I readjust my towel, trying to take it in. Tonya dead. Murdered. Found in the same marina where, the day before yesterday, we'd laughed after that stupid doll got hauled out. It seems unreal, like a cruel joke. I recall Josh's relief. Is he a suspect? "You want me to come to your police interview?" I ask. "Did they advise you to bring a lawyer?"

"No," says Josh. "But I think it'd be better if you came."

"Why?"

"The husband is always a suspect," he says dolefully. "And

we were getting divorced." I can hear him swallow. "God, it's so awful."

My mind is racing. I try to recall when Tonya went missing. I'm pretty sure she was last seen the Monday night before last, on the same day Josh first showed up in my office. My fingers move as I count. Nine days ago. When did Tonya die? I hope Josh has an alibi. "I handle family law," I say. "So if they charge you with anything . . . but there's no reason to think they will, right?" I cross the room and, phone wedged under my chin, scrabble through my underwear drawer.

Josh makes a weird croaking noise. "I . . . I guess not."

"Well, if they did, we'd find you a good criminal lawyer." I immediately think of Quinn's mom, Jackie Andriesen. I pull some beige panties and a matching bra from the drawer, then use my knee to shut it again.

"They asked me to come to the main station on Caledonia Avenue. Please, Toby," says Josh. "Please come with me. I could use some support." He sounds so worried I feel sorry for him.

"Hold on, let me find my schedule." I grab my calendar and my towel drops, my breasts too small to hold it up unassisted. After that, I check my watch and manage to drop the panties too. I curse silently.

"Toby?" asks Josh. "Are you still there?"

"Yes, just a second." I retrieve the towel from the floor and drape it around my shoulders like a cape, then reopen my underwear drawer. I toss in my beige bra and fish out one in pink lace, which I've never worn before. I dig out the matching panties. I'm not sure what inspired me to buy this set, much less wear it today. The color, although pretty, is much less practical than beige.

"Toby?" Josh's voice is breathless. The way he says it takes me back in time, me and him holding hands behind the canteen, him saying he'd been watching me for days, hoping I might like him. He'd seemed so sincere. Except that when the shit hit the fan, he hadn't stood up for me. Why am I even helping this guy?

I take a deep breath. So he let me down. So what? We were kids! It would have taken a strong man to do the right thing and he was just a boy. I'm being pathetic. "Yes, fine," I say. "I'll meet you out front of the station at eight forty-five. And stop worrying, Josh. I'm sure this is totally routine." A lie, of course, but it's best if he stays calm. "I'm sorry to hear about Tonya, but this is a murder investigation. The cops will talk to everybody."

When he thanks me, I hear relief in his voice. "I appreciate it," he says.

Judging from the thick clouds, it's set to rain all day long, which isn't unusual on Canada's West Coast. Josh is on the sidewalk under a big, black umbrella, pacing backward and forward like a caged animal. When he spots me, he rushes over, his red raincoat flapping. Despite the grey skies, he's wearing dark glasses and a red ball cap. He looks like a movie star in mid-scandal trying to avoid the paparazzi.

"Toby? Thank you so much for coming!" He leans forward to peck my cheek and our umbrellas become entangled. By the time we detach them my carefully blow-dried hair is soaked flat. Typical. I dab at my eyes, convinced my mascara has run.

We both apologize at the same time. I follow Josh under an awning. When he removes his sunglasses I see dark rings beneath his eyes. His cheeks are the color of clay. Tonya's death has obviously shaken him. I wonder if, despite their estrangement, he still loves her. He's staring out at the traffic.

"Are you okay?" I ask.

Josh shrugs. "It hasn't really sunk in." He gives me a wry smile. "I keep expecting her to call and start complaining about something. How can she be . . . gone? I was so sure she was off partying." He rubs his eyes. "We'd better go in," he says.

Entering the station I can smell disinfectant, roach spray, and burnt coffee. We stick our wet umbrellas in a rack and unbutton our raincoats. Josh removes his baseball cap. A pretty brunette in her mid-twenties is sitting behind the reception bench. Beside her computer stands a vase of pink carnations, a little plastic sign poking out to offer swirly *Congratulations!* I'm wondering what for when I spot her left hand—the diamond just-out-of-the-box shiny. Yet despite her recent engagement, faced with Josh, her eyes twinkle like her solitaire. She bats her eyelashes at him, my presence unnoticed. "Can I help you?" she asks hopefully. I turn away, irritated.

"I'm here to meet Detective Fitzgerald at nine," says Josh. Either he's ignoring the receptionist's flirtations or else he's so used to women coming onto him that her efforts don't even register. He sounds nervous.

Detective Fitzgerald arrives some minutes later.

In the overwhelmingly white milieu of Victoria, he could pass for a black man. He's got short, graying hair, gray-brown skin, and grey eyes so full of wretchedness that when he looks at me I imagine myself turning to black and white, like in an old movie. When Josh introduces me as his lawyer, Detective Fitzgerald's lip curls. "Right," he says.

We follow him down a long, brightly lit corridor. "In here." He holds the door for us.

Painted white, the room has fluorescent lights, a picnic-style table bolted to the floor, a large mirror, and no windows. I imagine someone standing behind this mirror watching us, the way they do on TV. Josh and I take one side of the table, Detective Fitzgerald the other. Then someone else enters the room. Turning, I see that it's Colin Destin.

I've met Colin at Quinn and Bruce's house, since Colin and Bruce studied together. Colin has actually asked me out for coffee a few times but I've never gone. It's not that he's not attractive— because he's extremely cute—but rather that it'd be weird to go out with one of Quinn and Bruce's friends and have it go wrong.

I wouldn't want to feel uncomfortable about going over to my best friend's place.

At the sight of me, Colin nods. He asks if Josh and I want coffee. Based on the charred smell in the lobby, I decline. Josh says no, too, so Colin fetches us two glasses of water. When he smiles at me I feel bad about not having had coffee with him. He probably hadn't meant it as a date anyway. Despite the fluorescent lights, Colin looks better than I remember, his jade green eyes ringed by lashes most women would kill for. I feel idiotic for thinking he was actually interested in me. I bet he's besieged by hot women.

Detective Fitzgerald starts by asking Josh about the divorce. Why were he and Tonya splitting up? Where were they both living? Was the divorce amicable? Having already covered this ground with Josh, I've heard all his answers before. I wonder if Tonya really was murdered. Given Detective Fitzgerald's grim demeanor, it looks that way. How did she die? And do the cops really suspect Josh? I think my presence has, if anything, increased Detective Fitzgerald's suspicion.

For some reason, I can't help but think of my mom's dumb tarot reading. Didn't she warn me about weird, negative events and rushing into things without proper consideration? I suppress a little shiver. There's no heat in this room. I wish I'd worn a thicker sweater instead of this flimsy (but flattering) lamb's wool one.

"When did you last see her?" Detective Fitzgerald asks Josh. The heavy bags beneath his eyes, together with his drooping jowls, give him the doleful look of a basset hound.

"Sunday, August 26th," says Josh, answering so quickly it's obvious he prepared in advance. "In the early evening. She came out to the marina. I'd just taken some customers salmon fishing. We were cleaning the fish and Tonya showed up."

"And how was she?"

Josh shrugs. "She was upset," he says. "But she was mad at me a lot, lately."

We all wait for Josh to explain. He runs a hand through his hair. I, too, would like to touch it.

"She wanted money," he says. "One of her credit cards got cut off. I was annoyed because she was yelling at me in front of my clients. We'd just had a great day fishing, and then she had to show up and cause a big scene." Josh shakes his head. "She could be really unreasonable, you know?"

"Then what happened?" asks Detective Fitzgerald.

"I gave her some cash and told her I'd transfer some more into her account," says Josh. "And I told her to watch her expenses." He takes a swig of water. "Her spending was crazy. She'd just buy anything that caught her eye without checking the price tag or even thinking about whether she really liked it. She's got boxes of stuff with the price tags still on! I told her she had a shopping addiction and ought to get help."

"How about the night of Monday, August 27th?" asks Detective Fitzgerald. "Where were you?"

Josh squints at a wall, looking baffled. "Um, I don't remember."

"You were seen at Oak Bay Marina around 7:00 p.m.," says Detective Fitzgerald. "Does that refresh your memory?"

"Oh yeah, I went out on my boat," says Josh. He nods, like it's just come back to him. "I cruised out toward Trial Island, tried a bit of fishing, and cruised back."

"At night?" Detective Fitzgerald's jowls quiver ominously. "Was anyone with you?"

Josh frowns. "No," he says. "It was still light out for about half the trip. I left the marina around seven fifteen and got back maybe ten forty-five. I remember because the eleven o'clock news was on when I was loading my gear into the car."

"Did you see Tonya?"

Josh swallows hard. "No," he says. "But I was looking for her."

This is news to me. Detective Fitzgerald looks equally intrigued. "How do you mean?"

"She called me around nine thirty. The mobile reception wasn't great. She said she wanted to see me. She sounded . . ." Josh frowns. "Upset and really insistent." He takes another sip of water, slips out of his jacket, and lays it across the bench seat. There's a dark patch on the back of his white shirt. I realize that, while I find the room cold, he's sweating.

"I told her I was on the boat and would be in by 11," he says. "She said she'd meet me at the marina. I told her to leave it till tomorrow, but she said no, it couldn't wait."

Detective Fitzgerald is sitting perfectly still. I have an unwelcome vision of a bird of prey, coasting without moving a muscle before it suddenly plummets. "Yet you say she wasn't there?" he asks quietly.

Josh shakes his head. "No. I tried to call her mobile a few times but it was switched off. I hung around for . . ." There's a guilty look on his face. "Maybe five minutes. I was tired and annoyed. See, it was just like Tonya to change her mind. I thought she'd found someone else to distract her and not bothered to call me back." He studies his hands. "I just didn't worry."

"But she sounded upset?"

Josh fingers his TAG Heuer diving watch. "Yes," he says, slowly. "But Tonya loved drama. I figured it was nothing." He pinches the top of his nose. "I should have gone by the house, tried to find her."

"So you didn't see her car?"

"No," says Josh. "I was parked near the front, but I'm fairly sure the lot was empty." He shuts his eyes. "Wait, I think there was a pickup truck over in the back right corner. Probably some kids making out. I didn't pay attention, just loaded my stuff into the back and sat listening to the news for a few minutes."

Detective Fitzgerald shuffles some papers. "Did anyone see you?"

"I doubt it," says Josh. "I didn't see anyone."

"And where did you go next?"

"I went home."

"You didn't stop at 7-Eleven or get gas?"

Josh shakes his head.

"Which way did you drive? You live in James Bay, right?"

"Yes," says Josh. "I'm renting a place on Montreal Street. Tonya is . . ." He swallows hard. "Was living in our house in Uplands. I took the scenic route along Beach Drive."

Detective Fitzgerald raises an eyebrow. "Why'd you go that way?" he asks. "It was dark, wasn't it?"

"It's a nicer road," says Josh. "And at night there aren't any tour buses or pensioners driving twenty."

Detective Fitzgerald scratches his chin. "Doesn't the scenic route pass by Hollywood Crescent?"

I wonder where he's going with this. Josh doesn't answer. I see something—annoyance, or maybe fear—ripple across his face. He grips the edge of the picnic table.

"Alana Mapplebee owns a place on Hollywood," says Detective Fitzgerald. "Did you stop off and see her?"

"No!" says Josh. He now looks openly irritated. "Like I told you, I went home. I was tired." I try to meet Josh's eyes but he won't look at me.

"What's your relationship with Miss Mapplebee?" asks Detective Fitzgerald. I turn to see Colin Destin staring at me.

Josh clears his throat. "We're friends," he says. "She sold me the house in Uplands."

"Nothing more?"

Seated at this picnic table, Josh suddenly resembles a small schoolboy squirming at his desk. He studies the table's scratched surface, then tugs at his shirt's collar. "We were, uh, involved," he says. "Romantically."

I feel my own face redden. So Chantelle Orker was right. When I'd asked Josh if he'd had an affair he'd denied it. He straight-out lied to me. Why did I believe him?

For the first time, I see satisfaction in Detective Fitzgerald's grey eyes, although his smile is as frozen as a crocodile's. "Were?" he asks. "You're no longer together? So when did your relationship with Miss Mapplebee start and finish?"

Josh sighs. "We're not together," he says. "We started, er, dating about six months ago." I cross my arms. That was back before he and Tonya were separated. He rubs his temples. "We saw each other for about four months. It wasn't serious. But Alana's going through a tough time, work-wise and . . ." He bites his lip. "Personally too, I guess. I never gave her the idea it was serious, but she's having trouble accepting I don't want to see her anymore."

Detective Fitzgerald wrinkles his nose. I feel like wrinkling mine too. "Are you still seeing her or not?" asks the detective.

"Not," says Josh. "The last time we, er . . . were, um . . ."

"Intimate?"

Josh nods miserably. Detective Fitzgerald clicks his pen. Josh takes a deep breath. "The last time we met was last month." He gives his collar a fresh tug. "But she's still been calling and following me."

"She's stalking you?" asks Detective Fitzgerald. His tone is so neutral it sounds ironic.

Josh shrugs. "Well, yeah, I guess you could call it that. Someone keeps calling me and hanging up. And she seems to turn up every-where I go. Plus she's sent me, um, photos of herself." He's being careful not to look my way. "You know, naked photos."

"But you didn't report any of this?"

Josh looks embarrassed. "No, of course not," he says. "I didn't want to make a big deal of it."

"Did Tonya know about the affair?" asks Detective Destin.

Josh hesitates. If Chantelle suspected, Tonya must have too. When did she learn about the affair?

Josh empties his water glass. "I'm sure she didn't know," he says miserably. "But I felt guilty, which is one of the reasons I decided to file for divorce." He gives me a pleading look. "I wasn't proud of myself, see? I hated that I'd turned into the kind of guy who was cheating on my wife. Alana was a wake-up call. It was time to admit that my marriage was a joke." He spreads his hands on the picnic table. I'm amazed by their size. I look away. I have an unwelcome vision of those hands throttling Tonya.

Maybe Detective Fitzgerald has the same thought, or maybe he'd been planning this attack all along. He leans forward, his face grim, and slides a photo across the table. I freeze in horror, as does Josh, the photo showing Tonya's body, bloated and bleached-looking, facedown on a metal table. She's wearing the tattered remnants of a tight, striped minidress, her legs and feet bare and mangled, like fish or crabs have been at her. Detective Fitzgerald slaps down another image: a close-up of the back of Tonya's head, a dark splotch in her wet, tangled hair, a large gold hoop in one hideously swollen ear.

Josh recoils in shock and presses a hand to his mouth.

"Did you do this?" rasps Detective Fitzgerald.

Josh leans back like he's been punched. "Of course not!" he says. "My God!" He turns away, his face ashen. "How could you even think that?"

When no one answers, he takes a deep breath, composing himself. I don't know if the detectives are convinced, but his shock and horror seem genuine. If this is staged, he should have been the one pursuing acting.

Josh rubs his eyes. "I was sick of Tonya's drama, but I never, ever wished her dead." His voice shakes. "I would never have hurt Tonya. Never. And I never emotionally abused her or any of that shit she accused me of."

"But you did cheat on her."

Josh's nostrils flare. He stands up. "Is this over yet?"

Detective Destin rises too. They're around the same height, and look equally fit. The two men glare at each other. If this were a bar, I'd be ducking.

I rise unsteadily to my feet. "Are you charging Mr. Barton?" I ask.

Detective Fitzgerald's grey eyes flick my way. "No," he says. "We're just doing our job, Miss Wong."

He turns back to Josh. "Stay where we can find you, Mr. Barton."

Josh is stepping out the door when Colin calls out to him. "Mr. Barton. Sorry, wait!" He sounds apologetic. "There's one more thing. It's important."

Josh swings around, nostrils flared. "What?" he asks, angrily.

"I know it's upsetting," says Colin Destin. "But could you look at those photos again? A possible motive is robbery, and we need to know if anything's missing. Some of Tonya's jewelry, perhaps?"

Josh's face loses even more color.

"We found a purse, with her ID, in the bay," continues Colin. "Orange and pink. Marc Jacobs?"

Looking shaky, Josh returns to the interview table. He doesn't look at Fitzgerald. I retake my seat beside him.

Detective Destin extracts the crime scene photos from their envelope, again. Josh's hands tremble as he leafs through them. At a close-up of a ravaged hand, he stops. His lower lip quivers. "She usually wore her engagement ring," he says. "A six-carat yellow diamond. It was square." His Adam's apple bobs. "Here, her left hand is bare."

Detective Fitzgerald makes a note of this. "Okay. We'll look for it," he says, curtly. "We haven't finished searching her residence. Can you think of anything else of value that's missing?"

Josh shakes his head. "I don't know. She had a lot of jewelry."

Colin looks thoughtful. "What was it worth, a ring like that?"

"I bought it for a hundred and forty thousand."

Colin blinks, as if blinded by just the thought of that much bling. "Canadian?"

"No, U.S."

I start to do the conversion in my head but give up. Who cares? Whatever the exchange rate, that's a lot of zeros.

Detective Destin thanks Josh for his time. It's a relief when he slides the pictures back into the envelope. "We'll be in touch," he says. He escorts us back down the long hall to the lobby.

I've stopped to say goodbye to Detective Destin when Josh rushes away, like he can't stand another second in this place. I turn to see him race into the street. It's raining harder now and he's forgotten his cap, raincoat, and umbrella.

With a last nod to Colin Destin, I retrieve Josh's and my stuff, then scurry after Josh. By the time I manage to raise my umbrella, I'm soaked again. Josh is at least half a block ahead of me, practically running. "Hey Josh! Wait up!" I call, but he doesn't hear. His car is parked in a pay-lot on Store Street. The wind keeps catching my umbrella. I stagger after him.

Josh reaches his car and stops. I hurry up behind him, but he doesn't react. He's just standing there, bareheaded in the pounding rain, with his keys in his hand. "Josh?" I ask again. The wind off the harbor is cold. I use my free hand to hold my jacket shut. I never got a chance to button it. Rain is blowing in under my umbrella, stinging my eyes.

It's only when I'm standing next to him that I can see what he's staring at: there's a big heart fashioned from red roses on the hood of his grey SUV. It's the kind of thing people put on wedding cars, except these roses have been splattered with black paint. Is this a sick joke? The effect is more sinister than romantic. "Jesus! Who did this?" I gasp. I look around. No one else is in sight.

A muscle in Josh's jaw jumps. Over by Value Village some seagulls are shrieking. A floatplane is chugging overhead, preparing to land in the inner harbor. I wait for the noise to lessen before repeating my question. "Josh?" I ask, but he doesn't turn. "Do you know who did this?"

When he looks my way, his face is as grey as the sky. He sweeps a hand through his wet hair. "Do you think A . . . Alana did it?" he asks hoarsely.

I shrug. Based on what he told Detective Fitzgerald it seems highly likely. How many romantic stalkers could the guy have? "Could it be someone else?" I ask, and Josh bites his lower lip. He barely seems to notice the water dripping into his blue eyes.

"No, I don't mean this," he says, nodding toward the grim floral display. He places a hand on his car's hood, as though suddenly dizzy. "I meant Tonya." He blinks, his eyes haunted. "Do you think Alana killed her?"

A cold wind is blowing in off the water, a sudden gust turning my umbrella inside out. I struggle to shut it. Rivulets of black paint drip off the roses on the SUV's hood.

Through a curtain of wet hair and rain, I see Josh grimace. Before I can stop him, he starts plucking handfuls of black flowers off the hood, his movements frenzied. "That bitch!" he says, tossing the flowers onto the pavement. "Oh God. This is all my fault!" He stops as suddenly as he began. He presses a fist to his lips, then bows his head. While black paint stains his fingers, his knuckles are bone white. Maybe that's rain in his eyes, or tears. His wide shoulders shake.

I want to comfort him, but don't dare. Faced with his furious grief, I feel helpless—and alarmed. That big fist pressed to his lips is like a grenade, ready to explode.

Out in the street a car honks. Josh shivers, then seems to remember where he is. He lowers his fist and turns to me, blinks. "I'm sorry," he says.

"Don't be," I say, although I'm not sure what the apology's for. Because he lost it? Because he lied to me? I nod toward the soggy flowers, now scattered on the wet pavement. "We need to tell the police about this," I say, then take a deep breath. "And Josh, if there were other women, the cops will find out. You have to tell them."

He shakes his head vigorously. "No! There weren't!" His face crumples, beseeching. "I'm not like that, Toby."

I nod. "Okay." But do I believe him? While his grief seems genuine, he lied to me about his affair with Alana. Again, I recall Chantelle Orker's warning, not to get sucked in by Josh's charm. Behind that handsome face, what else is he hiding?

CHAPTER NINE:

ON THE CASE

Quinn and I are in the baby section of The Bay, near a shelf displaying electric breast pumps. I've just finished telling her about finding the creepy rose-heart stuck onto Josh's car three days ago.

"That's insane," says Quinn. "I mean it rained all day Wednesday. What kind of person would stand out in the pouring rain sticking black flowers onto their ex's car?"

"Would you do it in the sunshine?" I ask, but Quinn ignores me.

"Did you call the cops?"

"I did," I say. "But not right away. By the time I called, Josh had already pulled all the flowers off his car."

Quinn gives me a disapproving look. "Seriously? But why? They were evidence supporting his claim about being stalked," she says. "There could have been fingerprints on the tape or something."

"He just saw them and freaked out," I say. "He said maybe Alana had killed Tonya and it was all his fault."

Quinn picks up a boxed breast pump. "Why would Alana Mapplebee kill Tonya?" When I don't say anything she snorts. "Ech. He was sleeping with her, wasn't he?" In the next aisle over, another pregnant woman glances our way, her face curious, yet disapproving.

"Shhhh," I say, and lower my voice. "Josh is my client. You know I can't discuss his private life."

"He *was* your client," says Quinn smugly. "He's not getting divorced anymore. But whatever, I can guess the whole story. Guys like Josh are so pathetically predictable. I mean, come on, Alana Mapplebee?"

"Well, Dan dated her, didn't he?" I ask somewhat defensively. The fact that Quinn's cool brother was with Alana makes me feel a tiny bit better about Josh having slept with her. Dan, after all, is proof that even nice guys can fall for bimbos.

Quinn rolls her eyes. "Exactly. My brother's a smart guy and Alana's, well . . ." She grabs another breast pump from the shelf, frowning as she scans the box's back cover. The front bears a photo of a blonde woman with what appears to be a set of plastic funnels festooned with rubber tubes clutched to her breasts. Japanese sex toy meets dairy farm.

"Alana's what?"

"A total idiot," says Quinn. "Her I.Q. is smaller than her bra size."

"But is she crazy?" I ask. "What was she like with Dan? Did he ever say anything?"

When Quinn replaces the box I catch sight of the price tag. Four hundred bucks for what looks like a torture device. I feel queasy.

Thankfully, Quinn has moved on toward a shelf of baby monitors. I follow shakily. At least the baby monitor boxes bear photos of babies sleeping like proverbial babies.

"She dumped him," says Quinn. "This was back when Dan was even more broke than he is now, back when he was waiting tables and writing screenplays at night. One minute they were all loved up, and then the next minute, she met some old guy with a mansion in Uplands and—poof—Dan was history."

"So she's a gold digger?"

Quinn hands me the baby monitor she's selected. She needs to keep both hands free to grab other purportedly essential baby items. I had no idea that reproduction required so much expensive paraphernalia. And we're not the only ones shopping. I've never seen so many women in various stages of pregnancy.

"For sure," says Quinn. "Like the guy she dumped Dan for was old . . . I mean *really* old, like eighty-something and totally decrepit." She examines a massive bottle-sterilizer and frowns. When I see the price tag I frown too. "I don't know how the old dude made his bazillions, but he was loaded." She struggles to remember. "I think he was in fertilizer or something. Or was it pest control? You know, roaches and—"

I break in. "So what happened?"

Quinn passes me the bottle-sterilizer. I balance it on one barely-there hip with the baby monitor set precariously on top. Quinn adds a box of breast pads to this stack. I look for some staff member to help, but there aren't any. They ought to supply carts in this section.

"The old guy died of a heart attack two weeks before their wedding," says Quinn. "It must have been a huge blow to Alana, since, if he'd held on for another fortnight, she'd have been entitled to major moola."

"Well, Josh is seriously rich," I say. "Maybe Alana felt that, with Tonya out of the way, she had a good shot at becoming the next Mrs. Barton."

Quinn peers at me. "Sounds possible," she says. "Or maybe Tonya and Alana got into some kind of argument. They'd be natural enemies, seeing as they were competing for the same section of the food chain. Dan did say that Alana has a vicious temper." She doubles back toward the breast pump section. The aisles seem extra wide in here, no doubt to accommodate the extra-wide pregnant women.

Quinn's finally made her choice when my cell phone rings. The mere sight of Josh's name on my phone's little screen gives me a thrill. I bite my lip, aware that this is getting out of hand. Having a schoolgirl crush on Josh was bad enough back when I was a schoolgirl; having one now is tragic. Time to nip this crush in the bud. First off, Josh is—or rather was—my client. Second, he has a clear preference for large-breasted blondes. And third, he is the prime suspect in a murder case.

I take a deep breath and answer.

If Quinn weren't busy talking to a woman who's expecting twins the week before her, I know she'd be eavesdropping. She'd be giving me a weird look too, because she knows me well enough to notice that my voice sounds strained. But luckily, Quinn's busy discussing the danger of soft cheeses, so at least I can pretend I sound normal. "Yeah, and no Gorgonzola," says Quinn, savoring every syllable.

"Or Camembert," says the other pregnant lady. I can hear the lust in their voices.

"Toby?" says Josh. "I've been trying to call you for the past half hour."

"Oh. Okay. What's up?" I try to zap the flutter of happiness that's resulted from Josh sounding so grateful to have reached me.

"The police have a search warrant to search my house and boat," he says. "They're going to start with the *Great Escape*. I'm on my way to the marina. Could you please meet me there?"

Her forbidden cheese-porn conversation finished, Quinn is now unashamedly eavesdropping. Seeing my shocked expression she looks quizzical. "Who is it?" she mouths. I shake my head and ignore her. I have to think here. Josh, clearly, needs a criminal lawyer. I'd better call Jackie.

When I tell Josh that I'll call him back in five minutes he sounds resigned. The second I hang up, Quinn is all over me. I hold up a hand. "Wait," I say. "I have to call your mom. It's important."

"Fine," says Quinn. "But could you call her from the food court? I have to sit down." She points to her Croc-encased feet. "I know it's the ultimate pregnant lady cliché, but my feet are killing me."

Luckily, there's no lineup at the till. Maybe all the pregnant ladies clogging the aisles are just window shopping. I dump all of Quinn's boxes on the counter.

"Let's go," I say, when she's retrieved her ready-to-combust credit card. I grab her bulging bags in one hand, and use the other to dial Jackie's number. As we stagger toward the food court, I fill Jackie in on Josh and Tonya. "He obviously needs a good defense lawyer, so I thought of you," I say. "Any chance you could help this guy?"

Jackie sighs. "You know I'm out of commission," she says. "I can barely make it down the hall to pee. And the reason it took me so long to answer is that I kept dropping the phone." She laughs wryly.

"Don't you have an assistant?" I ask. "An intern or someone who could run around for you?"

"I wish," says Jackie. "I'm starting to get addicted to Dr. Oz."

We've reached the food court. I dump Quinn's shopping bags on a table and take a seat. Quinn plods off toward Dairy Queen. I hope she'll buy me a Blizzard. "How about my partner Lionel?" asks Jackie. "He's every bit as experienced as I am. Want me to call him for you?"

"I guess so," I say. I had, I realize, been counting on Jackie's acceptance and can't help but feel that her refusal is bad news for Josh. I fight down a surge of worry. Why do I care so much about this guy? It's not like I even know him.

Jackie sounds thoughtful. "Is this man a friend of yours?"

"Mmm, sort of," I say. "We met as teenagers, at summer camp. Remember the year Quinn and I went to camp?"

"Yes," says Jackie. "And you don't think he did it?"

"No," I say. "I don't think he did." At the next table over two teenagers are making out. I'm reminded of me and Josh. The kids beside me look about the same age, fourteen or fifteen, max. Surely, they're too young for that much tongue-action! I look the other way.

When Quinn comes back—bearing, hallelujah, two Reese's Pieces Blizzards—I see her notice the amorous teens too. I wonder if it occurs to her that fourteen years from now the occupant in her belly might be just like them.

Jackie clears her throat. "Well, you know," she says. "I guess I could ask Mel and Philippa to loan you to me. If you're not too busy over there? You could act as second chair." She laughs. "If you have any interest in being my personal slave, that is. Your first task would be to remove the TV set from my house before what's left of my brains turn to mush."

"Are you serious?" I squeal. "I mean you taking on Josh's defense? And me helping?"

"I don't see why not," says Jackie. "Mel mentioned you were a tad underutilized over there, so far. She's worried you'll get too bored and jump ship, maybe head for one of the bigger firms in Vancouver."

This course of action has crossed my mind. But I don't say anything.

"So what do you think?" asks Jackie. "Or should I call Lionel? He really is excellent. Your friend Josh would be in great hands."

"No way," I say. "I'd much prefer you being involved."

Jackie says she'll call Mel and get back to me in a few minutes. Before signing off, she asks where I am. "What's all that noise in the background?"

Looking around, I see the food court has filled up. I check my watch: 11:45 a.m. I tell her I'm at the mall, baby-shopping with Quinn.

"Ah," says Jackie. "Well at least I'm spared that. I guess there's a silver lining to being laid up after all. Has she managed to decide on anything yet?"

"I heard that, Mom," says Quinn.

I wonder what else she overheard.

"Oops, gotta go," says Jackie. "I'll call you right back, Toby."

I turn to see the teen lovers still going at it. They make an odd couple, the girl wearing black and white striped leggings that emphasize her stocky legs, and the boy in the tall, gangly stage. I can feel Quinn staring at me. "So," she says, when I can't put off looking at her any longer. "Now you've roped my mom into this . . ." She shrugs. "This thing you have with Josh Barton."

I put down my Blizzard. "What thing?" I ask. "What are you talking about?"

"Oh, come on," says Quinn. "I know you're still totally attracted to him."

I don't know whether it's outrage or embarrassment or both that cause my face to go red, but it does. "So what," I say, trying to deflect attention from Quinn's latest insight. "You really think he killed Tonya?"

Before she can answer, Jackie calls me back. "Mel and Philippa are all aboard," she says. "We'll talk about fees and how Greene & Olliartee will be paid for your time later."

"Money's not a problem," I say. "Josh has plenty of it."

"Fine, then you'd better get down to his boat and see what the police are up to."

I promise to keep Jackie informed and to bring Josh over to meet her as soon as possible. Before hanging up she tells me to give her love to Quinn.

"I have to go," I tell Quinn. "Your mom has agreed to take Josh on as a client, and the police are searching his boat." I stand up. "I'll help you carry this stuff to your car."

Quinn hauls herself to her feet. My blush has subsided, but I'm still mad at her. We enter the parkade in silence. The elevator is small, old, and smelly. I hold my breath and feel claustrophobic.

Before she gets into her Mini, Quinn lays a hand on my arm. "Thanks for coming today," she says.

I nod. To say it was fun would be too great of a lie. "It was . . . no problem," I say. I wait for her to lower herself into her car, but she just stands there. It's obvious that she wants to say more, but I need to get going. I haven't even called Josh back yet. "Look, I have to go," I say. "I'll call you later."

Quinn tightens her grip on my arm. "Wait, Tob," she says. "I don't want you to take this the wrong way, but just be careful with Josh. Okay?"

"Careful how?" I ask, wondering if she knows something I don't. Has Bruce let something slip? Do the cops have new evidence that Josh did it?

Quinn looks hesitant. "Well, I know you were only a kid, but he did mess you around. And it's not like you've been with a lot of other guys."

This causes my chin to go up. I haven't, as Quinn just pointed out, had many relationships. Only three, for the record, none of which amounted to much—a couple of months with a hard-partying engineering major back in university; a holiday fling with a windsurfing instructor one summer in France; and about a year's worth of dates with a wine merchant who traveled a lot and turned out to be married with three children. Luckily, I never told Quinn about the wine merchant.

She releases her grip on my arm. "What do you know about Josh? Almost nothing, right? Except his bitchy wife was murdered and he was fooling around with Alana Mapplebee." She snorts. "It doesn't make him look good, does it?"

I shove my hands into my pockets. I know Quinn's right. The fact that I harbor *any* romantic hopes about Josh says something really sad about me. A: I am not his type. B: I should be glad of that.

"Quinn," I say, using my best lawyer's voice. "My interest in Josh is purely professional. That's it. You're totally wrong about this."

She eyes me suspiciously but is forced to nod. What can she do if I deny everything? "Good," she says. "Because I don't trust him."

I walk the one level up to my white VW Golf, a car that's plain but reliable. I'm approaching my car when, out of the corner of my eye, I see a man who, from behind, looks like my father. It isn't him, of course, because my dad is now completely bald, while this guy is much younger, with thick, sandy hair. He looks like my dad did when he left—tall, blond, confident, and good-looking. I'm shocked to realize he also looks similar to Josh Barton.

As I drive in tight circles down the parkade's exit ramp, Lady Gaga's "Bad Romance" comes on the radio. I wonder if my dad's desertion messed me up more than I think. Why else would I be attracted to a guy who's not just unobtainable, but possibly dangerous?

CHAPTER TEN:

THE BROTHER'S GRIM

In the bright light of midday, Oak Bay Marina is beautiful, the boats shining white against the dark blue ocean. I pull in past the killer whale statue and park. When I step out of my car, the wind pushes my hair into my face.

I walk past the gift shop and stop, shading my eyes against the sun as I stare down at the docks. Tonya's body was found under a section of the furthest dock, which is still blocked off by yellow police tape. Seeing it fluttering in the breeze gives me a strange feeling. How could someplace so pristine be the setting for a murder?

Descending the ramp, I spy the harbor seals that hang around begging for scraps. Two Asian tourists in matching orange hats are filming them, the creatures gazing up hopefully with their anime-character eyes. Resigned that no treats are forthcoming, one sinks to the bottom, where it lies, slug-like. Even here in the marina the water is clear enough to see the sea floor.

The bigger yachts lie toward the back. As I walk, I dial Josh Barton's number. "I'm here, at the marina," I say. "Where's your boat?"

His voice sounds strained as he gives directions.

The sun warms my face. It's a gorgeous autumn day, and being down on the docks takes me back to my childhood. As kids, Quinn and I spent a lot of time here, lying face-down on the bleached wood and peering through the cracks to watch the fish, crabs, and feathery tube worms that cling to the docks' undersides. I love the gentle sway beneath my feet, the tinkling of the yachts' lines, and the smells of salt and creosote.

I'm passing the Customs Station when I catch sight of Josh. He's standing midway down the last dock, staring at a large motor yacht, which bears the name *Great Escape* in gold letters. A few feet away sprawls a large black poodle, its coat sculpted like topiary. Is that

Tonya's dog? I'd forgotten all about it. Near the end of this same dock hangs a web of yellow police tape.

While I know nothing about boats, the *Great Escape* looks newer, sleeker, and much more expensive than the surrounding craft. White with dark blue trim, I'd guess it to be about seventy feet long. A uniformed cop is standing on the bridge, which is very high up indeed, watching my approach. Josh looks back my way. I wave to him but he doesn't respond, his expression grim. My stomach sinks. He usually seems pleased to see me.

When I get closer, I realize my mistake. It's not Josh but his younger brother, Mike, whom I haven't seen since that summer at camp. Over the years, they've grown more alike, except that Mike now looks older, instead of younger, with deeper lines around his eyes and mouth. I watch as he withdraws a pack of Marlboros from his jacket and lights one, his shoulders hunched against the wind.

"Mike?" I ask, and he looks up and scowls. He must not recognize me, or maybe he's mistaken me for a cop, or God forbid, a reporter.

"Hi," I say, and extend a hand. "I'm Josh's lawyer, Toby Wong. He asked me to meet him here. We went to camp together, way back when. Remember? Camp Wikwakee?"

"Oh, right," says Mike, with zero enthusiasm. He taps his cigarette's ash into an empty Coke can. I'm not sure whether to be relieved or offended that he didn't recognize me from that wretched camp. While I'd like to think I'm better looking than I was as a teen, I haven't changed *that* much. "Josh said you were coming by," he says, already squinting back up at the boat. He nods toward the policemen. "Can you stop these guys?"

"Not if they have a search warrant."

Staring up at the boat, I don't notice the approaching poodle. It now thrusts its pointy nose into my crotch. I try to side-step, but the dog is quick. I back up. "Hey! Down!" It ignores me, its puffball tail thumping happily. I say a silent curse. It's impossible to look dignified with a giant poodle sniffing your crotch.

"Claude! Lie down!" says Mike.

Claude. So it must be Tonya's standard poodle—the one that was with her the night she vanished. If only it could talk.

Mike points at the dog. "Claude! I said lie down!" Beneath its glam-rock hairdo, the dog blinks. Casting a last longing look at my crotch, it flops onto the deck, then embarks on some vigorous flea-scratching. With its close-cropped legs and puffy ankles, it looks utterly ridiculous.

"Er, nice dog," I say, trying to establish some rapport with Mike. "He was Tonya's, right?"

Mike nods. "Yeah, he's a good dog." He glances sideways at the poodle, as though embarrassed. "She got his hair cut like that," he says gruffly. I figured that. "I haven't gotten around to fixing it," he adds.

I wait for him to say more, but he just stamps out his cigarette and stuffs the butt into his Coke can. Moments later, he lights another one, his eyes never leaving the boat. I guess he's worried about his brother.

Following Mike's gaze, I see Detective Fitzgerald, who looks even less impressed by my arrival than Mike had. He summons me over to the boat's metal stairs and hands me the search warrant. It's bright out here and I forgot to bring my sunglasses. I squint at it, the judge's name a tangled scrawl. As expected, the paperwork seems in order.

"Where's Josh?" I ask, after refolding the warrant.

Detective Fitzgerald shrugs. Once again, he resembles an aging basset hound, slow-moving and doleful. "I think he went to the toilet." He gestures vaguely toward the public washrooms up by the coffee shop. I scan the entrance to the dock and, sure enough, there's Josh, descending behind a gaggle of selfie-stick-wielding Japanese tourists. He's got a coffee cup in each hand and a worried frown on his tanned face.

I feel a rush of sympathy. Whether he loved Tonya or not, her death must be a huge shock. And now the cops are searching his boat. How did they get a warrant that fast? The sooner Jackie and I can question Josh, the better.

When he spots me, his face lights up. My own smile is equally huge. I'm absurdly happy that he's pleased to see me.

I'm trying to stop grinning at Josh, when I notice a flurry of activity on board the *Great Escape*. I look up to see a uniformed cop hand something to Detective Fitzgerald. Various officers are gathered around, everyone looking grave yet eager. Over the regular sounds of clanking lines, sloshing water, and seagulls, I can hear low, urgent voices.

Craning my neck, I struggle to see what's aroused so much excitement. Mike is staring too, as is the dog, its tongue like a big, droopy slice of baloney. Being taller than me, I suspect Mike can see. There's a weird look on his face, a mixture of horror and vindication.

Fitzgerald appears at the top of the stairs, looking dour yet triumphant. In his hand, encased in a clear plastic bag, is a large black flashlight. A large and heavy black flashlight. I recall the photo of Tonya's head wound and feel ill. It would make an excellent murder weapon.

This thought has barely registered when I hear footsteps behind me. Turning, I see Josh storming toward us. He looks furious.

Two policemen step off the boat bearing a box full of stuff. I can see stacks of files and a laptop balanced on top. Staring at this box, the veins in Josh's neck stand out. He deposits his coffee cups on an overturned rowboat, rushes past us, and leaps onto the *Great Escape*. "Fitzgerald?" he calls out. "What does my paperwork have to do with Tonya's death?"

The detective materializes at the top of the stairs. "Probably nothing," he says, quietly. "But we're entitled to review it all."

Josh looks ready to answer back when he catches sight of the plastic-wrapped flashlight in the detective's hand. He trips on the metal stair and then catches himself. "Is that . . .? What is . . .?"

Detective Fitzgerald holds up the bagged flashlight. About thirty centimeters long and made of black-painted aluminum, it looks like the sort of thing a night watchman would carry. "Is this yours?"

Josh swallows hard. "No, I don't think so."

"Then how'd it get on your boat?"

Josh looks from me to the cop. He shrugs. "I don't know. Maybe someone else bought it."

Mike hops on board too, pushing past his brother. Seeing the mess the police have made on the back deck, he shakes his head angrily. "Jesus, you'd better not have broken anything." He glares at Fitzgerald. "Are you guys finished yet?"

Squinting against the sun, I see the detective smile, his sad hound-dog face transformed by a sly crocodile grin. "Almost. I think we got what we needed," he says smugly. Again, he raises the flashlight to show Mike. "Do you recognize this?" he asks him.

Mike's eyes skate to Josh, then down to his red sneakers. "No. I mean, I'm not sure. We had a big Maglite on board but who knows if it's that one?" His nervous tone makes it sound like he's lying.

Mike's about to say more but Josh cuts him off. "I'm sure that's not ours. The flashlight we had onboard was all black. That one's got a silver button."

Detective Fitzgerald licks his lips. "I see." Could he possibly sound more ironic?

Despite the warm day I feel cold all over. Josh, on the other hand, is sweating, his handsome features so transformed by anger that, for once, he looks ugly.

We watch the police haul various boxes away. Even the dog seems subdued, its tail thumping feebly, like it wants to remain upbeat but knows it's a losing battle. I give its crinkly ears a rub. The breeze has picked up, the yachts' lines humming eerily. My stomach growls, despite the recent Blizzard. Checking my watch, I'm surprised it's past 1:00 p.m. Is that flashlight the murder weapon? The smug look on Fitzgerald's face worries me.

Without thinking, I find my eyes sliding toward the yellow police tape, flapping in the wind. Except for a large wooden crate, the boards beyond the tape lie bare. While there's no visible sign of what happened, I know Tonya's body was found wedged under the dock. Did she die the Monday night she vanished? Thanks to Google, I've gleaned it's not unusual for a body in frigid water to take days or even weeks to surface. I walk to the tape and stop, then look back at the boat. Was she pushed off the *Great Escape*? I turn to look at the shore.

Scanning the bright green lawns and immaculate houses that line Beach Drive, it's hard to believe a murder happened here. Everything is clean and orderly. Perfect. Or too good to be true. I recall the old adage about Victoria being home to the newly wed and nearly dead. Poor Tonya. Both applied.

CHAPTER ELEVEN

PRIME SUSPECT

What a start to the week. First thing Monday morning, Jackie and I accompanied Josh to the police station for another grilling by Detective Fitzgerald. It went so badly I'm feeling panicky. During the interrogation, the detective gleefully informed us about the lab's findings. The flashlight is indeed the murder weapon. It was found in a box of tools in a locked cupboard in the yacht's engine room, bearing traces of Tonya's blood and tissue.

"I can't believe it," I groan, cutting my raisin snail into quarters. "This looks terrible." I mean the case, not the pastry. What have I dragged Jackie into?

Jackie shrugs. She's sitting in a wheelchair, in a near-empty coffee shop on Government Street. Outside, it's overcast and blustery, with brown leaves skittering along the sidewalk.

Josh is currently in the restroom, where, based on the color of his face when we left the police station, I suspect he's being sick. Jackie, meanwhile, looks perfectly serene. Her tall frame is clad in a navy blue Calvin Klein suit, this polished look only slightly marred by her sling, plaster-encased hand, Sasquatch-sized knee-high plastic boot, and the fluffy red sock covering her broken foot. Her uninjured foot bears a sedate navy pump and is now tapping gently.

"Plenty of people had access to that yacht," she says briskly. "Why would a smart man like Josh hide the bloody flashlight he'd just used to bludgeon his wife on his own boat instead of tossing it? It's not like he couldn't afford a new one."

"So you think he was framed?" I ask hopefully. I like this scenario much better than the one in which the object of my guilty fantasies is a cold-blooded killer. But who could hate Josh that much?

From the look on Jackie's face I know he's out of the bathroom. A minute later Josh takes a seat beside me, his face, beneath his tan, still drained of color. Jackie pushes a cappuccino into his hands and he takes a sip. He looks like he could use some booze in it.

"Why didn't they arrest me?" he asks woefully. His voice, like his eyes, lacks its usual sparkle. "I mean, it's obvious they think I did it. They don't believe a word I say. And now . . ." He swallows hard. "They found the murder weapon on my boat . . ."

Jackie places a consoling hand on his arm. I too, would love to touch him, except my motivations are far from professional. "You sure that Maglite wasn't yours?" she asks. I wait. It'd be bad news if the cops were to find a receipt for it in the papers they'd confiscated, or some CCTV footage of Josh buying it in Canadian Tire.

Josh shakes his hand. "I'm pretty sure mine was solid black and older-looking." He sighs, his temporary conviction evaporating. "But who knows? It was just a flashlight. I never really paid attention."

"Okay," says Jackie. "Who else had access to your boat?" She hands him a pen. "Make a list," she says.

Josh toys with the pen, considering. While he thinks, I look around. Housed in a former garage, this café lies on the edge of Victoria's quaint little Chinatown. Glancing out the window I spy an elderly woman going for a stroll. In her black satin trousers and quilted coat she looks like she stepped out of an old Chinese water-color. Watching this woman fondle some pomegranates outside an Asian grocer, I wonder if I've missed out on my heritage. The full extent of Ivy's Chineseness involves a love of playing cards and an addiction to Kung Pao Chicken. I try to picture myself married to a cute Chinese guy with adorable three-quarter-Chinese kids. Would I have more luck if I dated Asian men? Or am I not Asian enough to appeal to most of them?

This inane train of thought is interrupted by Josh's answer. He's come up with quite a list. "My brother Mike and Aden Macdonald crew for me," he says. "Aden's studying fisheries up at UVic. Young guy, but really solid. Ivan Jenkins—he's a mechanic—and his assistant were on board for a few hours the day after Tonya vanished. We were having engine trouble. And the next day, Louise Dobson came by to measure the front cabin. She's a designer friend of Tonya's I hired to redo the boat's interiors. Plus some guy—Phil or Bill?—installed a new depth-sounder on August 31st. And there are my clients, of course. This time of year the *Escape*'s booked most days. There were three guys from L.A. from August 26th to 30th, two retirees from the prairies from September 1st to 4th . . ." He continues down the list, then rubs his eyes. "I'll have to double-check about the 7th, that's the day before the cops searched my boat. I didn't go out that day." He attempts a smile. "Any idea how long my boat will be impounded? Canceling people's charters has been a nightmare. But that's the least of my problems, right?"

Jackie smiles sympathetically. "It depends what they find," she says. "The forensic team is there now. If it's clean, your boat should be released in a few days." She bends to sip at her latte via a straw, since holding the cup is problematic. I guess Alistair must have helped her to apply mascara and lipstick this morning.

Josh clears his throat. "And if they, you know . . . find something?"

Jackie frowns. "If it's a crime scene, the boat will be impounded for months."

I reflect on the implications. Was Tonya murdered on the boat? Or was she killed elsewhere? I can't imagine her killer carrying her body into the marina. Even at night, he might have been seen. Oak Bay is full of insomniac old people.

When Jackie lets go of her straw, her cast clunks against the table. When I meet Josh's eyes he gives me a wan smile. I fight the urge to reach out and squeeze his hand. Even now, in this grim situation, I feel a magnetic pull between us. I wonder if it's all in my head. Has two straight years without sex mushroom-clouded my judgment?

Outside the café, the elderly Chinese lady has been joined by an equally ancient man and a small boy on a tricycle. The child, who must be their grandson, is dressed like Superman. Watching his chubby peddling legs, I feel oddly wistful. Is Quinn's pregnancy behind this sudden awareness that everyone else my age is married with children? Thirty-three isn't old, but it's not *young* either.

Tearing my eyes off the little Superman, I scan my notes. I have the feeling I've missed something. At the name Louise Dobson I stop reading. Why does that name ring a bell? Then I remember: a pale freckly sickly girl from Camp Wikwakee. She had killer hay fever and was bullied relentlessly by Chantelle and Tonya, who dumped her week's supply of Claritin into the latrine. Was Louise really now part of Tonya's entourage? Talk about a sucker for punishment. And why did Tonya stay in touch with *everyone* from that shitty camp, like that summer was the pinnacle of her lame-o existence?

I rub my forehead. How ironic that I've spent going on twenty years trying to forget everything that happened at Camp Wikwakee only to end up with this case!

Thinking about Louise brings back my final evening at camp, her whine ringing in my ears. "Where are you going, Tobeeeee?"

"Nowhere," I said, just desperate to get away from the everyone, to escape the other kids' knowing glances and that last sight of Josh stepping off the dock into the dark, hand-in-hand with Tonya, her ass as shiny as a candy in its skintight wrapping.

"It's almost curfew!" squealed Louise. We were standing outside the latrines, Louise wearing a long frilly nightie and an expression of self-righteous horror. With that Victorian nightdress and her scant hair in a long skinny French braid, she looked like an extra on *Little House on the Prairie*. I cursed my bad luck at running into her. She was our group's self-appointed monitor, the one who'd be sure to tattle. I blinked the tears out of my eyes. Louise stuck her hands on her straight hips. "If you don't come up now, you'll get in big trouble."

"I'll be there soon!" I lied, already stumbling toward the bushes. My eyes felt hot and heavy with yet more unshed tears. I needed to run. Who knew where? It didn't matter. I couldn't go to bed, not yet. I'd just lie there and replay Josh's betrayal in my head and Tonya's victorious sneer, over and over and over again.

Louise was still calling after me. I spun around. "If Thelma asks, you didn't see me!" I yelled. I backed into the trees. "Go to bed! It's not your problem, Louise!"

While my thoughts are on Louise Dobson, I must be staring at Josh because Jackie throws me a questioning look. I force my gaze to my notes only to feel my eyes like an empty gas gauge determined to swing back his way. Jackie frowns. Does she suspect how I feel about him? Just the thought makes me blush, my face as red as the tacky lanterns the city has hung around Chinatown. "Toby?" she says.

I nod. "Yes?" I'm afraid of what she's about to say to me.

Jackie's deep blue eyes study me, then Josh. Maybe it's my guilty conscience, or maybe there's a warning in her gaze: I can't do my job if I'm emotionally entangled with this guy. "We need to get in touch with everyone who was on board recently," she says, this comment directed at me. I nod. She turns back toward Josh, who looks slightly brighter than a few minutes ago. I guess Jackie's calm, confident manner has reassured him a bit. "Is the boat guarded at night? Who has keys to the cabins? And the engine room?"

"The marina is locked at night, but everyone with a boat knows the code," says Josh. "As for the cabin and locker, well, me, Mike and Aden have keys. And Tonya had one."

Jackie perks up. "Tonya had a key? Do you know where she kept it?"

"On her Chanel keychain," says Josh. "It has a little Eiffel tower charm on it. The keychain also holds the keys to the house and her Mercedes. But she never went near the boat. She gets . . ." He studies his hands. "She got seasick. She hated being out on the water. That was one more thing we disagreed about."

I make a note to check on the whereabouts of the keys. I don't recall seeing them in the police photos of Tonya's purse contents. Jackie slurps up the remains of her latte. Josh checks his watch and looks shocked. "I have to go," he says. "I'm meant to be doing a Skype conference that started ten minutes ago. About my old company."

"Fine. Toby and I will stay and go over some things," says Jackie.

"Can you two meet up later today? There are some issues we need to clear up as soon as possible." She shifts her booted foot and looks from me to Josh. "Routine questions about your finances, Tonya's associates, etcetera."

Josh and I nod. "I'm free after three thirty," he tells me. "What time works for you?" I check my phone's day planner. I'm due in court this afternoon. It'll have to be after work.

"It'd have to be after six," I say. "Maybe dinner?" My heart has picked up speed. I know it's just work but can't help thinking of it as a dinner date. I start mentally flicking through my closet.

"Sure. Call me," says Josh.

He's gathering his things when my cell phone rings. It's my mother. I feel guilty. It's been days since I last called to check on her. "Have I caught you at a bad time?" asks my mom. When I say no, she asks if we're still on for dinner tonight. "Quinn said she'd be over around six," she says cheerily, and I curse my forgetfulness. Because my mom spent the weekend at a yoga retreat, we'd postponed our regular Friday dinner to today. "I thought I'd make paella," she continues.

When I say I can't make it tonight my mom sounds disappointed. I feel terrible. "I'm so sorry, Mom," I say. "But I'm with a client so can I call you later?"

"Why don't you just take Josh to your mom's?" asks Jackie, after I've stashed my phone in my purse. "Running through those questions should take an hour at the most." She turns to Josh. "Toby's mother is hilarious and a great cook." She bends to readjust the sock on her bad foot. "If Alistair hadn't booked us tickets to the symphony I'd invite myself over too." She winks at me. "It's been way too long since my last reading."

I ignore this last comment. Josh looks confused. "Reading?" he asks.

"It's a long story," I say. "You'd better get going."

"Right," he says. "So is that okay if I come for dinner at your mom's?"

I nod. Josh makes meeting my mom sound like no big deal, which it isn't, of course, except that I've never, ever brought a date home. Not that he's a date, I remind myself. He's a client. We're meeting for work. But I still feel thrilled. And nervous. I'm taking Josh Barton home to meet my eccentric mother. I hope she won't embarrass me too much.

When Josh has left, Jackie sighs. "This isn't good," she says. For a horrible, guilty moment I think she's referring to my crush and my face flushes again. But she's just talking about the evidence. "Access to the murder weapon. No alibi. And a great motive."

I nod glumly. "You don't think he did it, do you?"

"Beats me," says Jackie. "But it won't be easy finding a better suspect."

CHAPTER TWELVE:

MYSTERY PACKAGE

After helping Jackie into a cab I walk to Island Deco, the interior design company where Louise Dobson works, on Johnson Street. While the building's worn brick façade advertises its year of construction as 1927, the lobby is starkly modern, with curved white walls, a white desk, and white sofas. In the center of the lobby hangs a spiky red chandelier, and beneath this lies a round carpet printed with red and white swirls, as if blood were dripping off the crystals. It feels like the site of a recent seal kill.

Behind the desk sits a young, dark-haired man who regards me with as much joy as he'd view a stain on his white cashmere sweater. I say I'm here to see Louise and he performs a languid head-roll toward a white sofa.

When Louise steps into the room, I barely recognize her. Back at camp, she was bone-thin, with long, stringy dirty-blonde hair and an even longer list of food allergies. The woman now standing before me is about five-eight and shaped like a barrel, her hair cropped close to her skull and dyed the yellow of instant noodles. What hasn't changed is her coloring—her skin so pale she could pass for an albino were it not for her close-set eyes, which are hazel. Through yellow lashes, she slowly looks me up and down. "Yes?" she enquires. I remember her voice, now surprisingly high for such a large woman.

I stand. "Hi Louise. I'm Toby Wong. I called earlier."

She shows no sign of recognition but extends a cool, floppy hand. I supply the momentum required for a shake. "Oh. Right. This way." I follow her down a long white hall toward her office.

Not surprisingly, Louise is dressed in white, her white pant-suit—combined with her natural pallor—making her body all but invisible in this icy setting. Oddly, her shoes don't match, but are cheap, nasty-looking vinyl loafers the color of old mustard, which slap on the white tiles as she walks. I hurry after her, amazed that, like Mike, she didn't remember me from summer camp.

I step into her office and look around. More white on white. The lack of color is making me nervous. I'm sure to spill something.

"How can I help?" she asks, once we're both seated. She dons a pair of thick white-framed Lanvin glasses and blinks down at me. I wonder if she's near-sighted, far-sighted, or neither. Her expensive glasses might be for effect. She picks up a white and gold pen and twirls it around.

Since I haven't changed *that* much, I'm freshly amazed by her failure to remember me. After all, even though she's tripled in size, I'd still know her if we passed on the street. Is she just too self-absorbed to have really looked at me?

I explain that I'm Josh's lawyer, and that I'm looking into Tonya's murder. Louise's pale-lashed eyes fill with tears. "I . . . I'm finding it so hard to accept," she whispers. "It's so shocking. Who could hurt Tonya? She was such a sweet person." She sets down her pen and removes her glasses to pat the tears from her eyes.

I try to hide my incredulity. Tonya, sweet? Right, like strychnine. "I was hoping you might have some ideas," I say. "Josh mentioned you were friends. Were you close to her?"

Louise replaces her glasses. "We were very close," she says quietly. "After Tonya moved back here she didn't know many people. She missed Los Angeles." She grabs a tissue. "We spent a lot of time together."

"So she confided in you?"

"Oh yes." She gives me a sly smile, obviously proud of having been Tonya's confidante. I wait. Louise waits too. I wonder when she'll decide that enough suspense has built up. She twists the tissue around her big fingers.

Normally, I wouldn't take notes, but I get the feeling Louise would appreciate some props straight out of a TV drama. I pull my notepad from my purse and grab a pen. "Was there anything strange going on with Tonya recently?" I ask. "Anything that might be connected to her death?"

Louise gives a dramatic sigh. After making me wait a few more moments she leans forward, her voice like a stage whisper. "Someone was stalking her!"

Immediately, I think of Alana Mapplebee. "Did Tonya know who it was?"

Louise laces her fingers together. I note that her left hand, like mine, is bare of rings. So she's not married yet. Meanwhile, her other hand features a ring on every digit, including her thumb. There are two chunky silver bands, one ring with a giant turquoise stone, another with an even larger chunk of malachite, a diamond eternity band, and a cushion-cut citrine on her pinkie. What a weird mix! I wonder why she hasn't balanced her hands out a little.

"She thought it might be her ex-boyfriend, a man named Cage. They dated for a while in Los Angeles, before she married Joshua."

Joshua. Is that his full name? "So why would he stalk her now?" I ask. "Did he come to Victoria?"

"He got out of prison a few months ago and sent her an email," says Louise. "Tonya didn't want to see him, but he tracked her down and flew out here. He showed up at her house about a month ago. It really scared her."

Louise's eager tone intensifies my dislike for her. She sounds too excited, as though she's discussing a movie plot instead of the events leading up to her friend's death.

"I don't know why she was with him in the first place," continues Louise, breathlessly. "She said he was like Dr. Jekyll and Mr. Hyde. Really sweet one minute and then . . . psycho."

I perk up. This guy sounds like a great suspect. "Why was he in jail?"

"Cocaine," whispers Louise. "He was a drug dealer. He should have been in for way longer, but his lawyers worked out some deal." She says this last bit accusingly, as though, being a lawyer, I'm personally responsible for this scumbag's reduced sentence. "From what

Tonya told me, he had a violent past. He used to hit her." She bites her pallid lip. "She was petrified of him."

I ask what Tonya's stalking entailed and Louise shudders. "Late-night phone calls with nobody on the line. The theme song from *Halloween* on her answering machine. And someone put a Barbie doll covered with fake blood in her letter box."

I nod grimly. Tonya *had* borne more than a slight resemblance to Barbie. "Did Tonya tell the police?" I ask.

"I told her to," says Louise. "I don't understand why she didn't. Maybe she was worried about making Cage even crazier. She said the police couldn't protect her anyway. Or else . . ." She shrugs. "Oh, I don't know."

"Or else what?" I ask, doing my best to sound calm and patient. By now, I'm thoroughly tired of Louise's coy mannerisms. She seems to view Tonya's death as the most exciting thing that's happened in years. I bet Detective Fitzgerald wrote her off as a drama queen.

"Well, maybe Tonya didn't want the cops poking around in her business."

"What business was that?"

"Oh, nothing really." She plucks another tissue from her white snakeskin purse, which, if the discreet nameplate is to be believed, must have cost a fortune. Or is it a fake Chinese copy? "Tonya respected people's privacy." She smiles sadly and snaps the purse shut. "She was a *very* private person, you know."

I nod as though I'm buying this. I'd bet a kidney that Tonya was a huge gossip, and that Louise is too. Tonya would have loved describing her racy transgressions, while Louise would have lapped her tales up, eager to live vicariously and thrilled to be Tonya's trusted confidante. "So she didn't kiss and tell?" I ask.

Behind her designer glasses, she looks thrilled but indignant. "No! Of course not!"

I wait a few beats. "I know she was having an affair," I say. I know nothing of the sort, but figure Louise might bite.

Sure enough, her eyes widen. I can see the conflict in her face.

Does she say nothing and leave me to think that Tonya left her in the dark? Or does she tell all, thereby proving that she and Tonya were inseparable, after all?

"Tonya got hit on all the time, and it's not like Josh was there for her," says Louise. "She didn't want to move back here, remember? And he was always out on that stupid boat. She felt neglected, right?"

I nod like this makes sense. "Was it serious?"

"It wasn't like she was planning to leave Josh for him," says Louise. Interesting. So this relationship, like Josh's affair with Alana, must have preceded Josh and Tonya's separation. "She just needed someone to . . . you know . . . give her some attention," continues Louise. "She said he was sexy. And I guess it was exciting, keeping it secret, and all." She licks her lips. "He was devoted to her, buying her all sorts of presents."

I wonder how much of this is true and how much is Louise Dobson's fantasy. I bet she could use some romantic attention. Then I remember that, not having had sex in two years, I'm in no position to judge.

Louise looks wistful. I bet she's imagining herself in and out of Tonya's shoes (and clothes), while conveniently forgetting that Tonya's romantic tryst might have killed her.

"So who was it?" I ask, and Louise looks up sharply. For the first time since we've met, her eyes actually focus on me. "I . . . I thought you said you knew." She sounds petulant.

"I know she was having an affair," I say evenly. "But not the guy's identity."

Louise scowls. I realize that, like me, she has no idea who Tonya was sleeping with. She looks at her desk. "She called him, um, Package. Because he had a big, you know . . ."

"Package?"

Louise nods. She looks both annoyed at my failure to enlighten her and embarrassed that Tonya hadn't divulged all. I guess Tonya didn't trust her to keep her mouth shut, after all.

"Any idea how long they were together?"

"It started a couple weeks after she moved here," says Louise. "And she broke it off after Josh filed for divorce."

Having learned that I don't know the identity of Tonya's mystery lover, Louise seems less eager to talk. At any moment I expect her to look at her watch and claim another appointment.

"Why'd she end it?" I ask. Sure enough, Louise checks her watch. "This could be *really* important," I say, doing my best to sound as dramatic as possible. "Jilted lovers can turn violent."

Louise purses her pale lips. "You think Package might have killed her?"

I nod. I'm seriously *hoping* Package killed her. Or Alana Mapplebee. Or Cage. Or just about anybody, except Josh Barton.

Louise runs a hand through her cropped 'do. "Tonya felt he was getting possessive. She still hoped she and Josh could work it out and didn't want Pack, er . . ." She waves a hand. "This other guy to get his hopes up."

"So he wanted to, what, marry her?" I try not to sound too skeptical.

Louise nods sadly. "Yes. He was obsessed with her. When she broke it off, he was devastated."

I grit my teeth. While Josh and Tonya hadn't had much in common, apparently they'd both loved and left people who couldn't live without them. "Obsessed?" I ask.

Louise nods vigorously. "He couldn't understand why, now that her marriage was over, she couldn't be with him," she whispers.

I finish up my notes and close my notebook. It could be a motive. After I've picked up my purse and stood up, I turn back and ask if there's anything, anything at all, that might shed light on Package's identity.

Louise studies her fancy fountain pen and shrugs. For once, this gesture looks genuine. "She said he was almost as good in bed as Josh."

"Great," I say. "So we're looking for a handsome, generous, well-endowed man who's good in the sack and wants to commit."

For the first time, Louise actually smiles, which shaves a good decade off her face. "Ha! That should narrow it down," she says. "From what I hear, they're not so common."

I smile too. "But Tonya seemed pretty good at finding them."

There's a flash of something behind Louise's white frames. Anger? Contempt? She's not smiling anymore. I bet she was jealous of her friend. Listening to Tonya brag would drive anyone nuts. But crazy enough to bash her pal with a heavy-duty flashlight?

I thank Louise for her help, then hand her my business card. "If you do think of anything else, please call me."

Louise squints down at me. "Wait." She cocks her head. "Haven't we met before?"

I smooth down my jacket. "I don't think so."

"That's odd," says Louise. "Because I went to summer camp with this Chinese girl who looked just like you. She got expelled for—"

I walk out before she can finish.

CHAPTER THIRTEEN:

PARANORMAL ENERGY

After leaving Island Deco, I spend the rest of the afternoon in court for a child custody and support hearing. It's a relief when it's over, with both parents agreeing on shared custody.

I've been too busy to think about Josh, and am stunned to discover that it's 5:43 p.m. I'm supposed to meet him at my mom's place in seventeen minutes.

Luckily, I always stash my toiletries bag in my briefcase. After brushing my teeth and combing my hair in the courthouse's echoing washroom, I'm faced with a dilemma. Despite my just-for-court lipstick, I look washed out in the long bathroom mirror. Since I'll be seeing Josh, I'd like to apply some makeup but don't want to arouse my mother's suspicions. She's convinced that *all* cosmetics— no matter what the label says—are tested on animals, and won't put anything on her skin that she hasn't cooked up using herbs and berries.

After settling on blush and a little more lipstick, I study my face in the mirror: wide cheeks, small nose, plump lips, narrow eyes, heavy eyebrows. It's what my mom calls a "strong face," and while she means it as a compliment, I'd rather be described as "pretty." Re-checking my watch, I'm dismayed to see it's already five fifty-four. I stuff my cosmetics bag into my briefcase, give my hair one last, desperate fluff, and race for the staircase.

When I pull up in front of my mom's house Quinn's Mini is already there, as is a small black Porsche. It must be Josh's. Alarmed that he beat me here, I race up the steps. I ought to have been here to introduce him to my mother.

I needn't have worried, because when I push open the front door, I can hear Josh and Ivy laughing in the kitchen. "Oh hi honey," says my mother, when she notices me. "We were just talking about you."

The way she says it makes me cringe. What, exactly, has she been telling Josh?

"We were talking about Camp Wikwakee," says Josh smoothly. "How you and I met there."

I freeze. Doesn't Josh remember how I left camp in disgrace? Why would he mention Camp Wikwakee to my mom? She and I never talk about it. I'm sure it's something we'd both rather forget.

But now, rather than looking ill at ease or disapproving, my mom has a happy smile on her face. "I can't believe you've known Josh for so many years and never brought him home before," says my mother in mock outrage. My blush deepens. I go to the sink and help myself to a glass of water.

"We only met again recently," I say, just to fill the ensuing silence. "Josh is my client."

"Oh, you're getting divorced?" asks my mother cheerily. I cringe again. But Josh doesn't look remotely put out. He starts to say yes and realizes his mistake. Since I'd rather not discuss Tonya's death with my mom, I interrupt and ask where Quinn is.

"I sent her to the store for lemons," says my mom. "She wanted a walk." She checks a pot on the stove, allowing the smells of seafood and white wine to escape. Dressed in a blue tunic and denim shorts, my mother is lightly tanned, no doubt from working in her garden. I'm relieved to see how well she looks. Over the top of her tunic is a red apron that bears the words: *Only boring women have immaculate homes.* A quick scan of the kitchen confirms how interesting she must be.

"Can I help with anything?" offers Josh. In a long-sleeved white t-shirt and loose pants he looks summery and relaxed, like he's spent the day surfing instead of meeting with cops, investors, and lawyers.

I say no but my mom says sure. She hands him a bowl of romaine and instructs him to break it into small pieces.

"How about me?" I ask. Being near Josh leaves me unsure what to do with my hands. I may as well chop or mix something.

"You can spoon the blackberries in the fridge into four cups," says my mother. "Use the glass ones from Grannie Mei Li's cabinet."

Ivy's kitchen is tiny, so there's not much space, especially after Quinn gets back. At the sight of Josh, her eyes widen. "Oh hello," she says. "I'm—"

"Quinn," says Josh. "You haven't changed a bit." He gestures toward her belly and laughs. "Well, maybe a little."

"Toby told me you'd moved back here," says Quinn. She hands my mom the lemons. Dressed in a clingy yellow dress she looks a bit lemon-like herself. In the few days since I last saw her, her belly has had a major growth spurt. She turns back to Josh. "I was sorry to hear about Tonya."

"Thanks," says Josh. "It's rough, not knowing why she died." He looks at me when he says this. There are tears in his blue eyes.

Quinn, I know, isn't convinced, but my mom looks concerned. "Oh dear," she says. "Are you recently bereaved?"

"It was on the news," says Josh. "The woman who died in the marina? That was my wife . . ." His voice falters. "Well, ex-wife."

"I'm so sorry," says my mother. I watch her lead him onto the back deck, nodding in sympathy and patting Josh on the shoulder. I envy their easy rapport. People find my mom easy to talk to. I guess being a good listener is essential in her line of work. But why couldn't she have become a shrink or a counselor instead of a fortune teller?

Quinn hands me a glass of white wine. She peers at the label. "Did Josh bring this?" she asks.

I take a sip. I'm no sommelier, but it tastes a lot better than the plonk we usually buy. "Mmmm. He must have," I say. After we're both seated, I pass Quinn my glass. "You have to try it." She starts to protest but I cut her off. "One sip won't hurt the baby."

"Wow, that is good," says Quinn. She takes another sip. I pour out a quarter of a glass and hand it to her, then clink my glass against hers.

"Almost thirty-seven weeks," I say, because I've learned to talk in weeks instead of months. Quinn seems to know how many minutes there are between any given moment and her due date. "You're in the home stretch."

"Right," says Quinn. She stares glumly at her belly. "And we still haven't agreed on any baby names."

I take a larger swig. Is there no way to avoid this topic?

In recent months, Quinn has grown addicted to various baby name websites. She has spent weeks scrolling through name lists, her suggestions growing more and more desperate. I've received text messages at 3:00 a.m. featuring queries like: *Thomasina for a girl?* or *How about Igor?* I doubt there are *any* names she hasn't considered yet.

"If it's a girl Bruce likes the name 'Aurora,'" says Quinn. She makes a face. "I think it sounds like a hooker."

I nod. "Yup. Stripper name. What do you like?"

"I think it's a boy," she says sullenly.

I take another gulp of wine. We've had this discussion before. And before that. "Why don't you just get an ultrasound and find out for sure?" I ask. "At least that way you'd only have to trawl through half as many baby names."

"We want it to be a surprise," says Quinn. I roll my eyes. She takes another small sip of wine and scowls at me. "It's more fun that way."

I'm saved from answering by the return of Josh and my mom. "Who's hungry?" she asks. She lifts the lid off a pot on the stove. Josh carries a bowl of salad to the table.

"I'm starving," says Quinn.

"Same," says Josh. "It smells delicious."

My mother places a large pot of seafood paella on the table, then directs Josh toward the seat next to mine. After we're all seated, Josh proposes a toast to new and old friends.

"And to justice for poor Tonya," says my mother. We all sip from my mom's random assortment of wine glasses.

I hold out my plate and my mom spoons some paella onto it. "After dinner I'm going to try to contact her," she says cheerily. I fail to catch on. Quinn, too, is confused, because she asks my mom whom she's talking about.

Ivy looks up from the paella. "Tonya," she says matter-of-factly.

Something catches in my throat. "What?" I croak.

"I'm going to try to contact Tonya's spirit," says my mother. She talks slowly yet cheerfully, as though I'm a small child.

"You can't be serious," I say.

"Why not?" asks Josh. I turn to stare at him. "What could it hurt?" he asks.

My reputation, I think.

Quinn nods. "Yeah, I guess it's worth a try."

I look from Quinn to Josh to my mother, unsure whom I'm most disappointed with. Not my mother. I expect this from her. But isn't Josh supposed to be some savvy entrepreneur? I didn't think he'd go along with such idiocy. And Quinn should be backing me up. She *knows* how I feel about my mom's pseudo-psychicness.

"What?" asks my mother. She waves her fork, which has a prawn skewered on it. "No, no, don't say it. I know you're skeptical about the spirit world but . . ." She waves her other hand. "Ever since Josh came in I have sensed *strong paranormal energy.*"

How can I argue with *strong paranormal energy*? It's like talking to someone who thinks they were abducted by a UFO.

I spear a chunk of squid and chew. I can't help but feel annoyed about the upcoming séance. What's my mom planning to do, haul out the Ouija board? I wonder if Josh's acquiescence means anything. If he truly believes in this crap, I guess it's good news, since if he'd actually murdered Tonya he'd hardly be eager to contact her enraged spirit. But maybe he thinks it's total bullshit and is just pretending to give it a try so he'll *look* like he has nothing to hide. The thought makes my head hurt.

Josh volunteers to wash the dishes while I dry. Since we have some questions to run through, the séance will have to wait.

While we clean up, my mom takes Quinn on a tour of her garden. The days are starting to get shorter, but there's still a lot of light. When they open the screen door, the smell of petunias wafts in. Josh turns off the tap. "Your mom's so cool," he says.

I wonder if he's just being polite. "Do you really believe in psychics and ghosts?" I ask.

Josh raises a bowl out of the suds and wipes it. There's something sensual about this simple act, the fragile glass bowl cradled in one of his large, tanned hands while the other hand rubs it, carefully. I swallow hard. It was warm today and the kitchen feels stuffy. Even in a thin silk blouse I'm sweating.

Josh hands me the bowl and turns to look at me. When his eyes catch mine, it's all I can do not to drop the bowl. His gaze is so intense that I half expect my feet to float off the floor until our lips are level. His mouth opens and he leans closer to me, his eyelids closing. I feel my own eyes close and my chin tilt back. It's as though I'm a puppet and someone else is pulling the strings. I know this is a *terrible* idea but can't stop myself.

Josh's phone beeps. Both of our eyes fly open. Josh takes a step back and reaches for his phone. I shake myself.

When he checks his new message, his forehead creases. "Weird. A blank message," he says. "And I have no clue who sent it." He puts the phone back on the window ledge and plunges his hands back into the dishwater. "What were we talking about?" he asks.

"Psychics and ghosts," I say. My voice is thin from holding my breath. I can't believe I almost kissed my client. There are two dots of color on Josh's cheeks. I swallow hard. "I was asking whether you believe in them."

"I've never seen one, or anything like that," he says. "But who knows? There are lots of things we don't understand. I guess I'm keeping an open mind." He looks sideways at me. "I take it you're not a believer?"

"I'm not," I say, retrieving the list of questions we're meant to run through from my briefcase. I ask if he minds if I record his answers. He says no, so I pull out my tiny digital recorder, set it next to his phone, and press Play. We go through a list of Tonya's friends and associates, and the places she liked to go. It turns out that both he and Tonya held million-dollar life insurance policies on each other. For normal people, that'd be motive enough, but considering what Josh's worth, it hardly seems to make much difference.

When I ask whether Tonya told him about being stalked by Cage he nods. "Yeah, she told me about him. She even forwarded some emails he'd sent her." He shrugs. "He sounded like bad news."

I ask if he still has these emails and he says he'll look. Like Louise, he'd advised Tonya to notify the police. He didn't know if she had but doubts it.

I stand on tiptoes to replace a glass bowl on a high shelf. "Weren't you worried?" I ask.

Josh grimaces. "I know, it sounds like I'm an uncaring bastard because my estranged wife is getting stalked and I do nothing, right?"

I shrug. "No, I didn't—"

He cuts me off. "It was like this. Tonya loved drama. The whole reason she went out with that loser in the first place was because he seemed exciting. He's some drug-dealing thug who impressed her with his designer suits and flashy car."

I think of the small expensive-looking Porsche parked out front.

Josh shakes his head angrily. "I was mostly just concerned she'd be dumb enough to get back together with him."

"Do you think she did?" I ask. Was Cage the mystery lover Louise was talking about?

Josh rubs his chin, thereby depositing a soap sud on his face. I fight the urge to wipe it away. He must notice me staring at it because he swipes it off himself. Talking about Cage has clearly upset him. I wonder if he was jealous.

"Who knows?" he asks. "He hit her a few times when they were together. I don't know why she'd have gone back to someone like that. But why be with him in the first place?"

When I tell Josh about Tonya's scary phone calls, the horror movie soundtrack, and the butchered Barbie doll, he looks alarmed.

"She never mentioned that," he says. "But I doubt Cage is that creative."

He passes me a plate and our hands touch, an electric tingle traveling down my arm to the small of my back. I wonder if he felt it too. Out of the corner of my eye I can see him staring at me. Recalling the last time our eyes met, I keep my gaze fixed on my dishtowel, which bears the slogan: *Trust me, I'm psychic!*

I ask if he knows Cage's real name and he snorts. "Yeah. It's Lewis James Flice. I guess Lewis just didn't have the right tough-guy ring to it."

"There's something else Louise said." I watch Josh closely. "She claimed Tonya was having an affair, starting back before you guys separated."

I'm expecting some visible reaction but there isn't one. "I told you that all along," says Josh. He overturns the washbasin and rinses it, then refills it with clean water.

"Who with?"

Josh turns off the tap. "I don't know. Didn't Louise tell you?"

"She claimed not to know either."

"And you believed her?"

I nod. "Yes," I say. "Can you think of any reason she'd lie?"

"She's a little out there," says Josh.

I recall my suspicion that Louise was jealous of Tonya. Does she have a crush on Josh too? I imagine her meticulously applying roses to the hood of his SUV. She's definitely creative. "Has she ever seemed interested in you?" I ask. "Romantically?"

"Louise Dobson?" He smiles as he hands me the last pan. I wonder what's so funny.

Seeing my expression, Josh shakes his head. "Louise is a lesbian," he says. "If she had a thing for anyone, it would have been Tonya."

By the time my mom, Quinn, Josh, and I convene in the living room, it's dark outside. My mother lights candles and incense and turns off all the lights. Outside, the streetlights have come on. Looking out the window, I can see an older man walking a black dog that reminds me of Tonya's giant poodle. When it gets closer to my mom's, the dog lunges into her yard, the old guy staggering as he drags it back. I see my mother's fat cat, Pudding, shoot up a tree, eyes blazing green in the glow of the streetlight.

I'd decided not to join my mom's "session," but curiosity won out. Plus we have to hold hands—a good excuse to touch Josh.

Quinn and I are sitting on the sofa. Josh is on a hard chair to my right, and my mom is on an ottoman to Quinn's left. Holding hands, we form a squashed circle.

"Shut your eyes," says my mother. She starts to chant, a weird droning noise that makes me cringe with annoyance and embarrassment. She sounds like a cross between a Tibetan monk and a vacuum cleaner. This goes on for a few minutes. I'm tempted to stand up and walk out. *What* is my mother doing? I can't believe people fall for this shit.

What keeps me from leaving is the feel of Josh's hand. He has a firm grip. My mother's chanting rises to a climax and Josh squeezes my hand. I open my eyes to find him looking at me. Quinn, whose hand I'm also holding, has her eyes shut. She looks so peaceful I wonder if she's napping.

"Close your eyes," says my mother. Both Josh and I smile guiltily. As far as I can tell, my mom's eyes have stayed shut the whole time. I wonder how she knew. When I look back at Josh his eyes are shut again.

"I'm looking for a woman who has crossed over," says my mother in a hushed voice. "Her name is Tonya Dawn Barton."

We all wait. I worry that my palms are sweaty. "If Tonya's there, please send us a sign," says my mom. I hold my breath. In a weird, crazy way I almost want something to happen, because if nothing does, my mom will look even loonier than she already does. We all wait. There's dead silence.

"Tonya?" asks my mother. Her voice has changed. She sounds much older now, and terribly tired. "It's all right. I can feel you. We want to help find your killer. Can you help us?"

Despite myself, I shiver. I'm tempted to open my eyes, but something holds me back. There's a loud thump outside in the front yard. Quinn clutches my hand. I open my eyes. Like me, Josh and Quinn are staring out the window. I look up and down the road. The yard and the street appear empty.

I clear my throat. "Was that the cat?" I ask. There's no sign of Pudding in the tree where I'd spotted her earlier. Quinn has released my hand and placed it on her belly.

"Let's try again," says my mother. We all dutifully clasp hands and close our eyes. Even though I don't believe in any of this, I worry it's bad for my mom's health. She sounds so drained. For a moment, she hums, only to break off and say Tonya's name. "Yes, it's all right. We're here," says my mother soothingly. "Can you tell us who attacked you?"

We all wait.

"I . . . I missed that," says my mom. "We should look where? Where should we look? Tonya?"

At that moment, Josh's cell phone beeps. I open my eyes. He releases my hand and removes his phone from his pocket. "Oh God, sorry," he says. "I forgot to turn it off."

"It's alright," says my mother, her voice flat. Looking at her, I feel freshly alarmed. There's no shine to her eyes and her skin appears equally dull, like all the sparkle has been sucked out of her. Quinn looks tired too. I know she's been going to bed early of late. She stands up and stretches, then sits down and rubs her belly. I guess the baby's been kicking a lot.

When Josh opens his text message his forehead furrows. "Any idea what this means?" He extends the small screen my way. I lean closer to read it.

"CLOuD CoLOr," I read. I shrug. "Means nothing to me. Who sent it?"

Josh brushes a curl off his forehead. "That's what's really weird," he says. "Check this out." He hands me back the phone. The *From* line is blank. I click on *Message details* and a box pops up. Empty.

"What is it?" asks Quinn. I hand her Josh's phone and she squints at it. "Cloud color," she says.

"There's no record of the phone that sent it," I say. "I guess it's some network error."

A loud thump causes Quinn to gasp. Something hit the window directly behind us.

"Was that a bird?" I ask. We all stare into the dark yard. Some thick cedar bushes lie directly below the window. I peer down but can't see anything.

"Creepy," says Quinn. She hands Josh his phone and shakes herself. "This is going to sound crazy," she says. "But that message . . . you don't think it could've come from Tonya, do you?"

My first thought is that pregnancy has zapped her intellect. But then I recall how Josh's phone beeped back in the kitchen, just when it seemed he might kiss me . . . That message, like this one, had no sender details. Was that Tonya too, trying to stop Josh from kissing me?

It's such a crazy idea that it makes me mad, firstly with myself, and then at my mother. *This* is what happens when people go along with her stupid paranormal delusions. Everyone ends up scared and totally irrational. It's like Salem. One minute, a couple of preteens are having fits, the next, nineteen "witches" have been hanged. Next thing you know, we'll convince ourselves that Tonya is tapping out messages with her phantom acrylic nails or cruising around the yard in a spectral Mercedes.

My mom and Josh are now rereading the text message together. My mom runs a hand over her eyes. "I don't know anything about text messaging," she says. "But spirits have been known to communicate in all sorts of ways, like via photographs or recordings, or flashing lights and ringing phones, even turning the TV on and off." She reaches for her mug of by now cold tea. "So it's possible."

She studies Josh's face. "Cloud color. Does it mean anything to you?"

"Maybe it's the name of a boat," says Quinn. She too is holding her mug of cold tea as though she's trying to warm her hands on it.

I stand up. "I'm making fresh tea." I say. If I have to listen to this lunacy for another second I'll end up yelling at my mother, my best friend, and the man of my warped dreams.

CHAPTER FOURTEEN:

DEARLY DEPARTED

Tonya's memorial service is being held at the Horizon Chapel, a soulless flat-roofed building down on Fort Street. Listening to a guy who sounds like a TV evangelist and looks like a ventriloquist's dummy describe Tonya as a modern-day saint, I'm finding it hard not to roll my eyes. Clearly, he never met the woman.

Jackie, Quinn, and I are sitting midway back, near the side aisle, where we can escape if needed. This seat also gives us a good view of the crowd. I figure there's a high chance that Package might show up.

Quinn nudges me in the ribs. "Is that Louise Dobson?"

I nod. Louise is in the front row, dressed in a black pantsuit and sobbing into what looks like a Versace hankie that matches her yellow hair. I told Quinn about our weird discussion down at Island Deco. Louise is sitting next to Tonya's mom, who's an older version of her daughter: a heavily made-up woman with a bleached blonde perm, an Indian wedding's worth of gold jewelry, and a trout pout. Despite the good weather, she's wearing a fake fur coat and knee-high boots. Giant black sunglasses cover her eyes, giving her the look of a mafia widow. Beside her sits Tonya's brother, Ryan, whom I remember from camp, except he's now stockier and jowlier. A year older than us, he was the kind of kid who squished snails for fun. Even now, at his sister's funeral, he looks like a cocky creep, dressed in a too shiny suit with a mobile phone glued to his ear.

From Ryan, I turn my attention to Josh, who's sitting beside his brother, Mike, across the aisle from Tonya's family. Dressed in dark suits, both brothers look stiff and uncomfortable, their curls combed flat and their arms crossed tight against their chests. They're neither talking nor looking at each other, both staring at the spiky floral arrangements.

Quinn jabs me again. "Oh my God. Is that Chantelle Orker?"

I follow Quinn's gaze to see the latecomers: Chantelle herding a scowling preteen boy down the aisle, her muscular body packed into a tight black dress and a black hat covering half of her face. Painted bright red, her downturned lips scream of discontent. "Yup. That's her," I say, recalling our run-in in Safeway. Chantelle looks slightly less tacky today, but only because black's more forgiving. Did Tonya still dress like that, or had money improved her sense of style? Somehow, I highly doubt it.

Quinn's eyebrows are scaling new heights. "Look! I don't believe it! Who's that guy? Oh my God, it's Josh's brother!"

I look up at Chantelle in time to see her press those red lips to Mike's ear. "Whoa," I say, trying to take this in. What are the chances that both Barton brothers would end up with the nastiest girls from that nasty camp? Bad taste must run in the family.

Quinn's eyes are almost as round as her belly. "D'you think that's their kid?" she asks.

I study the blond boy, now slumped into Mike and Chantelle's pew, a set of jumbo-cinnamon-roll-sized headphones clamped over his ears. The kid has Mike's piercing blue eyes and Chantelle's big chin. He's got her snarling lips too, minus the lipstick.

"Yeah, must be," I whisper.

"Holy crap," says Quinn. "Mike has a kid with Chantelle Orker?" She shakes her head. "Jeez, I hated that girl. Remember when she mixed blue Kool-Aid crystals into your sunscreen and the color wouldn't come off?"

I nod grimly. My nickname was "Baby Smurf" for a couple of days. Before it became something far worse . . . This memory brings a jab of actual physical pain under my ribs. I grip the edge of the wooden pew and try to breathe slowly. Quinn shoots me a worried look. "You okay?" she mouths.

I nod, except I'm not. Being around these people stresses me out to the point that I'm scared I'll have a panic attack. The last one I had was in a hotel bathroom, in a basement, when the power went out. It was the sudden darkness and lack of space and air that triggered it. Quinn hands me her water bottle. "Thanks," I say, gratefully, and take a swig.

She drinks some too, before recapping the bottle and stuffing it back into her giant bag. "I wish it were booze," she mutters.

"Same!" She's made me smile.

At a sign from the funeral director, Josh rises from his seat and walks toward the closed coffin. Chantelle stops whispering in Mike's ear and throws Josh a poisonous look. As he passes, Tonya's brother glares and mutters under his breath. Tonya's mom raises her dark shades and gives Josh the evil eye, like she's cursing him. Interesting. Do they all think he killed her?

Josh walks across the stage and stops. Gazing down at his extended family, he sways a little, then pulls himself together and adjusts the microphone. He looks pale and haggard, his slicked-back hair making him seem older and unfamiliar. He clears his throat and the room falls silent. "Thank you for coming," he says, being careful not to look down at Tonya's family. "It means a lot to me." He looks at his hands and blinks, then continues. "We're here today to remember Tonya, who brought so much happiness to so many of us." At this, Louise Dobson emits a strangled wail. Quinn nudges my foot. "One of the things I'll never forget about Tonya is how much she loved to dance," says Josh. Until now, he's been reading from a small page, but he folds it and keeps talking. "When I met Tonya, I was very young. I liked her for what were probably the wrong reasons, because she was attractive and pretty." He lowers his eyes and then raises them. It feels like he's looking straight at me. "There was a lot more to Tonya than that." He gazes over our heads, as though looking out to sea. "But some people never got to see it. When she danced, it wasn't about how she looked, but how she made people feel. I fell in love with her dancing." He twists the paper in his hands. "She was free when she danced." His voice breaks and he hangs his head. "I hope wherever she is, she's dancing."

As Josh talks about Tonya, my mind wanders. I think of the last time I saw all these people together—Josh, Mike, Chantelle, Louise,

Quinn, and Ryan. And Tonya, of course. It's weird to think she's gone, only enduring in people's memories. The room is stuffy. I feel tired. I close my eyes, remembering my last night at camp, how I'd crept up to my bunk, depressed and exhausted, and found the note on my pillow:

Toby—I'm sorry. I made a mistake. I don't want Tonya. I want you. Please meet me at midnight in the Nature Hut.

I'd held it inside my sleeping bag and turned on my flashlight, the batteries so feeble I was scared I'd misread it. The printed letters seemed to quiver, the handwriting shaky, like it had been scrawled in a hurry on a soft surface. Heart pounding, I grabbed my jacket and climbed down the bunk's ladder again. I could hear the counselor's snores and Louise's loud allergic wheezing. Below me, Quinn's hair was spread gold on her pillow, like a kid's drawing of the sun. I found my shoes—still wet—and tiptoed to the door. Not even Louise stirred. I opened it as slowly and as quietly as possible.

The moon was almost full. I crept off the balcony, feet crunching on gravel. My hand shook as I reread the note. Oh my God. It was true. *I don't want Tonya. I want you.* He'd changed his mind, after all.

I didn't have a watch but knew it was sometime past eleven. I'd heard the cuckoo clock in the camp office on my way back to the cabin, maybe fifteen minutes ago. All around, the trees were tall black plumes. I skirted the edge of the trail, ready to press myself into the bush if anyone came. My steps were as quick as my heartbeat. Was he already there, waiting for me? It was downhill all the way to the Nature Hut.

Quinn whispers in my ear, causing me to jump. "Did you know Tonya danced?"

I blink, shake my head. I push my hair behind my ears, push the memories of that night away. "I didn't," I tell Quinn.

Josh is describing the dance shows in which Tonya starred, the competitions she won: jazz, modern dance, even ballet. An injury had ended her hopes of a career as a professional dancer, after which she'd focused on acting. "She was so lovely when she danced," said Josh. "So free."

He looks so sad I feel true sorrow that Tonya is dead. It's so strange to reconcile the mean, trashy girl I knew with the joyful dancer Josh is describing. Maybe she grew up and changed, after all. Did she ever feel remorse for what she did to me?

"Again, thanks for being here," says Josh. He descends the stage and stops beside Tonya's coffin. His face crumbles. I look away. The moment is too private.

A line has formed leading to the coffin, its silver top heaped with pink lilies. With a shudder I recall the crime scene photos: what a week underwater had done to her. There's no way I'm going up there. It's not my place, anyway. I can forgive her now, but we were never friends.

"Where are Josh's parents?" whispers Quinn.

Jackie shifts in her wheelchair and smoothes down her skirt. Her chair is parked so as not to block the aisle. I'm sitting next to her and Quinn is on my other side. "Josh's parents divorced in his late teens," says Jackie, leaning in so we can both hear. "He's estranged from his mom, who lives with her new husband in Bermuda. And his dad died of a heart attack about a decade ago."

"That's awful," I say, wondering how Jackie knows all this.

"Who's that guy in the purple shirt?" asks Jackie, nodding toward a terrifically fit-looking man with a goatee.

"No idea." I study the guy in purple. "Why? You think he could be Package?"

"Trust me, he's not," says Quinn flatly. "That's Xavier Donaldson. He's a tennis coach up at the Oak Bay bubble. See the good-looking guy right beside him? That's his boyfriend, Patrick."

As if on cue, the guy on Xavier's left turns to reveal perfect cheekbones and a discreet earring. I recall Josh's claim that Tonya had a lot of handsome gay friends. I scan the crowd for other men who might be Tonya's mystery lover. A high percentage of the mourners look like they work out a lot. There are plenty of potential Packages.

After the service, I'm standing near the refreshment table when someone calls my name. I turn to see Mike with a shot of whisky in one hand and a sausage roll in the other. While he seemed cold down at the marina the day Josh's boat was being searched, after a few drinks, he's the life of the funeral party. "Hey! Hello again!" he says, his face flushed above his tight collar. "Toby, right? We don't see each other for what, twenty years, and then meet twice in two weeks. How's it going, eh?" He looks from me to Quinn, who's standing beside me holding a glass of orange juice. "Whoa, another Camp Whacky alum." He smiles at Quinn's belly. "They're everywhere," he says in mock horror. "And multiplying . . ."

Still clutching her yellow hankie and a small black purse, Louise materializes beside Mike, who nods at her and mock-grimaces. "Aghhh . . . Another one," he says, still pretending to be scared. Louise looks taken aback. "We're talking about Camp Wikwakee," explains Mike. "Do you all remember that dump? And the food? Those mystery meatloaves." He pretends to gag. "There's no friggin way it'd pass Health and Safety today." He downs the rest of his whisky.

Louise looks from Mike to me, her eyes narrowing. "I knew it was you, from camp. You *are* the same Toby."

I give a reluctant nod. "Er, right." I point to her handbag, eager to change the subject. It's quilted black, with a gold chain and inter-locking gold Cs. "Ah, nice purse."

Louise smiles tightly and shifts it to her other arm, like she's scared I might steal it. She turns back to Mike. "I enjoyed camp," she says haughtily, which totally figures. She brightens. "D'you all remember the camp song?" She starts to sing tunelessly, one be-ringed hand fluttering. "At Camp Wikwakee we respect our friends. At Camp Wikwakee the fun never ends . . ." I'm so stunned by this nineteen-year-old display of camp spirit that I just stand there, open-mouthed. How can Louise remember that place as fun? It's like she was brainwashed.

Quinn meets my eyes. She looks ready to burst out laughing.

Thankfully, Louise's singing peters out when Chantelle Orker joins us. Stopping beside Mike, she peers down at me like I'm a speck of lint she'd like to brush off. "Oh. It's. You," she says, this statement including Quinn in its disdain. "What are you guys doing here?"

"They're with me," says Josh, materializing on my right.

Chantelle's frown deepens. "That figures." Between those bright red lips, she bares horsey teeth at Josh and lowers her big head as if preparing to charge. He glares right back at her. They're like mountain goats, ready to push each other into a ravine.

Quinn gives me a look. Yikes! What do Chantelle and Josh have against each other?

I gesture toward Mike and Chantelle. "So, how long have you been together?" I ask. "Is that your son over there?"

Chantelle manages a tight smile. "Yes, that's our Cayden." Her smile widens as she looks at Mike. "We've been married twelve years now."

"Wow," I say, genuinely amazed. "It's incredible, how you met all those years ago at camp. And Josh and Tonya too."

At this mention, Chantelle's smile flips upside down. She scowls at Josh again.

Oblivious to his wife's ire, Mike turns my way and squints. "Heeeeey, weren't you kicked out of camp?" he asks, like he's struggling to remember why I left. Looking at me, more of the story must come back because his confused look morphs into a leer. "So was it true that you—"

"What time is it?" interrupts Quinn, her voice sharp. I know she's wearing a watch.

"Just past four," says Louise.

Before Mike can turn the conversation back to my expulsion from camp, Quinn asks Louise about her work. They talk about Louise's design studio for a while, then switch to Quinn's job, leading to a long discussion between Josh, Mike, and Quinn about whales and pollution. Mike contradicts everything Josh says, and Josh grows increasingly irritated. I wonder if Mike resents that his brother's his boss. Finally, Mike heads back to the bar, allowing Chantelle to take over as Josh's nemesis. After listening to them snipe at each other for a few more minutes, I retreat to the restroom. Quinn's right behind me. "Jeez," she says, when we're out of earshot. "Were they *that* bad as teenagers?"

"They were worse!" It's amazing how little everyone has changed in the past two decades. Chantelle is still a bitch. Louise is still weird. Mike remains socially inept. And Josh is still too cool, handsome, and accomplished to be true. I study Quinn in the bathroom mirror. She's the same too—pretty, curious, kind, and funny. So what about me? In Toronto, I was able to forget Camp Wikwakee, but being around these people brings it all back. I feel like a loser, all over again.

We've just exited the restroom when I hear Josh's voice coming from the men's room. He sounds aggravated. "With those kinds of possible returns you knew the risks," he says. "It wasn't a safe bet and you knew it!" Both Quinn and I pause outside the men's room door. I assume he's talking on the phone, until another man answers.

"That's such bullshit!" he says. While Josh sounded annoyed, this guy sounds furious. "You sold it as a sure thing, then wiped me out! Why didn't you lose your shirt when it all went to shit?"

"I lost a lot," says Josh. "But I spread my investments around. I never told you to put everything you had on it!"

Now the man's voice becomes pleading. "So how about a loan?" he asks. "To help me get back on my feet again."

"You never paid back my last loan," says Josh. "And I still haven't seen a viable business plan. Come up with a great idea and really sell it to me. Right now, you're just asking for another handout."

"No! Wait!"

"No."

"Don't you—"

The door opens with a bang. Quinn and I both take quick steps back as Josh strides out. Without glancing in our direction he storms off down the hall. Quinn gives me a questioning look.

A moment later, the bathroom door bursts open again to disgorge Tonya's brother, Ryan. While Josh's face was pale, his is an angry red. Seeing us, he blinks, then turns away, his hands balled into tight fists. We watch as he stomps toward the reception hall.

Quinn raises an eyebrow. "Interesting." She fingers the cuff of her black dress. "I wonder if other investors feel like Josh ripped them off."

I nod, having had the same thought. I need to look into Ryan's accusations. Did Josh get rich by cheating people? "You think someone could have killed Tonya to get back at him for a bad business deal?" I suggest.

Quinn shrugs. "Doubtful, given that they were getting divorced." She shakes her head. "Unless they did it to frame him." I picture Detective Fitzgerald's sly grin upon finding the flashlight on the *Great Escape*.

"Oh there you are!" We both turn to see Jackie wheeling herself down the hall, one-handed. I feel a pang of guilt, and walk over to help push her. She waves me off. "No, no. Pushing myself is no problem if it's flat." She studies our faces. "What are you guys doing out here?"

"We heard Josh and Tonya's brother arguing about money," I say, then fill Jackie in on Quinn's latest theory.

"Seems like a long shot, but we'll look into it," says Jackie. "Anything else interesting happen?"

"Well, Josh and Mike seem pretty tense," I say. "And Mike's wife Chantelle kept giving Josh the evil eye. Plus Tonya's mom looked like she was ready to call out a hit on him."

Jackie rolls her eyes. "Families." She checks her watch. "Are you two ready to get going soon?"

We both nod. Hell yes.

After saying our goodbyes, the three of us exit the Horizon Chapel. The parking lot is set on a slope, and my high heels aren't helping, but because of Quinn's belly, I have to push Jackie to her car.

While the past few days were warm, a cold wind has blown in. Stopping to catch my breath, I gaze back at the funeral chapel, dark curtains drawn in every window, a place of never-ending mourning. Behind a dumpster, I can see the back of a hearse sticking out. "You know how in movies the murderer always goes to the funeral to gloat?" I ask, shivering. "Do you think he was there today?"

"Or she," says Jackie, twisting in her wheelchair to look back at me. "It could be a woman, after all."

"Or she," I concede. "But I don't get it. Who besides Josh really benefited from Tonya's death?" A curtain twitches in one of the funeral home's ground-floor windows, as if someone is watching us. I rub my hands to warm them.

"That," says Quinn, pulling up her hood, "Is the million dollar question."

"Or multimillion, in this case," says Jackie. She raises a hand and squints up at the sky. I feel a raindrop hit my cheek, cold and wet, and roll into my collar. "Oh no! We're going to get soaked," says Jackie. "You push, I'll wheel!"

Sure enough, we're only halfway to our cars when the heavy rain sets in.

CHAPTER FIFTEEN:

PERSON OF INTEREST

'm just outside the office when my first client of the week calls to cancel. She has pink eye. Resisting the urge to rub my own eyes, I take advantage of my unexpected free time by heading up the street to Starbucks.

After securing a double latte, I remove my jacket, take a seat near the window, and unpack my laptop. When I check my emails I find one from Josh. He's forwarded the correspondence between Cage and Tonya. I enlarge the font before reading.

In his first message, Lewis, aka Cage, comments on the breakdown of Tonya's marriage and claims to miss her. This email ends with a promise—or a threat—that he'll see her soon. His spelling and grammar are atrocious. Tonya's response, titled "Leeve me alone," makes it clear she's not keen—and has equally lousy spelling. She tells Cage to stop calling her and claims to have moved on and be getting engaged. Interesting. Cage's final message is just one line: "As if. You cant live without me." I have to stop myself from correcting that missing apostrophe.

Looking up from the screen, I rub my temples. Although it's close to nine, I still don't feel fully awake. Last night, after Tonya's funeral, I found it hard to sleep, and had repeated nightmares. While I can't remember the dreams' details, a panicky feeling has stayed with me. I test my forehead for clamminess, worried I'm coming down with something. My eyes feel gritty too. Oh no. What if it's pink eye?

I fight the urge to Google my imagined symptoms and reach for my latte. Following a fortifying swig, I refocus on Tonya and Cage's exchange. What have I learned from them?

I should make a list of what I do and don't know.

1) Does Cage sound threatening? It could be read either way. Has he stalked/assaulted other women? Where is he now?

2) He called Tonya more than once, or at least she thought he had. Can we get her phone records?

3) She claimed to be getting engaged. Was she just trying to dissuade Cage or was this true? If true, to Package or to someone else? Someone must have seen her & her lover/s together.

4) Why did she send these emails to Josh? Did she expect him to be her knight in shining armor? Was she trying to make him jealous about the new boyfriend/fiancé?

I'm wondering what else to add when someone says my name. I look up to see Detective Destin. "Hey Toby," he says, looking pleased to see me. "Mind if I join you?"

Maybe it's his day off because he's dressed in tan cotton slacks and a blue polo shirt. He's holding a raisin scone and a regular coffee, and has a brown leather laptop bag slung across his shoulder. His expression is so friendly that to say no would be churlish. Plus he's already halfway into the seat across from mine. I nod and close the cover of my laptop. Colin deposits his bag onto the spare chair between us, and sets his cup and plate on the table.

At this time of day the café is full of retirees. Surrounded by gray hair, Colin looks incredibly fit and healthy. Again, I'm surprised by how good-looking he is. With his short, dark hair, green eyes, and pale skin, he reminds me of an old-fashioned matinee idol. Then he smiles and his smoldering, movie star–looks morph into those of a mischievous schoolboy. "How are you finding island life?" he asks. "A bit slower-paced than Toronto?"

"I love it," I say, then wonder if this is true. I miss the energy of a big city, the sense that everyone is busy. Most people in Victoria seem to be on holiday, retired, or both. But was my life in Toronto that great? I often left the office at 10:00 p.m. And I probably wouldn't be sitting in Starbucks with a cute guy on a Monday morning chatting about things that are totally non-work-related.

"Are you from here?" I ask, and Colin shakes his head.

"No, I grew up in Saskatoon," he says. "But I went to UVic and stayed. It'd be hard to go back to those prairie winters."

I wonder why he stopped by to chat. Is he looking to impart or obtain information about Josh Barton? Is he truly, like Quinn has hinted, interested in me? Or is he just being friendly?

"Quinn mentioned that your mom is recovering from breast cancer," says Colin.

I nod. Just hearing the word "cancer" brings a lump to my throat.

"My mother's a cancer survivor too," says Colin. "She's been in remission for four years now and it's a huge relief." After he says this, he looks embarrassed, like he's worried he's being too personal. "What I wanted to say is that, well, I know how tough it is. So if you ever want to talk to someone who's been through it, well . . . just let me know." He gives me a crooked smile, then gestures toward his raisin scone. "Would you like some?"

I start to say no, then reconsider. I've had too much caffeine. Some food might make me less jittery. I nod and he cuts the scone in two. He looks genuinely happy that I've accepted half his scone. I thank him and break off a chunk.

Since we're both busy chewing, neither of us has to talk. I wonder what to say. I want to ask about progress on Tonya's case, but I know that's a bad idea. But then Colin raises the subject. "I heard you were old friends with Josh and Tonya," he says.

I almost choke. I guess he had a reason for stopping by, after all. I feel mildly disappointed this wasn't purely a social visit. "You heard wrong," I say. "We went to summer camp together when we were fourteen. It was up island, just past Sooke. Quinn was there too. And so was Mike and his wife, Chantelle. And Tonya's brother, Ryan. Plus Louise, the interior designer. But I didn't stay in touch with any of them, besides Quinn, of course."

"Oh," says Colin. He extracts a raisin from his scone. "So you and Josh never dated?"

I'm so surprised by this question that I slosh some latte onto the table. Colin hands me a napkin. "No," I say. "Where did you get that idea?"

Colin hesitates. "Ah, Louise Dobson suggested you were more than just friends."

I feel myself blush and shake my head in bewilderment. "I don't see how she could have gotten that idea." I break off another chunk of scone. Was Louise deliberately trying to mislead the detectives? But why? "When were Josh and I supposed to have dated?" I ask.

Colin shrugs. Along with curiosity, I see a flash of humor in his eyes. "Recently."

"Well, Louise is delusional, I say. "Josh is my client." I know I sound defensive, but I can't help it. "I'm single," I add, then wonder why I'd felt compelled to say so.

Colin gives me a big smile. "I find that hard to believe."

I'm about to reiterate my single status when I realize he might be teasing me. Or does he not believe me about Josh? I wonder if I look guilty. Should I mention that Josh and I shared a few moments back at camp? But surely, it's not worth bringing up. We held hands and kissed a few times—and that was nineteen-plus years back. I take another sip of my latte. I can feel Colin watching me.

"So the first time you saw Josh again was when he came into your office, the day before his wife was reported missing?"

"Yes." I give an involuntary shake. "Did Louise tell you about Tonya's ex-boyfriend Cage? Did she mention that someone was calling Tonya and hanging up and that she'd been sent a bloody Barbie doll?"

Colin nods. "She did," he says. "We don't know if Cage was involved, but the guy is definitely trouble." He hesitates. "He has a history of violence toward women."

I can't help but take this as positive news.

Seeing my expression, Colin gives me a warning look. "Don't get too excited. We don't even know if he was in town the night Tonya died. He came and went a lot, and the dates are hard to match up. We're still trying to find the guy."

"So he's gone?" I ask. "You don't know where he was staying?"

"A cheap motel in Esquimalt," says Colin. "The Sea—." He clamps his lips shut and narrows his eyes. "Don't you go looking for him," he says. "Like I told you, he's bad news. Stay away from this guy."

I open my eyes as wide as they'll go, as though the thought hadn't even occurred to me. I figure I may as well ask if he's followed up about Alana Mapplebee.

"What about her?" asks Colin. There's a mosquito bite on his right wrist and he scratches at it. Despite the recent sunny weather, his skin is very fair. I guess he's been working long hours. He drains the last of his coffee.

"Remember how Josh said she was stalking him?" I say, and Colin nods. I remind him about the black-painted roses stuck onto Josh's SUV, and his suggestion that Alana might have killed Tonya.

He makes a face. "It seems a bit farfetched, doesn't it? I mean, yes, Alana's kind of extreme but . . ." He waves a hand. Something about his expression makes me pause.

"Do you know Alana Mapplebee?" I ask. And I mean *know,* in the biblical sense. Colin shrugs. Recalling Alana's overdone smile, hair, and boobs, I feel my stomach sink. If Colin has been with Alana too, I may as well enter a nunnery. Do men *really* want someone that artificial? I know it's none of my business, but I can't help but ask if he dated her.

Colin's dark eyebrows wiggle. "Me and Alana?" He looks as surprised by this concept as I had at his earlier suggestion that Josh and I were an item. "No. She went out with Quinn's brother Dan a few years ago." He brushes some crumbs off his pants. "Dan's an old friend so that's how I met her."

I smile weakly with relief. I'd forgotten that Colin and Dan were friends. "And?" I ask. Based on Colin's thoughtful expression it's clear he has a story to tell.

Colin shifts in his seat. He looks uncomfortable, like he'd love to divulge all but knows he shouldn't. He shrugs. "Let's just say it was a volatile relationship." He checks his watch and frowns, which reminds me that I've got an appointment at ten thirty and had better be off shortly. I wait and Colin meets my eyes. "Alana seemed pretty nuts," he admits.

I give him an encouraging smile. "How nuts?"

He scratches his ear. "Like not long after she and Dan got together, Alana saw Dan with Quinn. She didn't realize Quinn was his sister and thought Dan was seeing another woman."

I picture the scenario. "And?" I ask again.

"And she went apeshit and smashed all the windows on Dan's car."

"Wow," I say. "That is nuts. And Dan didn't break up with her?"

"Well, she claimed she was drunk and said she was really sorry." Seeing my face, he raises his hands in an expression of surrender and laughs. "Hey, it's not like I dated her," he says. "I don't know what Dan was thinking."

I use my spoon to scrape out the last of my milk foam. "So maybe Josh has a point."

Colin shrugs. "We haven't charged anyone yet," he says carefully.

"But Josh is still the prime suspect?" Given that the murder weapon was found on Josh's boat, I'm guessing the answer is yes. But why hasn't Josh been charged? I insert my laptop into its case and zip it.

"He's a person of interest," says Colin. He studies my face for a moment, the green of his eyes seemingly darker than just moments ago. A glance out the window reveals the sky remains blue, the sun unshadowed. Colin frowns. He runs a hand through his silky dark hair. "I don't like that you and Jackie are working for this guy." He clamps his lips shut, as though he's said too much. The way he's looking at me makes me uneasy.

"Why not?" I get the weird feeling that Colin's jealous. While Josh must inspire jealousy in a lot of guys, I wouldn't expect this from Colin. He's obviously not as rich as Josh, but he seems to have a job he loves and is good at. Plus he's extremely attractive. So maybe it's not jealousy that I'm sensing but something else, like worry. I wonder if Colin knows something scary about Josh he can't tell me. I recall Chantelle's claim that he's a sociopath. Being married to his brother, she'd be in a position to really know him.

Colin bites his bottom lip, which is full and pink. "Forget I said anything," he says, gruffly. "I just . . . well, guys with that much cash are used to getting whatever they want. The guy seems like an absolute narcissist to me . . ." He shrugs. "But like you said, he's just your client."

I shove my crumpled-up napkin into my empty mug. Quinn said more or less the same thing, I recall. And Chantelle. I struggle to remember what I learned in Psych 101, regarding narcissism versus sociopathy. Both are bad but sociopaths are worse. But lots of people use those terms for people they don't like. I bet loads of people are jealous of Josh.

I tell Colin I have an appointment and thank him for the scone.

He laughs. "Next time, I'll buy you a whole scone for yourself." When I stand to go he stands too. There's a brief awkward moment when we're both figuring out what to do, but then he leans forward and kisses my cheek. He smells like he looks: fresh and healthy.

Next time, I think. As I maneuver around a young mother with a tiny baby in a stroller the size of a Smart car, I realize I like the sound of that.

Looking back, I see Colin watching me. I raise my hand and he waves. The young mom gives him an appreciative once-over. Those clean-cut good looks coupled with that naughty grin are hard to ignore. And he seems like a great guy. Or was he just trying to charm me in hopes of digging up dirt against Josh? My client.

As I exit Starbucks, I chide myself for being so suspicious. Even though Colin and I are on opposite sides of this case, I really like him. Sticking to the sunny side of every street, I find myself smiling all the way back to Greene & Olliartee.

CHAPTER SIXTEEN:

MOTEL SEX

After my 2:00 p.m. client has left, I get out the phone-book and search through all the motels in Esquimalt. It doesn't take long to pinpoint the Seabreeze. I update Jackie, who sounds worried, despite my reassurances that I won't actually try to talk to Cage—just work out if he was in town when Tonya vanished.

It's close to four when I leave the city center and drive through a run-down neighborhood of low, aging strip-malls. The Seabreeze lies between a 1950s-style laundromat and a false-fronted appliance repair shop, its dusty window crammed with TVs and stereos that have been obsolete for decades. Opposite the motel lies a used car lot, its faded triangular flags hanging limp for want of a breeze. There's no sign of the sea either.

The Seabreeze is an old-style, two-story motel, its rooms arranged in an upside-down U around the almost empty parking lot. I pull into a visitor's slot. Built in the 1970s, the motel hasn't been changed since, its orange and green paint now faded to dull tones of peach and pistachio. A neon VACANCY sign is struggling to glow in the bright sunlight, an arrow pointing to the room that serves as reception. Dusty lace curtains fill the windows. Someone has stuck a Grateful Dead sticker onto the OPEN sign.

When I push open the door a bell jingles. Behind the counter stands a blonde woman with the tight clothes of a teenager and the tired face of a forty-five-year-old. If I had to bet, I'd wager she's my age. Sucking on a cigarette, she eyes me suspiciously. "You here about the chamber maid job?" The room smells of stale cigarette smoke and hairspray.

"Ah, no," I say. I start to reach for my card but stop. She doesn't seem the type to appreciate lawyers. "I'm looking for someone," I say, and the woman nods. She doesn't look surprised. I doubt there's much that'd surprise her.

"Oh yeah." She takes a long drag of her smoke. In the room next door someone turns on a TV. I hear canned laughter.

"An American guy named Lewis Flice," I say. "But some people call him Cage."

Her mouth tightens, just for an instant, and she stubs out her cigarette. "Cage. Yeah, he was here." She tugs at one of the three gold hoops she has in each ear. "You a cop?"

"No." I hesitate. "A woman got murdered," I say. "And the cops think my friend might have done it."

The woman stares toward the parking lot. "Who's your friend?" she asks.

"It's not important," I say. "But this guy, Cage, was the murdered woman's ex-boyfriend."

The receptionist snorts. "So what?" she asks. "You think Cage killed her?"

"I don't know," I say. "But it'd help to know where he was the night of August 27th. That was a Monday."

She fingers her hair, which is piled in a plastic banana clip. I wait as she taps on a computer keyboard and squints at the screen, pulls a fresh cigarette out of a pack on the counter. She lights it, then gives me a grim smile. "August 27th. He was here," she says. "And he wasn't murdering nobody."

"How do you know?"

Smoke writhes out of her nostrils. "Because he was with me," she says bluntly. "All night long." She inhales again, studying me through eyelashes caked with mascara. Despite the lines around her eyes and mouth, she has a hard-edged sexiness.

"Did you tell the cops?" I ask.

She taps ash from her cigarette. "Why would I?" Her tongue flicks around her lips. "I don't need no trouble."

I nod. I wonder why she decided to tell me. Or is she lying to protect Cage? I meet her eyes, which are a pretty shade of blue.

Periwinkle. For some reason, I believe her. "Do you know where Cage is now?" I ask, and she throws back her head and laughs.

"It's not like we made plans to meet up in Paris," she says. "I was just a fling." Her voice isn't so much bitter as tired. Clearly, this lady isn't counting on happy endings. She sucks on her cigarette and eyes me speculatively. "This girlfriend of his, the one who was murdered, you wouldn't happen to have a picture of her, would you?"

I pull a photo from my purse. It's one of Tonya and Josh, dressed up for some wedding or ball. Tonya is in a shiny turquoise gown and Josh is wearing a tuxedo. Jackie instructed me to pass this photo around the spas, shops, and bars where Tonya was a regular in hopes that someone would recall seeing her with another man. So far, nobody has remembered seeing her with any men at all, just with various girlfriends, including a pale one with short blonde hair who must be Louise Dobson.

"Why?" I ask, and the woman shrugs.

"Just curious. He talked about her."

I hold my breath.

Seeing my hopeful expression, she shakes her head. "Didn't say nothing important. Just that she had nice tits." She gives a harsh laugh. "What a romantic, eh!"

I hand over the photograph and her mouth opens. I can see her crooked bottom teeth. She runs her tongue over them. "Her?" She lays the photo on the desk and taps it with a chipped teal fingernail. "*That's* Cage's girlfriend?"

"That's her," I say. The woman adjusts her bra strap.

"Well I'll be damned," she says. "I know her."

When I ask how, she responds with a sly smile. She might not tell me, or might demand money. A truck pulls into the lot and her attention shifts. She flicks back the lace curtain and frowns. I see a big guy with lots of tattoos and a beer gut climb out of the cab. His jeans are so tight he has to move slowly.

I recall Colin Destin's warning about Cage being dangerous. "Is that Cage?"

"No," says the woman, obviously amused by my error. "That's my boyfriend, Mitchell." The truck door slams and she turns back to the photo of Josh and Tonya. "I've seen her here," she says flatly. "She was a regular."

"Here?" I ask, unable to keep the skepticism from my voice. "You saw Tonya here?"

"Uh huh," says the woman. "She'd come in once, maybe twice a week. Starting, oh, about a year ago." She leans forward to study the photo more closely. "Haven't seen her for a while though."

She hands me back the photo and I replace it in my purse. "Who was she with?" I ask.

The woman runs a hand through her bangs to fluff them, then lifts a powder compact to her nose and swipes on another layer. "She was with him." She nods toward the photograph. "That cute guy in the tuxedo."

After leaving the Seabreeze I call Jackie and tell her what I've learned: some lady in Esquimalt swears Josh and Tonya were enjoying clandestine get-togethers at a low budget motel. Jackie groans. "Huh. Just when we thought this case couldn't get any weirder," she says. "I'm at Quinn's place. Can you meet me here?"

I drive straight over there.

Quinn opens the door with a glass of milk in one hand. "My mom's in the nursery, putting the crib together," she says. "Don't distract her!"

I roll my eyes. "This is important, Quinn!"

"So's my crib," she says.

Quinn instructs me to help myself to a drink, which I do. Bruce stocks my favorite brand of beer, brewed right here on Vancouver Island. While Quinn is foraging for snacks in the kitchen, I walk down the hall to the baby's room. Sure enough, Jackie's wheelchair is surrounded by disassembled crib parts. She's staring at an instruction booklet with a frown on her face.

"Hey. How's it going?" I ask.

Jackie looks up and sighs. "Not well," she says. Seeing my beer, she brightens. I hand her my can and go to fetch another. "Can you figure this out?" she asks, when I'm back. She passes me the instruction booklet.

I take a seat on the floor and flip through pages full of tiny text. If there was ever an English version, it's now missing. I look in the box. Nothing. "This totally figures," I say. "There's a choice of Spanish, Italian, German, Portuguese, and what I think is Korean. No English. Or French." With our schoolgirl French we'd have a shot, at least.

"Well, between the three of us, surely we can figure it out," says Jackie. "How hard can it be? Two lawyers and a professor . . ."

I peer at the diagrams and shrug. The crib has a lot of parts. The main drawing bristles with arrows. You'd need an aerospace engineering degree to even know where to start. "I don't think so." I hand her back the leaflet and pop my beer's tab.

She squints at the instructions for another minute before tossing them onto the pine floor. "Let's let Bruce deal with it," she says. "Quinn's doing more than her share, and you and I have other things to think about."

I drink a little of my pale ale. "We sure do," I say. I lie down on the floor. The ceiling, like the walls, has been painted a nice gender-neutral yellow. There are cheery orange curtains with a white bird print. In the center of the yellow ceiling hangs a colorful jungle-themed mobile. Jackie finds the remote and pushes a button. A tinkly rendition of "Twinkle Twinkle Little Star" starts up and the mobile starts spinning. I stare up at it, my thoughts turning back to the Seabreeze Inn.

Jackie must be thinking about my latest discovery too. "So this motel receptionist," she says. "You believed her?"

"I think so," I say. Again, I wonder why the woman decided to tell me about her and Cage's tryst. A weird sense of pride, perhaps? Or did she view cheating on her tattooed boyfriend as such a minor deal she saw no reason *not* to tell me? I replay my recent visit to the Seabreeze in my head. "I don't get it," I say, admiring a fuzzy lion on the baby mobile. "Why would Tonya and Josh be meeting at a cheap motel? They were married, for God's sake. And they had a palatial house in Uplands."

"Maybe they found it exciting," says Jackie. She takes a swig of beer. "You know, role-playing or something?"

I make a face. "What?" I ask. "They enjoyed pretending to be poor? And even after they separated they still met twice a week for sex?" I shake my near-empty beer can for emphasis. "It doesn't make sense, Jackie."

"You just never know," she says. "Maybe the sex was still good. As a divorce lawyer, I imagine you hear all kinds of craziness." She takes another gulp of beer. "I sure as hell do."

"Maybe the receptionist was wrong," I say. "Maybe the couple just *looked* like Josh and Tonya." Even as I say it, I realize the chances are slim. Neither of them would exactly blend into a crowd, unless they were at a casting call for a *Baywatch* remake.

Jackie smoothes back her hair. "Alana Mapplebee looks a bit like Tonya," she says. "Or at least they're the same type. Maybe Josh was at the motel meeting Alana."

I consider this. While both women had big blonde hair, boob jobs, and fake tans, their features aren't that similar. Alana's mouth is smaller, while Tonya's nose was more snubbed. Different face shapes too, with Alana's being longer than her rival's. The Seabreeze's receptionist seemed awfully sure that the woman in my photo was Josh's lover.

"Maybe it wasn't Josh," says Quinn. I turn my head to see her standing in the doorway, balancing a tray on her belly.

I sit up and glare at her. "Have you been eavesdropping?" The endless rendition of "Twinkle Twinkle" has gotten to me. I grab the remote and turn off the mobile.

Quinn shrugs. She doesn't look remotely contrite. She sets her tray onto a low table and pops an olive into her mouth. Besides the olives, the tray bears corn chips and salsa. At the sight, my stomach growls. It's almost time for dinner.

"It's not like you were keeping your voices down," says Quinn. She lowers herself into a white rocking chair and starts rocking. She's wearing a pair of Bruce's jean cut-offs and a long blue top, which has ridden up to reveal that a pink hair-elastic is holding her shorts shut. Her belly button, which used to be an innie, is sticking out. I can't help staring at it. "It could have been Mike," says Quinn.

"Mike?" asks Jackie.

I bite back a groan. The thought of Josh and some other woman made me so jealous I missed the obvious. It has to be Mike. I think back to the day I mistook him for Josh at the marina. "Quinn's right," I say. Then I shake my head. "Ew. It's like something off a bad daytime talk show."

"Nasty but possible," says Quinn. "Remember back at Camp Wikwakee? Mike had a huge crush on Tonya."

"*Every* teenage boy had a crush on Tonya," I say. Just like every teenage girl—besides Quinn, and possibly Louise—had a crush on Josh.

"It would explain why Tonya wouldn't even tell her friends who she was seeing on the side," says Jackie. She sips her beer. "Sleeping with your husband's brother is not . . ." Words fail her.

"I guess I'd better go back to the Seabreeze," I say. "Maybe the receptionist will remember their cars or something." I lie back on the floor. Along with the lion, the mobile features a zebra, a giraffe, an elephant, an antelope, and a kangaroo. I wonder who thought the kangaroo was a good idea given that it belongs on a different continent.

Staring up at the mobile, I try to imagine Josh's taciturn younger brother as Tonya's well-endowed, ardent lover. It seems so twisted. I recall what Louise Dobson said, about Tonya breaking it off with Package because he'd become too clingy. Could Mike have killed her because she dumped him? Was he planning to divorce Chantelle to be with Tonya? Does Chantelle know? I guess not, given that she and Mike seemed to be getting along fine at Tonya's funeral.

"Do you think Josh knows about Tonya and Mike's affair?" asks Quinn. She's drinking iced tea and eyeing her mom's beer enviously.

"He couldn't," I say, shocked at the thought. "Mike's still working for him. If Josh knew, would they even be speaking?"

Quinn rubs her belly. "Maybe Josh's just biding his time before he takes revenge," she says. "It's not like he can do anything now, with the cops all over him trying to get him for Tonya's murder."

I blink. Quinn has always had a great imagination. What she's saying is that Josh bludgeoned Tonya and plans to kill Mike too. When I turn to Jackie, I expect her to look incredulous. Instead, she looks thoughtful. I set down my beer. Is Jackie actually considering Quinn's crazy revenge theory?

"You'd better get back to the Seabreeze," says Jackie. "And for God's sake, don't say anything to Josh about any of this. If Tonya was sleeping with Mike, we'd better find out if Josh knew or not, because if he did . . ." She shakes her head. "Well, the cops would be thrilled. Even *without* all that money at stake, discovering your wife and your brother having an affair is one hell of a good motive for murder."

CHAPTER SEVENTEEN:

MOTHS

Jackie and Quinn talked me into staying for an early dinner. By the time I get back to the Seabreeze, darkness has fallen.

The chain-smoking receptionist looks neither surprised nor pleased to see me again. "Did you send the cops?" she asks. She's now wearing a hooded sweatshirt over her tank top and has applied what must be her evening makeup: metallic blue eyeshadow up to her brows and even more mascara. The odor of fast food has joined the smells of old cigarette smoke and hairspray. There's a crumpled McDonald's bag in the trash, while a half-empty box of fries lies open on the desk near an old-fashioned dial telephone.

I shake my head. "No," I say, alarmed. "Why? Were they here?" The woman nods.

I bite back a groan. Do they know about Mike? "What did they want?"

She shrugs, like it's not worth getting into. Faced with her hard blue stare I feel nervous. It looks as though her patience has worn thin. I expect her to tell me to get out of here.

Instead, she offers me a smoke. I guess my company must be better than nothing. "Same as you," she says, handing me her lighter. "They wanted to know about that blond couple."

I manage to light the cigarette and start coughing. The last time I smoked was in high school.

The receptionist picks out a crispy fry. There's a ring with a row of colored stones on her ring finger. I've seen similar ones advertised in the backs of magazines. You can select your birthstone and those of your loved ones. I study hers: Peridot—August. Garnet—January. Aquamarine—March. Opal—October. I wonder who the stones are for. Her mom and dad? Or her kids, perhaps?

Outside, a car honks. The woman flicks back the lace curtains.

Satisfied that nothing of interest is happening within sight, she turns back to me and stifles a yawn. "Where you from?" She wipes her hands on her jeans and taps out a fresh cigarette.

I stub mine out, gratefully. "Here," I say. "Born and raised in Victoria."

Beneath frazzled bangs, she frowns. Even before she says it, I know what's coming: "No, where are you *really* from?"

How many times, over the years, have I heard this question, or worse? The first half of the hateful rhyme Tonya invented at camp floats into my ears: *Me Chinese, me a slut* . . .

I bite down, hard, to block my ears and to stop myself from shooting back an answer the receptionist won't like. I can't afford to offend her. I want her to keep talking to me. Plus she doesn't mean to be rude or ignorant. I just look different from her—so can't *really* belong.

"My great grandparents came from China," I say. "On my mom's side."

She nods. "I got nothing against immigrants myself," she says. "Most of the chamber maids we got here are Mexican. We got one from El Salvador too. She's only got one hand but works really fast." She lights her smoke. "I don't know how she does it."

"I'm Toby," I say, since I don't know how else to respond.

The woman nods. "I'm Anastasia," she says. "Not that I'm Russian. My mom was a bit of a dreamer, thought it sounded romantic." She gives a tight smile. "Most people call me Stacy."

"Nice to meet you, Stacy," I say. Once again, she's peering out of the lace curtains. I wonder what time her shift ends. She must get really bored in here.

I'm wondering how to turn the conversation back to Tonya and Mike when Stacy does it for me. "The cops got really excited when I ID'd Cage's ex," she says.

I nod. "Do you remember what kinds of cars they drove?"

Stacy looks incredulous. "The cops?" she asks. "Unmarked but you can always tell." She snorts. "I can spot a cop a mile off."

I shake my head. "No, what cars were Cage's ex and the guy she was with driving?"

"Oh them." She picks up another French fry. "She drove a little gold Mercedes convertible. Hard to forget. And the guy had a Ford truck, same model as Mitchell's, which is why I remember it. Except Mitch's is black and his was blue." She eyes me curiously. "Why? The cops think that hot guy she was doing here might have killed her?"

"I don't know," I say. I feel both exhilarated about having unearthed some new info and mildly sick. Mike drives a blue Ford truck. How will I tell Josh that his wife was sleeping with his brother?

My alarmed expression must register because Stacy gives a knowing nod. "That hot guy, Mr. Smyth, he's your old man, isn't he?" She exhales a cloud of white smoke. "I knew he was cheating on *someone*." She looks me up and down. "That uppity blonde bitch stole him from you, didn't she?" She purses her lips. "And now the cops think you offed her?"

I shake my head and laugh. I bet she watches a lot of soaps. "No," I say. "I'm single. Smith? Is that what they called themselves?"

"Yeah, with a 'y,'" says Stacy. "Tricky, huh? 'Course I knew it was a fake name." She twists at her ring, studying my black pants and cream sweater. From the pitying look in her eyes, I think she's still convinced I'm a scorned woman. "If you want that guy back, ya might want to dress a little sexier," she says. "Like, tighter clothes. Guys are visual, ya know?"

I'm too amazed to respond. I bet she got that straight out of Cosmo.

"And heels. Guys love a woman in heels." She pulls a powder compact from her purse and swipes on a fresh orangey layer. "You can do a lot with makeup."

I bite my tongue. A woman who makes Chantelle look classy is giving me fashion advice. But she seems sincere. I sigh. That's why it's so sad. She's just trying to help me.

A few units down some drunk guy starts to yell. A door slams. Stacy rolls her glittery eyes. "Jesus, I got to go tell that asshole to keep it down." She snaps her compact shut. Before preceding me out the door, she turns to give me one last bit of advice. "That guy, Smyth or whatever he's called, forget about him. Find someone else. He's not worth it."

I start to say she's got it wrong, that I don't want him, but his brother. Then I shut my mouth and nod. It's pathetic, either way, and the truth is, Quinn might be right. Maybe I've spent all this time wanting Josh because I know I'll never get him. What if I'm one of those people who's just happier on my own?

I follow Stacy outdoors. Outside of the office hangs a light. A moth is banging against the bulb as though hoping to burrow inside it. I consider flicking it away. Maybe it'll go someplace else. But I know it's a lost cause. That moth and that light bulb are fated.

CHAPTER EIGHTEEN:

OH BROTHER

Jackie and I are sitting in her kitchen, which offers a view of their hilly yard, rooftops, and Cadboro Bay, in the distance.

It's raining, the ocean like dull pewter. I get up and help myself to another cup of coffee. Jackie's house is warm, and despite, or maybe because of, the gloomy day, the kitchen feels bright and cozy. From the living room I can hear the sound of a vacuum cleaner. Jackie's twice-a-week cleaning lady, Mary, is in today. Over the top of the vacuum Mary is singing a Beatles song.

Jackie pries another slice of date square out of the pan sitting between us. "Another slice?" she asks.

I hold out my plate. Ever since Jackie's accident, friends have been dropping off cakes and casseroles. Her extra-wide freezer is packed. I take a bite. The date square is still warm from the oven.

Jackie glances at the wall clock. "Josh should be here soon," she says. "Are you going to tell him?"

I shrug. We need to tell him about his brother's affair, but the thought leaves a bad taste in my mouth. How betrayed will he feel? I take another sip of coffee. "I guess so," I say, reluctantly.

With the vacuum still going, we didn't hear Josh's car. Mary must have let him in, because all of a sudden, he's standing in the kitchen doorway. "Sorry, I'm late," he says. Dressed in a red raincoat, a navy sweater, and jeans, he looks like he just hopped out of a Ralph Lauren ad. Maybe it's my imagination, but I catch a whiff of the ocean. He heads for Jackie first, kissing her on both cheeks, then turns to me and says, "So what's the bad news?"

I look at Jackie, willing her to fill him in, but she just asks if he wants some coffee and a date square. Josh eyes the pan and smiles. "Please. It smells fantastic." I jump up to fetch him a mug and a plate. He hangs his raincoat on an empty chair and takes a seat next to Jackie.

After he's got his coffee and cake, I can't put it off any longer. I take a deep breath. Josh looks from me to Jackie, then back at me. As usual, I feel self-conscious in his presence. Is my top too tight?

"We know who Tonya was sleeping with," I say.

Josh runs a hand through his damp hair and frowns. "Okay. Who?"

I tell him about my visit to the Seabreeze Inn. "The receptionist recognized a photo of Tonya," I say. "And your brother. They were meeting there."

Josh's face hardens. "Mike?"

I nod, trying to analyze his reaction. Did he already know? While he looks genuinely upset, I'm not sure he's surprised. His eyes, normally aquamarine, appear almost as dark as his sweater. I wait for him to question me, but he doesn't.

"She ID'd their cars too," I say. "Sorry."

Josh stares out of Jackie's picture window. A red squirrel saunters across the lawn, freezing when it catches sight of us, only to dart off, chirping loudly. Jackie folds her arms. Like me, she's waiting for some reaction.

Josh turns back to us. "I wish I could say that's impossible, but unfortunately it sounds . . ." He massages his forehead. "Plausible."

"Really?" I say, shocked that he could even imagine his brother sleeping with his wife. White trash overload.

"You don't know Mike," he says. He meets my eyes, then looks away. "We've never gotten along that well."

"But he's married," I say. "And he works for you!"

"Yeah," says Josh. He grimaces. "Ever since we were little he's resented me, and I've always felt guilty about it. Whenever I try to help him he accuses me of showing off or interfering. But then he's always asking for money, and if I say no, I'm a selfish bastard." He clenches his jaw. "I can't win, basically."

"Did you suspect them?" I ask. The police will be eager to prove that Josh knew about Mike and Tonya.

Josh takes a deep breath. "I knew Tonya was being unfaithful before we split," he says carefully. "But no, like I said, I didn't know it was with . . ." He swallows hard. "My brother."

"How did you know she was having an affair?" asks Jackie. Like me, she's watching Josh intently.

"Louise Dobson told me."

I can't hide my surprise. "Why would she do that?" I ask. "I thought Louise was Tonya's friend."

Josh shrugs. "I'm not sure Tonya had any real girlfriends."

I think back to my meeting with Louise and how she'd struck me as a drama queen. Was telling Josh a way to get back at Tonya for years of being bullied and belittled? How deep did Louise's dislike of her so-called friend go?

"I thought she was making it up," continues Josh, "but then I started paying attention." He looks thoughtful. "Tonya seemed different, more secretive and excited."

"Did you confront her about it?" asks Jackie.

"No." Josh studies his plate. "At the time I was seeing Alana, and it made me feel less guilty to find out Tonya was cheating on me, too." When he meets my eyes, he looks embarrassed. "That's when I knew our marriage was unfixable."

"According to Louise, Tonya broke it off with Mike," I say. "And he didn't take it well."

At this fresh mention of Mike, Josh's face darkens. "Well, he wouldn't," he says. He stands up and starts pacing around the kitchen. "He was sleeping with her to get back at me," he says. "This wasn't about Tonya. Mike didn't even *like* Tonya. He was always complaining about her, saying what a ditz she was. He thought Tonya was a bad influence on Chantelle too, always taking her shopping."

"Apparently Tonya told Louise he was in love with her," I say.

Josh rolls his eyes. "Tonya would think that," he says sourly. "She thought everyone was in love with her."

He looks so disdainful that I can't help but wonder why he'd married her in the first place. "Did *you* love her?" I ask.

Josh looks surprised. I'm surprised I voiced the question too. Is it any of my business?

"I . . . God, I don't know." He sighs. "When we met up in L.A., I was working all the time. I was stressed and lonely, and Tonya was a familiar face, someone from home. We had fun together and . . ." He looks wistful. "I'm not sure it was love," he says. "But I wanted it to be." He meets my eyes, then turns to gaze out the window. It's raining harder now, the lawn sodden.

For a few minutes, nobody speaks. Then Jackie clears her throat. "Josh," she says. "Right now, we don't know if the police know about Mike and Tonya's affair. But if we figured it out, so will they, and at that point they're going to ask whether you knew, or not." Jackie's voice is solemn. "If you did, they'll see it as yet another motive for killing her."

Josh spins toward her. "I already told you I didn't do it." His eyes narrow. "Do you think Mike could have . . ." He swallows hard and stops talking.

"Do you?" I ask.

Josh makes a fist, and for a second I think he'll hit something. But he just takes a deep breath. "I'm going to kill him," he says. He looks angry enough to be serious.

In the living room there's a loud clattering noise. Mary must have dropped something. The vacuum is turned off. Seeing my expression, Josh exhales. "I don't mean that literally," he says. "But I need to talk to him . . ." He reaches for his mobile.

"No," says Jackie. She lays a hand on his arm. "You will not discuss this with Mike until after the police have questioned him."

Josh starts to respond but Jackie cuts him off. "This is important," she says firmly. "You hired me to ensure you won't be charged, tried, and convicted of your wife's murder. Let me do my job and let the police do theirs. You do want to know who killed Tonya, don't you?"

Josh's shoulders slump. "Yes," he says.

But looking at his tight lips, I'm not sure I believe him.

CHAPTER NINETEEN:

NAME GAME

One of the places I've been asking people if they recognize photos of Josh and Tonya is the Oak Bay Marina. Maybe someone will recall seeing her here with somebody besides Josh on the night she died. Or confirm Josh's story that he jumped off his boat and headed straight to the parking lot.

Since Quinn is already on maternity leave and the weather is brilliant, I invited her to join me this morning. After poking around, we can have an early lunch in the café.

While I'm dressed for work, I have left my heels in the car and am wearing flip-flops. Quinn is clad in shorts, one of Bruce's massive t-shirts, and a bucket hat. Although it's a Wednesday, the docks are busy, with fishermen lugging coolers to and from shore, and pedestrians, like us, out enjoying the Indian summer. It's warm, with no clouds, bright sunshine, and a fresh breeze blowing in off the water.

I have a stack of photocopied color prints in one hand and a paper coffee cup in the other. Due to he/she who cannot be named, Quinn's coffee is decaf, but I've gone all out and ordered a double espresso.

I've just told Quinn about the fashion advice I got at the Seabreeze Inn.

"Ha! She told you to wear tighter clothes?" Quinn laughs. Her eyes glint beneath her green hat. With her tan, plus all that extra blood, she looks bronzed and luminous. Pregnancy, like everything else, suits her.

"Yup," I say. "And high heels."

Glancing back at the ramp, I see a young guy laden with rods and tackle checking out Quinn's toned legs, only to do a guilty double take when he spots her belly. Ogling pregnant ladies isn't kosher. I feel the urge to laugh at him.

Quinn looks me up and down. "Oh please. You dress fine," she says. "This is Victoria. Everyone dresses casually. You wear tight clothes and high heels in the daytime and people will think you're a hooker."

Given that most of Quinn's wardrobe hails from the Mountain Equipment Coop, it's not like she's about to be hired by *Vogue* as a guest stylist. Maybe Anastasia was onto something. If I want Josh to fall for me—after his name's been cleared and I'm no longer on his payroll, of course—I might want to up my style quotient.

"This receptionist . . ."

"Anastasia."

"She's called Anastasia?" asks Quinn. I can see her brain ticking over. Anastasia is clearly one baby name she's failed to consider yet.

"Yes," I say. "But she goes by Stacy."

"I don't like either of those names," says Quinn. She pouts. "Still no name . . ."

"Wait until the baby's born," I say. "I'm sure as soon as you see . . . it, the perfect name will pop into your head."

"I don't see how," says Quinn glumly. "I've already thought of *everything*."

I bite my tongue. I'm sick to death of this topic. "Why don't you ask my mom?" I ask, in desperation. "Maybe she could, like, consult the cards to find you a name. Or her Ouija board."

"Hmmm, maybe," says Quinn. Then she sees my face and realizes I was joking. She looks indignant. "Ye of little faith!" she says. "Mocking your own mother!"

I roll my eyes. "She makes it so easy."

Quinn puts her hands on her hips. "Come on, you have to admit that séance was creepy! That knocking against the window!" She shivers happily. "And that weird text message when Ivy asked for help to find Tonya's killer! What was it? Cloud Color?" Quinn looks around. "Hey, what if it's the name of a boat? It sounds like a boat's name—the *Cloud Color*."

I shrug. There's no point in even answering. Quinn knows what

I think about that dumb text message. If some part of her (clearly not the part that got a PhD) wants to believe it was a missive from beyond the grave, I can't stop her.

"Let's go this way," she says, and I sigh. She's now scanning the name of every boat we pass. I show my photocopies to a couple of ancient mariners, who, after finally locating their reading glasses, say they don't recall either of them. Quinn and I walk on in silence for some minutes.

Finally, we reach the last dock, where the *Great Escape* is usually moored. I'm surprised it's not here. Having impounded it for ten days, the police released it yesterday, which means Forensics found nothing suspicious. Tonya wasn't killed on the boat. At least some good news for Josh. I gaze along the dock. Down where Tonya's body was found, the yellow police tape has been cleared away.

Quinn takes my arm as if to steer me away from these grim thoughts. To our right lies the *Sweet Maria*, a white and green sailboat with a small American flag at its rear.

"How about Maria for a girl?" asks Quinn.

"I don't love it," I admit.

Her face falls. "Yeah, me neither."

I'm wondering what I'd call my kid, if I were pregnant. Will I ever get the chance to have a family? All those years I was studying and working sixteen-hour days I never thought about kids, and now, nearing my mid-thirties, I'm back in a place where most of the single guys are either students or retired widowers. I doubt I'd be brave enough to be a single mother.

Maybe Quinn senses a cloud of gloom hovering over me, or maybe, like usual, she's got great timing, because she turns and asks if I'll be her baby's godmother.

"Me?" I ask, genuinely surprised and flattered. "Are you sure? I mean, I know nothing about kids."

"And I do?" asks Quinn.

We both laugh. I tell her I'd be honored.

"Great, your first job is to help me to think of a name," she says.

"Something that isn't too popular so there won't be three or four of them in the kid's class."

I nod. Quinn has outlined her baby-name manifesto at least as many times as my mom's asked if I'm seeing someone.

"But it can't be too out-there either," continues Quinn. "Like no made-up names or Pixie-Apple-Tigerlily kind of thing. And definitely no bizarre spellings."

"Like Smyth with a Y," I say.

"Exactly." She readjusts the strap of her maternity bra, which is about as wide as the Trans-Canada. "My mom knows someone who named her kid D-apostrophe-A-R-C-I-E-E."

I shudder. Call me anal—and Quinn does regularly—but people who stick signs outside of their homes reading THE BROWN'S are slowly driving me toward vandalism. Misplaced apostrophes are bad enough, but that unnecessary apostrophe in what ought to be DARCY makes me want to slap someone. "Shouldn't be allowed," I say.

A stereo is playing on one of the boats, Bob Marley telling us not to worry. I inhale the cold sea air and sing along in my head. It's a nice thought. But then I remember how Bob ended up dying of some obscure cancer. Immediately, I think of my mother, then try to divert my attention back to the scenery.

We pass the *Dora*, the *Saltspring Gal*, and the *Esmeraldo*. Even Quinn fails to consider this last name for her offspring, although she gives "Dora" some serious thought. Despite myself, I'm on the lookout for a *Cloud Color*, too. I spot a *loud* on the side of a large catamaran and my heart jumps, another step revealing it to be the *Laugh Aloud*. I feel freshly annoyed at my ridiculous mother.

Quinn's eyes slide along the hull of a sailboat with brass portholes only to stop at its moniker, the *Abby Lucas*. "Those are both cool names." She stops walking and repeats them to herself.

It's hot in the sun, and bright. Even with sunglasses, I'm squinting. Shielding my eyes from the glare I recognize the large black poodle ambling toward us. A long piece of broken kelp trails from its mouth, leaving a squiggly wet line on the dock. "Hey, that was Tonya's dog," I tell Quinn.

"Cute," says Quinn, who loves dogs. She bends down and extends a hand. "Here boy," she says. "What's his name?"

"Claude," I say. "His last owner was French." The dog's ears jerk forward and its puffy tail thumps. It ambles closer.

"Here Claude," says Quinn, bending to scratch its throat. Claude leans up against her, clearly thrilled. Quinn's great with animals and babies.

Watching Quinn pet the dog, I know she'll be a wonderful mother. I can't believe how fast time's going. My oldest and best friend will soon have a baby. And part of me, I'm ashamed to admit, is jealous—and scared of losing her. Will our lives become too different when she's a mom, until we have nothing in common?

I'm standing there, pondering this huge shift in Quinn's life and how it'll affect me, when a stray thought flits through my head. I shut my eyes but the thought's gone. The dog's tail thumps against the dock. I gaze out toward Cattle Point, a half dozen sailboats in view, pristine against the navy blue water. Straight ahead I can make out the ghostly shape of Mount Baker. Claude's collar jangles. And then I catch it.

Tonya couldn't spell for shit, even in the afterlife.

I crouch down and peer at the dog's collar. Quinn gives me a weird look. She's still rubbing the white patch at Claude's throat. I see a dark, crusty spot on the stainless steel dog tag.

"What are you looking at?" asks Quinn.

I shake my head. It's probably not dried blood. And if it is, it's just an incredible coincidence. Luck. Chance. A total fluke. I bite my lip. This is too crazy.

"Toby?"

I hear a male voice and firm footsteps. Detective Colin Destin is striding toward us, dressed in grey pants and a white shirt. Although he's squinting against the sun he looks good. I wish I'd followed Anastasia's advice and applied some makeup, instead of just clear chapstick.

Colin smiles and I smile back. In his office clothes he looks out of place on the docks. As do I. He cocks his head, shyly. "Hi," he says. "What are you guys doing here?"

I hold up a photocopy of Tonya's face. "Asking around," I say.

For a second, Colin's face tightens. Quinn says she's just out for a walk and Colin nods. "Perfect day for it." He sounds wistful.

"You working?" asks Quinn.

"I am." He sounds resigned. "I'm looking for Josh's brother, Michael Barton. Have you guys seen him?" Then he notices the poodle and bends down. "Hey big fella. Do you remember me?" Claude gazes up at him adoringly. "Too bad he couldn't tell us what happened to Tonya, eh?" he says, patting the dog's wooly rump. He ruffles Claude's ears. "You could be the star witness."

Maybe I've gotten too much sun, or too much caffeine, because all of a sudden, I feel dizzy. I feel guilty too, like I'm privy to a secret I'd rather not know. I blink. Quinn is looking at me strangely.

If there's anyone I know who's psychic, it's my best friend. At least she can read *my* mind. "Claude's collar," she says. She gives me a hard look and lowers herself carefully to a crouch. She peers at the dog's collar.

"Look!" she says excitedly. "There's blood on it!" She points at some dark crusty flecks on the metal dog tag. Colin looks perplexed. The poodle rolls onto its back and stretches, clearly hinting at a belly rub. "I can't believe it!" says Quinn.

Colin starts to ask what she means when she grabs his arm, hard, and tugs on it. From the startled look on Colin's face, it's obvious he thinks she's in labor. "Claude's collar!" she says again. "The dog was with Tonya the night she died! That's Tonya's blood! There might be fingerprints!" She waves her hat. "You have to test it!"

Colin has known Quinn for years. He and Bruce did their basic police training together. He knows Quinn is smart, sane, and sensible, yet I can see him wondering. Is she suffering from some sort of pregnancy-induced mania? Is it sunstroke? She waves her hands like a crazy person.

Unimpressed by Colin's failure to grasp the situation, Quinn turns to me. "Ha!" she says, as though she's just won a bet. "It worked! Your mom's séance worked! She really did contact Tonya. Cloud Color. You knew the dog's name. I can't believe it took you so long!"

Now Colin is staring at me. Meeting his doubtful gaze, my face colors. I wish I'd gone to the office. Or come here without Quinn. "Toby?" asks Colin.

I want to tell him this is a misunderstanding but where would I start? How can I explain without mentioning my mom's purported gift? I wonder how, even when she's not physically present, she still manages to embarrass me. My blush has spread. I study my feet. Even my toes appear scalded.

When it's obvious that no response is forthcoming, Colin turns back to Quinn. "What are you guys talking about?"

I resent his use of the plural. "It's nothing," I mumble.

Quinn throws me an incredulous look. "What do you mean—nothing?"

I use the photocopies to fan myself. Quinn won't let this rest. I look toward the marina's coffee shop and long for a cold drink, preferably a strong alcoholic one. Then I try, despite the blush, to adopt the measured, *sane* persona I employ in court. "Colin?" I ask. "Could you do us a favor and test the dog's collar for blood, DNA, and fingerprints?"

Colin bends to look at Claude's collar. "I guess it could be blood." He straightens up and shrugs. "Or it might just be crud, you know, old dog food, dirt, grease . . ." He gives me a tentative smile. "But what the hell. We'll test it." He looks back at the dog. "But I need to find his owner."

"That's me," says a clipped voice. We all turn to see Mike Barton, dressed in cargo shorts, a faded green t-shirt, and a Canucks cap. He whistles and Claude jumps up. The dog looks guilty, like it's been caught cheating.

"Michael, I've been looking for you," says Colin Destin. He reaches into his jacket pocket for his badge and Mike frowns.

"I know who you are." He looks unimpressed. "What do you want?"

"I have some questions," says Colin. "And I'd like to take your dog's collar."

For an instant, Mike looks surprised. But then he just shrugs. "Sure, whatever." He passes the fishing rod he's holding from hand to hand. "Is this about Josh?" he asks.

Colin looks from me to Quinn. He wipes his hands on his pants. I guess Claude slobbered all over them. "It'd be better if we talked alone," he tells Mike. "Will you walk up to my car?" Seeing Mike's look of alarm, Colin raises a hand. "You don't need to come to the station. I just have a few questions. And there are evidence bags in my car." He nods toward Claude. "For the collar."

"Fine," says Mike. He squints at Quinn and me. "You two into boating?" he asks.

I'm fairly sure that's sarcasm in his voice. While I don't bother answering, Quinn says we're out for a walk, enjoying the perfect weather.

"Yeah, it's a nice day," says Mike, looking straight at me. "But if you're looking for my brother, he's not here. He's out with some girl." He pretends to smile. "Who can keep track?" he asks.

Faced with Mike's mocking stare, I feel my eyes water. Did he mention that other girl just to see how I'd react? I glare back at him. Does everyone know about my crush?

Colin smiles at me. "So, um, see you soon?" he asks.

I nod. I hope Colin didn't understand that Mike's last comment was directed at me. Or am I just paranoid? "Uh yeah, bye Colin," I say. "Have a good day." Ew, how lame did that sound? It's like I work at McDonald's.

"Don't forget about the collar," says Quinn.

They're about twenty feet away when Quinn smacks me with her bucket hat. "What's going on between you two?" she whispers.

"What?" I ask. I have no idea what she's talking about.

"You and Colin." She tilts her head. "All those lingering looks you exchanged."

"We didn't exchange any lingering looks!" I say. "You really are crazy!"

"Ha! And this is coming from you?" asks Quinn. She bends to tie her shoe but can't manage it. I offer to do it for her.

When I've straightened up, Quinn picks up where we left off. "I know Colin's had a thing for you for a while, but I didn't realize he stood a chance." She smooths her shirt over her belly and smiles. "I like it," she says. "You'd be great together."

"Quinn," I say. "You're insane. This baby has done something to your head. I mean, first that thing with my mom being able to talk to spirits and now this . . ." I turn toward the ramp and see Colin and Mike walking up the stairs. The dog has stopped to sniff at a garbage can. I watch a seagull dive bomb it. Claude starts barking.

"What?" asks Quinn. "You think Cloud Color was just a coincidence?" She snorts. "Oh please, Toby! Even for someone as . . ." She stomps on Claude's abandoned piece of kelp. "As in denial as you, that's too much."

"Denial?" I ask. "What am I in denial about?" By now I'm hot, thirsty, and genuinely fed up with Quinn.

"Everything!" she says. "Starting with your dad leaving and you never, ever wanting to date anyone who's actually available!" She throws up her hands. "Just because your mom's sometimes wrong doesn't mean she's never right! And just because your parents' marriage didn't work out doesn't mean every relationship's doomed. There are no guarantees, you know!"

There are real tears in her eyes. All those pregnancy hormones, I guess. I'm tempted to yell at her, or storm off, but also afraid to. Plus I'm stunned. I can't believe she sees me this way. My best friend thinks I'm a coward.

I start tearing up, too. I try to step back, but Quinn is too fast and her arms are too long. Before I know it, I'm crushed against her big round belly. "I'm sorry," she says. "That sounded harsh, but you're not a kid anymore. I *know* you want a partner." She squeezes me tighter. "You just have to give guys a chance. Real guys, I mean."

"I do," I mumble. It's hard to breathe with my nose squashed against Quinn's shoulder. "I just haven't met the right guy yet."

She releases me and leans back. There's something motherly about her expression, at once indulgent and stern. "Maybe you have," she says flatly.

I think of Josh, and the feeling I get when he looks at me—hope mixed with hopelessness, the percentages forever shifting. I think of my dad and his new family, the two stepbrothers I've only met a few times, and how, after they arrived, my dad stopped making any pretense of maintaining contact with me.

In one of the boats, Bob Marley's now singing about freedom. *None of them can stop the time.* I look toward Mount Baker. Some of the mist has burned away, the mountain appearing so close, and so perfect, that it takes my breath away. If only I could see the future so clearly.

CHAPTER TWENTY:

DIRTY LAUNDRY

The majority of the tenants in my building are senior citizens, mostly widows. The guy across from me, Mr. Garlowski, is one of the building's few widowers, his wife, Martha, having suffered a brain aneurysm thirteen years ago, shortly after their youngest son announced his plans to drop out of med school and sit in a tree for two years to raise awareness about the plight of the marbled murrelet.

Mr. Garlowski told me about Martha's demise when we first met in the building's communal laundry room. The first few years were hard, he'd said, but he's gotten used to being single again. Then he'd leered at my ass and winked at me.

Despite being short, bald, and scrawny, around here, Mr. Garlowski's a hot commodity. So hot, in fact, that every other time I pass his door I can hear a different woman's voice in there. Sometimes I peek out of my little peephole and see them loitering in the hall, clutching casseroles or trays of cookies and fixing their hair one last time.

All this female attention has gone to Mr. Garlowski's liver-spotted head, because he's convinced he has a chance with me—despite being forty years older *and* a few centimeters shorter than me.

I think he watches my front door, because whenever I go to do laundry, he shows up. I'm separating my colors when he hobbles into the room, his laundry basket full of plaid garments. Everything the man wears is checkered. Year-round, he favors brushed flannel.

As usual, Mr. Garlowski feigns surprise upon seeing me, doing a comic double take and pushing his glasses up his nose. "Hey Doll!" he says, my name being alternately Doll or Sugar. Sometimes he calls me China Doll, which I especially hate. By comparison, Doll is almost acceptable.

I say hello and keep sorting.

"I thought you'd be out on a hot date," says Mr. Garlowski. "It being Friday night and all."

I ignore this comment. Mr. Garlowski starts patting at various plaid pockets in search of quarters. Finally, as expected, he asks if I have change for five dollars. As usual, I do, and as usual, I resent giving it to him. Why am I organized enough to get change in advance when I'm working full-time, whereas Mr. Garlowski can't get it together despite being at home all day long?

Not that he's at home much. What with lawn bowling, golf, tennis, and going to the Oak Bay Seniors' Center, he's a busy man. Plus he's out constantly with his string of lady friends.

"Perfect night like this, I figured you'd be out with your man," says Mr. Garlowski. He stares up at the laundry room's only window, which, given that we're in the basement, barely counts as one, as though he were gazing through the gates of Paradise.

Through this cell-like opening I can see the base of a rhododendron bush, visible despite the late hour because a floodlight is shining on it. "Stars out, soft breeze, perfect night for a drive . . ." He tugs at his pants' elastic waistband. "Ah, if only I were young again."

He dumps his entire load into a machine and tosses in some detergent. It's all I can do to stop myself from saying something. How has he lived so long without learning how to do laundry? No wonder his clothes look like they do.

He nods toward my laundry piles. "Ya know, Sugar, in all my years I've never met anyone as careful about separating colors as you."

I toss a light blue sock into my pale colors pile and shrug. "How so?" I ask.

"Light and dark I get. And colors too. Martha did those separately. But you, you got white and black plus light, bright, *and* dark colors." He nods toward my various piles. "That's five categories." He scratches his bald head. "I can see why you'd make one hell of a lawyer."

"I hate it when colors run," I say. Since the laundry room's walls are bare cement there's an echo in here and my voice comes out sounding weird and prissy.

"Uh huh," says Mr. Garlowski. He shoves his hands into his plaid pants and looks me up and down. Something about his expression, combined with Quinn's recent assertion that I'm a control freak, leaves me wanting to throw something at him. A dirty sock, maybe. Definitely nothing sexy or he might take it the wrong way.

"Take it easy, Doll," he says, heading for the exit. In the doorway, he stops. "Oh, I forgot. You had a visitor, Sugar."

"A visitor?" I parrot. I'm holding a mauve nightie that's a bit too purple for the light pile, but too pale for the brights.

"A young man," he says. "He stopped by this afternoon. When you were out."

"Oh," I say. Naturally, my first thought is Josh, quickly followed by Colin Destin. The Japanese takeout I had for dinner shifts in my belly. Josh or Colin? I imagine them both standing outside my door, waiting.

A bell dings. I tell myself to get a grip. There's a high chance it was neither of them. My idea of young might not match Mr. Garlowski's. "What did he look like?" I ask.

Mr. Garlowski fingers a loose button on his shirt. I bet that by tomorrow, some lady will have offered to fix it. "Tall, blond, not bad looking," he says.

Josh? Fighting back a smile, I take a chance and toss my nightie into the bright pile. "Did he say what he wanted?"

"No idea," says Mr. Garlowski. "But he slipped a note under your door. You didn't see it?"

"Uh, no," I say. "But thanks for telling me." It occurs to me that Mr. Garlowski might be pulling my leg. Maybe, like everyone else in town, he's aware of my crush on Josh. Maybe he thinks it's fun to torture me. I grit my teeth and chastise myself. Paranoid much?

Mr. Garlowski is still hanging around in the doorway. When I look up at him, he gives me a sly smile. "So, is he your boyfriend?"

I shake my head. "No," I say firmly. "Just someone from work." The last thing I need is to fertilize the building's gossip vine.

"Right," says Mr. Garlowski. He gives me a big wink. "Whatever you say, Sugar." He cocks his head. "I don't want you to take this the wrong way, Doll, but the guy looked like a bit of a player." He taps the bag beneath his left eye. "I know. I got the eye, Sugar."

"Takes one to know one," I say, and Mr. Garlowski laughs. I grit my teeth. That slipped out. I wonder if I ought to apologize.

Above us, someone is walking around. Whoever it is is obviously wearing clogs, or some type of heavy orthopedic shoes. I say a little prayer of thanks that my unit is on the top floor. The reason my apartment was available, and a great deal, is that this building has no elevator and most residents can't reach the fourth floor.

Mr. Garlowski taps a plaid slipper against the floor. "You know, life is short," he says. "You gotta have fun, Sugar."

I expect that to be the end of it, but Mr. Garlowski hesitates. Beneath his square glasses, his eyes are solemn. "I wish Martha were still here," he says. "I really do. But she's not, so I gotta be grateful for the years we had and make the most of what I've got now." He gives his pants' elastic waistband another tug.

I see a flash of checkered boxers and raise my eyes, fast. Mr. Garlowski meets them. "You know what I'm saying, Doll?"

"Yes," I say. Talking about Martha he looked so wistful that I almost liked the man.

"You got your whole life ahead of you," he says. "So get out and enjoy it. You hear me?"

All of a sudden, I fear I might cry. Instead, I focus on measuring out the correct amount of detergent, and wish Mr. Garlowski a good night.

"Sweet dreams, Sugar," he says. And then he gives my ass a once-over and winks at me.

After he's gone, I'm tempted to chuck everything into one machine and race upstairs and find the note. But I don't, because that would reveal a lack of willpower. Plus, if it's not from Josh, or really dull, I'll feel even more stupid for having rushed up there.

When my five loads are in the machines I head back upstairs.

Just like Mr. Garlowski said, there's a folded note in my tiny front hall, bearing my name in slightly messy male handwriting.

I pick it up and open it.

Dear Toby,
I've been trying to call but your phone is off. So I stopped by.

A quick check of my phone reveals that it powered down, the battery down to zero. I set down my empty hamper and carry the note into my bedroom, where I keep my phone-charger.

Are you free for brunch on Sunday? We could go out on the boat around 10:00 a.m. and have a picnic on my favorite deserted island—smoked salmon, strawberries, and champagne.

Let me know! I hope you can make it.

Call me!

Josh

I plug in my cell phone and sit on my bed. Josh Barton is asking *me* on a date. A warm feeling spreads through my chest. I study the painting on the wall across from me, a watercolor of two little girls, rock-pooling. One of the girls has dark hair, and the other is fair. The dark-haired one holds a red bucket. The painting was a gift from my mom a couple of Christmases ago. She said it reminded her of Quinn and me.

I reread the note. A date with Josh Barton. A picnic. Smoked salmon and champagne. I feel like hugging a pillow or jumping up and down. One of the most desirable men I've ever met is asking me out. I imagine the two of us clinking glasses and gazing into each other's eyes. I feel exultant. Then I remember that Quinn's baby shower is Sunday at 4:00 p.m. Can I go out with Josh and make it back in time?

My phone beeps. It's my eight o'clock alarm, reminding me to feed my fish. Still holding Josh's note, I walk into my living room. When I moved here, my mom bought me a fish tank, for lucky feng shui. There are currently eight goldfish in residence. I started out with twelve. Don't tell Ivy.

Watching my fish, I wonder if I've turned Sunday's lunch date into something it isn't. Maybe Josh wants to discuss the case. Or maybe he sees me as a friendly ear. His intentions might not be romantic.

My elation soon morphs to worry. I don't want to make a fool of myself. I don't want to get my hopes up. I consider texting Josh to say sorry, I have other plans. I could just relax and do regular Sunday chores, like cleaning the fish tank and reorganizing my junk drawer. I should exercise too, and wrap Quinn's shower gift. Plus I have a ton of ironing to get through.

But then I think of Mr. Garlowski, and his advice to live a little.

I imagine calling Josh to say sure, I'd love to go boating with him. I'd sound relaxed and he'd sound relieved. "I can't wait to see you," he'd say.

I'm so wrapped up in this fantasy that I drop the fish food. The jar rolls under the couch and little pellets scatter. I curse, then get down on all fours to retrieve the jar.

By the time I've swept up the mess, I've decided to text rather than call. It's just easier.

Sunday brunch sounds fun! Quinn's baby shower is at 4:00 p.m. Can I get back in time? What can I bring?

I spend an anxious five minutes before he texts me back with instructions. He's moved out of his rental and back into his palace in Uplands. It's got a private dock, where the boat is moored. The fantasies rev up again.

I'm so distracted that I forget about my laundry. It's past ten by the time I remember and run downstairs. All the machines have stopped running, the laundry room dead quiet. I transfer everything into the dryers and insert more coins, then stop. Where's my pink bra? I recheck the machines and bend to search the floor. My one and only piece of sexy underwear has vanished!

My first thought is Mr. Garlowski. But would he really steal women's underwear? He's chauvinistic, but I doubt he's *that* twisted. None of the building's few other male tenants strike me as the type either. Was it one of the women? I picture some elderly floozy in my hot pink bra. It seems unlikely.

Long after my clothes are dry, it's still annoying me. What happened to my pink bra? What's the world coming to if my delicates aren't safe in a seniors' building in Oak Bay, a suburb so sedate, orderly, and refined I can't think of a single house with an overgrown yard? Most residents probably think "graffiti" is a type of Italian flat bread. Missing cats make the local news.

I was planning to spend tomorrow at my mom's. But maybe I should go downtown and buy another pretty bra to wear on my date with Josh. But no! I'm getting carried away. My underwear will be well hidden beneath layers of warm clothes. This might not even be a date. I don't need sexy undies.

After getting into my pajamas I call Quinn and tell her about my missing bra.

"Someone must have picked it up by accident," she says. "Some of your neighbors can't see so well." I can hear her drinking something, probably milk, since she's trying to consume lots of calcium. She swallows. "What did it look like, anyway?"

"It was pink," I say. "And kind of lacy."

"Lacy pink?" asks Quinn. "Since when did you start wearing *any* gonch that's not beige?" She laughs. "And lacy? What else are you not telling me?"

"Nothing," I say. "It was on sale."

"Uh huh," says Quinn. She sounds suspicious. I wait and sure enough, a second later, she asks what I'm doing this weekend. Don't ask me why, but I can't keep anything from Quinn. Lying's not possible. Even over the phone she'd be onto me.

"I'll go see my mom," I say.

"Nice. What else?"

This is the moment of truth. I fiddle with the phone cord. I could tell her I have no plans except for her shower. But I'd better not risk it. "I'm having brunch with Josh," I say. "On his boat. A picnic."

I fluff my pillow, waiting for Quinn's response. "A date?" she asks. "And you weren't going to tell me?"

"It's not a date," I say. "He's still my client. Well, technically he's Jackie's client. But I'm working for Jackie . . ." I stop talking.

"Right," says Quinn, her tone making it clear she's not buying any of this. "Is it just you and him?" she asks.

"I'm not sure," I admit. I hope so. But maybe it's a group excursion. I hope Mike won't be there, or Chantelle. That'd sure kill the mood. I wait for Quinn to repeat her warnings about Josh. I didn't tell her that Mr. Garlowski had pegged him as a "player."

"Right," she says again, her disapproval filling the line, like static. "Okay, well sleep tight. And see you at the shower, right?"

"Of course," I say. "But that's it?" I can't believe she has no further comments about my outing with Josh Barton.

"That's it," she says. There's a pause. "Well, the reason I was asking was because Colin called to get your home number. Apparently he wanted to take you out for lunch on Sunday but your mobile was off." I feel my stomach sink. "Toby?" ask Quinn. "Hey, are you there, Toby?"

"Yes," I say. I study the painting of the two little girls on the beach. It really could be Quinn and me, the dark-haired girl short and skinny and the blonde taller. I feel inexplicably sad. I will never regain the childish wonder I felt upon capturing a bullhead or finding a pale pink sea anemone. I turn away from the painting. "Colin wanted to ask me out? As in a date?"

"Yup," says Quinn. "But if you and Josh are together I'll get

Bruce to let Colin know. There's no point in Colin getting his hopes up if you're really into Josh, right?"

"No," I say. "We're not together. This boat trip isn't even a date, remember? I already told you that. It's just brunch." I look up at the ceiling.

"Okay," says Quinn. "So Colin still has a chance?"

A chance, I think. Like I'm a prize in a raffle. Does he have a chance? I smile. "I . . . is he really interested in me?"

"Apparently," says my best friend dryly. "Not that you take my word for *anything*."

"Well, sure. It'd be fun to go out with him," I say. "Some other time. Why not?"

"Fine," says Quinn. She gives a long-suffering sigh. "I guess he'll call you."

"Great," I say. I try to keep the smile from my voice.

"You really *do* need some new underwear," says Quinn. "Nice ones, I mean. Not beige."

"Right. I'll get some," I say. And I really mean it.

CHAPTER TWENTY-ONE:

HATE MAIL

Since my building's parking lot is tiny, and a few more residents will have to die before I manage to get a space, I have to park in the street, nearby. Last night, the only free spot was beneath a massive oak that's home to a murder of crows. One of them is now hiding overhead, screeching at me. I reckon that long ago, someone substituted the term "flock" with "murder" because they wanted to murder those creepy birds, which take an evil delight in dropping small items and crap onto anything within range. I scurry toward my car, holding my purse over my head.

I lower my purse, dig out my keys, and stop. A small parcel has been tied to my driver's side view mirror with yellow rope. Weird. It wasn't there last night. I lean closer. That's a lot of knots. It'd take some serious Girl Guides' skills to undo it.

I look around and take a step back. Why would someone tie a package to my car? Could it be dangerous? I wonder who I should call, then decide on Bruce and Quinn. I fish my mobile out of my bag.

It turns out that Quinn's still asleep and Bruce is running late for a meeting. He advises me to call Colin Destin. I'm hesitant, but Bruce insists. "Swear you'll call him," he says. "I'm not joking, Tob."

I cross my fingers and promise.

I'm heading indoors to fetch scissors when I reconsider. I can't lie to Bruce. Quinn would never let me forget it. Before calling Colin, I phone my mom to say I'll be late. "Take your time, Sweetie," she says. "I'm going to pop over to Thrifty's to get some groceries. The parking's not so crazy when it first opens." She asks if I need anything, and I say no, then change my mind and ask her to pick up granola, cranberry juice, and frozen yogurt.

Overhead, the first crow has been joined by a colleague. They both sound like they're laughing at me. I walk around the car, just in case a note is lying around. I peer under the car too, and under the cars parked nearby. Should I really bother Colin? I hope he won't think I'm crazy.

He answers on the first ring.

"Hi Colin," I say. "This is Toby Wong. Bruce gave me your number. Sorry to call you so early, but I need your help with something."

Luckily, Colin sounds both wide awake and pleasantly surprised to hear from me. I recall Quinn's claim that he wanted to ask me out for lunch tomorrow. The thought that he's interested in me causes a warm, full feeling in my belly, as though I've just eaten a big bowl of tomato soup and drunk a mug of hot chocolate.

"No problem. I've been at work for a while," says Colin. "How can I help, Toby?"

I explain about the mysterious parcel and remind him how both Tonya and Josh had received unwanted "gifts." "I'm sure there's some simple explanation," I say. "I just wanted to double-check, you know?"

"Where are you?" he asks.

I give him my address and he says he'll be right over. "Don't touch it," he says. "Just in case."

I retreat from beneath the crows' lair and take a seat on the low wall that fronts my building. Luckily for me, it's not raining, although it's early enough in the morning to be too cold for the light jacket, cropped pants, and flat sandals I'm wearing.

I'm reluctant to go up to my apartment in case someone removes the parcel from my mirror. If Colin gets here to find it missing, he might decide I'm nuts after all.

By the time Colin drives up in an unmarked police car, my legs have the mottled, blue-veined look of uncooked sausages. I've taken to pacing the length of the wall to keep warm. This has earned me odd looks from various neighbors, who, having been up since daybreak, are heading home following early bird breakfasts down on Oak Bay Avenue.

Colin pulls into a Loading Only zone and parks, then strides over to me. He's wearing a dark blue jacket and holding a camera.

Again, there's an awkward moment when we're figuring out how to greet each other. Perhaps because this visit is professional rather than social, Colin opts for a handshake. While his hand feels reassuring and warm, I wish he'd kissed my cheek instead.

"Whoa, your hand is freezing!" he says. "Do you want to sit in my car and warm up?"

I shove my hands back into the pockets of my summer jacket and say I'm fine. Cold as I am, I'd rather see what's inside that mysterious brown-paper parcel.

I watch as he photographs it in its current location, then withdraws a pair of scissors from his jacket pocket. He tugs on some plastic gloves. "Has anyone threatened you recently?"

I shake my head. "No. Never."

Frowning, he struggles to snip through the sturdy rope. "Can you think of anyone with a grudge against you? The spouse of one of your clients or former clients, for instance?"

I shrug. "Back in Toronto I can think of a few people who were fairly bitter about their spouses' settlements," I say. "In Victoria, I haven't been practicing long enough to have upset anyone."

Colin deposits the parcel into a plastic bag. I feel a surge of disappointment. "You're not going to open it?"

"Well, there's no real reason to think it's dangerous," says Colin. "But we may as well get the guys back at the station to double-check, especially given what happened to Tonya."

"Can I come too?" I ask. I want to know what it is. I hope it's nothing embarrassing. Maybe I should have mentioned it to my mom, just in case she decided to come by and leave me a gift in the middle of the night. Although surely, even someone as offbeat as Ivy would just use my building's drop box.

Colin's holding the plastic bag containing the package from one corner. "Of course."

"Great," I say. "I'll follow you to the station."

At the station, I call my mom's number again but nobody answers. She must still be at the grocery store.

After it's been ascertained that my parcel is neither a bomb nor full of anthrax, Colin fetches me from the lobby and leads me to one of the interview rooms. While this space is as claustrophobic as it was when I was here with Josh, at least it's heated today. I take a seat and Colin smiles at me. "You ready?" he asks. I watch as he snaps on a pair of rubber gloves and opens the Ziploc bag.

It's only when Colin is peeling back the brown paper that it occurs to me: I may have made a bad decision. What if the parcel contains evidence relating to Tonya's murder, evidence that someone wishing to remain anonymous wanted Josh's defense, rather than the cops, to have? What if the contents hurt Josh's case? Maybe I should have taken the parcel to Jackie.

Colin tears a hole in the paper wrapping and something falls out and lands on the table. I go to reach for it, then freeze. Colin picks it up and shows it to me.

Lying in his hand is the head of a dead rose. It's been spray-painted black, then splattered with bright red paint. I recall the black floral heart left on Josh's SUV. Is Alana Mapplebee behind this creepy offering?

Colin peers inside the package and frowns. I hold my breath. He tilts the parcel and its contents slide out, a dozen dried black and red roses spilling out of a pink lace bra.

I feel my cheeks turn hot. Spread out on the interview table, under harsh fluorescent lights, my bra looks elf-sized. I bet Colin has never seen a bra that small. I consider pretending it's not mine, then tell myself to stop being pathetic.

Colin peers into the empty parcel, then sticks two fingers inside. He pulls out an envelope-sized slip of paper and lays it onto the table. Although the words are facing the wrong way, I have no trouble reading it. Fashioned from letters cut out of newspaper, the note reads: LEAVE VICTORIA, BITCH.

Tonya had received a similar note with her red-paint-flecked Barbie doll.

A muscle in Colin's jaw jumps. He looks angry. "Who could

have sent this?" he asks. "Do you have any bitter ex-boyfriends? Guys you might have rejected? Anyone who came on too strong?"

I shake my head. I'd rather not tell Colin that it's been nineteen months since my last date, with a guy I met in a Toronto doctor's office who spent our entire date describing—in vivid detail—his recent hernia surgery.

"How about social media?" asks Colin. "Are you active on dating sites? Have you gotten any similar sorts of messages? Anyone seem obsessive? This kind of stuff can start online and then escalate."

Again, I say no. My few attempts at internet dating were so lame I swore never again. The real world is weird enough. "There's nothing like that." I survey the bra, wishing the label weren't sticking out, those AAs on full display. "But it's my bra," I admit. I explain how, just last night, it vanished from my building's communal laundry room.

Colin's frown deepens. "Last night? That means whoever sent this was in your building." He tugs at his collar, clearly agitated. "This isn't good, Toby. How could they have gotten in?"

I think of all the times the front door is propped open to allow Mrs. Von Dortmund's incontinent cat to go in and out, and how often senile and half-blind visitors are granted access to the building after pushing the wrong button. "It's not exactly high security," I say. "But we could ask around. Maybe one of my neighbors saw someone."

Colin promises to send someone over to question my neighbors. "Any chance you'd consider staying with a friend until we figure this out?" he asks.

I cross my arms. "No way," I say. I could go and stay at my mom's, of course, or at Quinn's. But it seems unnecessary. I like my own space. It's not like I was attacked, after all.

I say this to Colin and he shakes his head. "I still don't like it. Given that Tonya received a similar message, we have to assume it's related. Something you're doing is upsetting someone, and they're trying to scare you."

I push my hair from my eyes. It's hard to equate a dead-flower-stuffed bra and a nasty note with murder. "You really think Tonya's killer sent this?"

"I don't know," says Colin. He pinches the skin between his eyebrows. "Your questions are obviously rubbing someone the wrong way." He gives me a pointed look. "I know you went to the Seabreeze, by the way. Remember how I told you that Cage was dangerous?"

I start to defend myself but Colin cuts me off. "I know," he says. "You were just doing your job." He lays a hand on my arm. "My job is to protect you. We think this guy Cage is in town, and from everything we've found out, he's real trouble." His voice softens. "Please Toby, let me handle this."

I study the threatening note. LEAVE VICTORIA, BITCH sounds like something a woman-beating thug would write. I recall Cage and Tonya's misspelled email exchange. Would Cage have inserted that comma?

Glancing up from the note, I meet Colin's eyes, clear celadon green, rimmed by those thick—almost feminine—lashes. He looks so serious I feel uneasy. I promise not to try to find Cage.

"Good," says Colin. "But he's not the only suspect. You really need to watch your back, Toby. Pay extra attention to what's going on around you. Get someone to walk you to your car after dark." He searches my eyes. "And if you feel uneasy about anything, anything at all, even if it's in the middle of the night, promise you'll call me."

CHAPTER TWENTY-TWO

THE OTHER WOMAN

I walk from the police station to Capital Iron, where my car is parked. The Chinese grocers' and tourist shops are just opening up. I pass shopkeepers arranging boxes of fruits and veggies on the sidewalk. The more I think about the parcel, the humiliation of seeing my bra laid out on the interview bench, and the nasty message, the madder I feel. Josh seems convinced that his stalker is Alana Mapplebee. I think it's time I came face to face with this woman.

The hot dog stand across from Value Village isn't open yet. I sit on an empty bench and fish my phone out of my purse. Having copied her number off the realtor ad next door to Quinn's place, I don't have to call directory assistance. After two rings a woman picks up, her perky "Hello, this is Alana Mapplebee speaking" sounding more than a little forced. Although it's past 10:00 a.m., it's as if she just woke up. I highly doubt she'll agree to see me.

I explain that I'm Josh's lawyer and that I'm trying to learn more about Tonya's death. Sure enough, Alana's reaction is far from friendly. "So why are you calling me?" she asks.

I take a deep breath. "Well, I heard you knew Josh," I say cautiously. "And that you sold him and Tonya their house. I figured you might have some insight into their relationship."

"Look, the cops already came by," says Alana. "And I told them exactly what I'm going to tell you. Tonya was a bitch, and Josh is a lying bastard." Her emphasis on the word "bitch" sends a shiver down my spine. Following a pause she asks me to repeat my name again.

"Toby Wong," I say.

For some reason, Alana seems to have a change of heart because her next words come out sounding more tired than angry. "I don't know anything about Tonya's death, but if you want to meet me, why not? Can you come to Ye Olde Tea Shoppe around three?"

"Sure," I say. "That'd be great. Thank you."

I'm as surprised by Alana's choice of venue as I am by her agreeing to meet me. Decorated in a dim, faux-Tudor style, Ye Olde Tea Shoppe plays off Victoria's reputation for Olde England charm, an image kept up by the city's red double-decker buses, copious antique and curio shops, and boutiques peddling Irish lace and Scottish tartans. I wouldn't have pictured Alana as a big fan of crumpets, chintz curtains, and tea cozies. But Ye Olde Tea Shoppe is a convenient choice for me, lying just a few blocks' from my mom's place.

A bum from the nearby homeless shelter shuffles past, then decides to join me on my bench. Despite the early hour, he's staggering drunk. "Washyouzname?" he says, in a blast of beer breath. This query is quickly followed by: "Yagottanychange?" Time to go. I find my keys and hurry to my car. It's parked near a large mural of some bears that the artist dedicated to his little sister, who succumbed to cancer. As always, reading the inscription brings a lump to my throat.

En route to my mom's, I stop at Harry's Flowers and pick up a pot of red cyclamens, Ivy's favorite flower. Before getting out of the car, I call Jackie and fill her in on this morning's events. "That note's a clear threat," says Jackie, sounding worried. "Are you sure you should be meeting this Mapplebee woman? Josh suspects she might be involved." I can hear Fleetwood Mac playing in the background and Jackie's husband, Alistair, singing along. Jackie asks him to turn the music down, then gets back on the line. "I really don't like the sound of this, Toby."

"It'll be fine," I tell Jackie. "We're meeting at Ye Olde Tea Shoppe." I try to lighten the mood. "What's she going to do, smother me with a Royal Wedding tea towel?"

"Hmmm, I guess you're right," concedes Jackie. She wishes me luck and tells me to keep her posted.

"I will," I say, then repeat Colin's warning about being extra cautious. If someone thinks I'm a threat, they might see Jackie the same way.

"Good point," says Jackie. "I'll get Ali to turn on the alarm system. Be sure to order one of the raisin scones," she adds. "They're really good. With clotted cream. And jam!" I wouldn't have picked Jackie as a Tea Shoppe regular either.

Just as I'm hanging up, I see my mother pull up. She's had the same yellow Honda hatchback since I was in law school. I retrieve the potted cyclamen from my passenger-side foot-well and wave at my mom.

She collects two paper bags of groceries out of the back and lowers the car's hatch. "Hey honey. Perfect timing."

"Hi Mom. Let me help with that." I take the bigger bag off her and follow her up the front steps. We both set our bags on the kitchen table. There are fresh flowers in the center: a terra-cotta jar full of sunflowers today.

My mother turns, her bright dark eyes upon me. I hand her the potted cyclamen and she smiles. "Oh. Pretty! Red. My favorite. Thank you!" Then her smile falters. "I'm getting bad vibes," she says.

I can't hide my skepticism. "Off the cyclamen?"

She shakes her head and sets down the plant. "No. Off you." Her dark eyes narrow. "What's happened?"

"Nothing!" I say, more emphatically than I intended. "Nothing at all! Everything's fine, Mom! I'm just busy with work and . . . Quinn's baby shower." I busy myself putting groceries into her fridge, then prattle on and on about the quilt I bought for Quinn's baby. "It's cream with yellow embroidery," I say. "And super soft and squishy."

From the concerned frown on my mom's face, I know she's not listening to a word I'm saying. She nods and smiles, like a troubling question's been answered. "Agate and carnelian," she says. "Let me go find my crystal box."

I open my mouth to protest, but she's already gone. I put a tub of organic ice cream into her freezer. Moments later, she's back with a giant lacquered jewelry box. It's bigger than some microwave ovens. She sets this massive box on the kitchen counter and starts pulling out strings of beads: shiny, dull, faceted, cabochon, in every color of the rainbow. The sunlight catches them, sending multicolored sparks around the room. Draped in beads, my mom looks like a vendor in an Arab bazaar. More strands clatter onto the counter. "There," she says, when she's finally found what she wanted. She stands on tiptoes and hangs one brown and one red strand around my neck. "Perfect. That's just what you need. Protection from the evil eye." She rearranges the beads against my chest. The stones feel cool and heavy against my skin.

I look down: lumpy opaque red and brown rocks, each bead the size of an acorn. They are so not my style.

I start to protest, then stop. The beads clash with my top but so what? Wearing them is a small price to pay if it will ease my mom's worries.

On a Saturday afternoon, Ye Olde Tea Shoppe is almost empty, with just three tables of grey-haired women and a couple of loud American tourists. One elderly man is sitting alone in the far corner. Compared to Mr. Garlowski, he's George Clooney. The old ladies can't stop gawping and giggling behind their veiny hands. I'm freshly reminded how, with each passing year, my odds of finding romantic fulfillment slip lower.

I take a seat at a table for two near the window, facing the doorway. At three on the dot Alana steps inside. It's a windy day and her hair has been blown into her face. I watch as she smoothes it back and checks her watch to be sure she's on time. I'd expected her to be late. Yet again, she's surprised me.

Alana removes her sunglasses and looks around. At the sight of me she gives a tentative smile. I nod and she heads my way. Dressed in jeans, tan suede boots, and a pale pink sweater, she looks softer and prettier than on her real estate signboard. Her hair has been trimmed to shoulder length, and she's toned down the blonde streaks. A big cream tote bag hangs from one slender arm. She looks much classier than the way I envisage Tonya. Maybe Josh doesn't have such dreadful taste after all.

Alana sticks out her hand and we shake. "Thanks for coming," I say. I see that her nails are painted the same shade of pink as her sweater, and she's got one ring on each hand, one with a bright blue topaz and the other with a pretty lemon quartz. Thanks to my mom's obsession with crystal energy, I can't help but notice gemstones. I'm still wearing the chunky beads she insisted on this morning.

Alana takes a seat and signals the waitress. Like Jackie, she recommends the raisin scones.

I wonder how to approach things. But before I can say a word, Alana apologizes for her earlier outburst. "I know it sounds brutal to call Tonya a bitch after what happened to her," she says. "But just thinking about her and Josh gets me so upset . . ." She leans back and sighs. "I wish I'd never met him."

I'm about to ask what happened, but there's no need. Alana is off and running. "I didn't know he was married," she says. She shakes her head. "I know. How could I not have known, right?"

I think back to my own relationship with the wine merchant, Jorge, and how shocked I'd been to learn he was married with three kids. "I don't understand," I say. "Didn't you sell Josh and Tonya their house in Uplands?"

"Yes," she says. "But Tonya was back in L.A. at the time, and Josh conveniently failed to mention that he had a wife." She twists the yellow ring on her finger.

The waitress sets down a teapot, and Alana pours two cups. Her hand is shaking. After taking a sip, she continues. "The crazy thing is I really fell for him. When we first got together I didn't even know he had so much money."

Given that Josh was buying a multimillion-dollar home, this is debatable, but Alana seems to have convinced herself.

"So how did you find out he was married?"

Alana studies the floral tablecloth. "He told me," she says. "He said he couldn't live with the guilt and felt so horrible that we had to stop seeing each other." Her mouth tightens. "I was beyond furious."

Looking at this woman I realize my first impression was wrong. She might look fragile, and even sweet, but I bet she's a tough adversary. Had Alana Mapplebee been with us at camp, she might have usurped Tonya as Camp Wikwakee's queen bee.

Without even realizing what I'm doing, I find myself rubbing my mom's agate beads. I grit my teeth. My mother has brainwashed me. But they do feel comforting, smooth and cool beneath my fingertips. I need to ask Alana about the stalking incidents.

I describe the bloody Barbie doll and the threatening phone calls that Tonya received. I'm about to bring up the roses on Josh's SUV when Alana cuts me off. "So what, you think I did that?"

"I didn't say that," I say. "I just . . . well, do you have any ideas?"

"Well don't look at me," says Alana. "Tonya's the one who was hassling *me*."

"She was?" I ask.

"Yes. Not long after Josh dumped me I started getting prank calls." Alana pours some more tea into her cup. "And then someone stuck a dead crow splattered in red paint in my mailbox." She wrinkles her nose at the memory. "I guess he told Tonya about me and she wanted to get even."

"Did you tell the police?"

"It was my private life!" she says, then adds, "Would you tell the cops you'd been sleeping with a married man?" She adds some sugar to her tea and stirs angrily. When I look sympathetic she softens a little. "One of my ex-boyfriend's best friends is a cop," she explains. "The last thing I want is for news of my affair with Josh to get back to him."

I think of what Colin told me about Alana and Dan and lower my eyes. Over the top of her teacup, Alana blinks at me. "I've made mistakes," she says. "But who hasn't?" She lowers the cup with a jerk, causing some tea to slosh out. "I really loved Josh," she says. Her voice quivers. "He used me."

I smooth out my napkin. "So why did you keep calling him and sending him photos of yourself?"

Alana's cheeks flush. She reaches for her tote bag. I think she might leave, but at just that moment, the waitress reappears. Clad in a long skirt, a frilly apron, and a ridiculous bonnet, she lowers two plates bearing massive scones and a pot of cream onto our table. "Can I get you some more hot water?" she asks.

I hand over the pot. When the waitress is gone, I meet Alana's eyes. She sets down her purse and sighs. She looks angry and embarrassed.

"It was stupid," she says. "I just . . . I couldn't believe it was over. I'd never been dumped before. I know it sounds crazy, but I thought he'd change his mind. He said he . . ." She breaks off and shrugs. "Who cares what he said, right? We did get together after we broke up. I kept thinking that . . ." Again, she stops talking. There are angry tears in her eyes. "I was so dumb," she says. "He just saw me as an easy booty call." She rips a hefty chunk out of her scone.

I study her. She's definitely upset, but is she also a stalker? "Did you leave the rose heart on his SUV?" I ask.

Alana raises a perfectly plucked eyebrow. "A heart on his car?" She gives a tight little laugh. "Oh please. I was desperate but not that desperate."

"How about a bra stuffed with dead roses?"

She snorts. "Someone sent Josh a bra full of dead flowers?" She smiles grimly. "I guess I'm not the only girl he pissed off."

"It was my bra," I say. "Someone stole it and sent it back to me, along with a nasty note." I'm watching Alana closely.

"That's freaky." She studies her plate. "You think the bra is related to what happened to Tonya?"

"I do." I take a small bite of scone and chew slowly. Jackie and Alana were right. The scone is delicious and the jam tastes home-made, with entire uncut strawberries in it. For a few minutes we both eat in silence. I consider Alana's responses. I'm inclined to believe her.

Alana pats her mouth with a floral napkin. "So you're Josh's lawyer?" she asks. She licks her lips. "I'm not surprised." I ask what she means and she rolls her eyes. "He wouldn't hire some wizened old man, would he?"

"I have a lot of experience," I say, then wish I'd sounded less defensive.

"I wasn't implying you don't," says Alana dryly. "But it figures that Josh would hire someone young, female, and beautiful." I blink and Alana laughs. She leans forward. "Has he come onto you yet?"

I try to keep my face neutral.

"Let me guess," she says. "Perhaps an outing on his yacht? A picnic in his garden. Champagne and strawberries." She pushes her hair behind her ear and smiles bitterly.

I'm not sure whether to be more shocked by her use of the adjective "beautiful," or the fact that, as described, Josh has promised me strawberries and champagne on his yacht tomorrow. Is he a rampant womanizer? Or has Alana been keeping tabs on me? How could she know about my date with Josh? I suppress a shudder. "He's just my client," I say tightly.

Alana shrugs. While she doesn't say "whatever," it's written all over her face. She takes another bite of her scone. We sit in silence for a few moments. I wonder if I should cancel my brunch date with Josh tomorrow. But for all I know, it's just a friendly excursion. I feel unreasonably angry at Alana Mapplebee. She's tainted something I was really looking forward to.

I remind myself to focus. "Do you know if Tonya had any enemies?" A quick sip of tea. "Besides you?" I can't help adding.

Alana's eyes narrow. "I only met her a couple times." She squints out the window. "She seemed like a stuck-up bitch." That word, again.

"But you didn't kill her?"

Alana wields her butter knife. "Ha!" she says. "If I was going to kill anyone, I'd kill Josh. He's the one who lied to me."

Looking into her eyes, I wonder if she's telling the truth about how her affair began, or whether she's just managed to convince herself that she's not the home-wrecking type.

She must notice me studying her because her expression turns challenging. "If you want to find someone with a *really* good reason to hate Tonya, why don't you look at your client?"

"Because of the money, her share?" I ask.

Although the café is practically deserted, Alana lowers her voice. "What would you do if you caught your wife having an affair with your brother?"

I freeze. "You knew?" I say. "How did you know about them?"

Alana looks smug. "Some time after Josh dumped me he asked me to meet him at his boat. Like an idiot I ran over there. Josh and I were in the parking lot and we saw Mike and Tonya on the dock."

I freeze. "And?"

"They were all over each other."

I feel cold. Yet again, Josh lied. He told me and Jackie he didn't know. "What did Josh do?"

Alana shrugs. "Nothing," she says. She breaks off another chunk of scone only to set it down again. I wait. "After that we, you know, made love. The sex was really rough." She shakes her head. "I didn't like it. Josh was . . ." She shudders. "It was angry sex." She picks up her napkin and twists it. "That was the last time we were, um, together."

When the waitress brings the bill, Alana reaches into her tote and withdraws a black quilted purse. "No, let me," I say. "I asked you here."

"Thanks." She shuts her purse. She's putting it back into her tote when I spot the Chanel logo. She must sell a lot of properties in the Uplands. Or was it a gift from Josh? I can't resist asking.

"What? This?" Alana looks at her purse in surprise. "No, that wasn't Josh's style at all. He knew nothing about brands. I bought this second-hand from a girl I know through work." She slides it back into her oversized tote bag.

After the waitress brings my change and we've both stood up, Alana turns to me. There's a little half smile on her face. She toys with a strand of shiny hair. "So . . ." She bites her glossy lip. "Is Josh seeing anyone?"

I tell her I don't know. Her smile hardens. Maybe she doesn't believe me. Or else she thinks I'm lying. Does she think *I'm* with him? Maybe I'm just imagining the hostility in her pale blue eyes.

I thank her for coming to meet me.

"Right. Good luck," she says. I'm not sure if she's being sarcastic or not.

At the door, she stops to allow a group of Japanese tourists to enter. Seeing Alana, they all look impressed. I guess she meets their vision of a Western babe: tall, slender, blonde, and busty. Nobody seems to notice me, except for Alana.

Before she slips through the door, she casts one last backward glance my way—a cool appraising look, like I'm a run-down house in a less-than-desirable neighborhood. Am I a fixer-upper? Or a teardown? She spins and strides away from me, her golden hair swaying.

Watching her walk up Oak Bay Avenue, I feel uneasy. Talk about mixed emotions. No matter how much she claims to hate Josh, I think she'd kill for the chance to get back together with him.

CHAPTER TWENTY-THREE:

THE GREAT ESCAPE

I pass through the ivy-clad gateposts of Uplands, the most desirable neighborhood in Victoria. Massive Gary oaks spread over the small lanes, which are lined with giant rhododendrons and bright flower beds. The closer I get to the water, the bigger the estates, many of the waterfront properties built by timber and coal barons at the turn of the twentieth century. I pass a house that looks like a castle.

A brass plaque marks Josh's driveway. Compared to some nearby manors, his house is almost modest—with maybe four or five bedrooms. Fashioned from dark stone, it has a black tiled roof, a centered front porch, and two rows of front windows. Ivy covers most of the stone. The lawn looks like a golf course.

I drive down a driveway flanked with hydrangeas, more blue than pink, and thick rosebushes. Their scent wafts through my open windows.

Faded white lines indicate where visitors should park. I pull up, resist the urge to check my appearance in the rearview mirror, and collect the box of zeppole I'd brought off the passenger seat. On the way over I stopped at the Italian bakery. Smoked salmon, strawberries, and champagne sound great, but there's no beating fat and sugar.

Through the trees and bushes, I can see blue glints of the ocean. I smell salt and kelp. It's cool in the shade. I zip up my jacket. While there's barely a cloud in the sky it'll be cold on the water.

The stone path leading to the front porch lies in sunlight. When I press the doorbell the resulting ring sounds very far away. Since I don't want to look like the nervous, preening women who linger outside of my neighbor Mr. Garlowski's place, I resist the urge to fix my hair and just stand there. Nothing happens. I press the bell again and check my watch. Josh did say ten, right? I wonder if he's popped out for a minute. But no, he's probably out back, preparing the boat. I follow the path toward the ocean.

Behind the house, the lawn is rimmed by a slim, pebbled beach. The tide is high. In the bay, the *Great Escape* is moored to a narrow dock, like a big Christmas bauble hanging off a skinny twig. The yacht shines white in the sunlight.

Admiring this idyllic view, I think of Tonya. How could she not have loved this place? Is Josh right that she hated it here, and was bored with small town life? It's hard to imagine being unhappy in this house, but who knows? Maybe her life only looked perfect seen from the outside.

Still balancing my box of zeppole, I descend the wooden stairs to the beach. More rosebushes border the stairs, their sweet scent cloying. I find myself comparing their scarlet blooms to the dead flowers I saw at the police station yesterday. But no, I'm being para-noid. Practically every yard in Victoria has some rosebushes. After all, it's dubbed "The Garden City."

I step onto the dock, the wood bleached blond-grey. I can just make out a fading trail of wet paw prints. Are they Claude's? Is Mike joining us? My spirits sink a little.

Halfway along the dock, I turn back to admire Josh's garden and those of the neighboring houses. The weather is perfect, the sky as blue as a cornflower. A cool breeze lifts my hair. I shiver.

On the dock near the boat lies a cooler. I'm tempted to peek inside but it seems presumptuous. Instead, I call out to Josh, expecting his head to pop up at any moment. All is silent. When repeated yells fail to rouse him, I decide to phone him. Maybe he ran out to get some-thing, after all.

His mobile is off. I check my watch. It's now ten past ten. I con-sider going back to wait on his porch, but decide to sit on the dock, in the sun, admiring this unfamiliar view of Uplands' coast. The landscaping must require an army of staff and yet it's dead empty. Do the gardeners work at night? And where are the homeowners? Probably in London, or Beijing, or the Cayman Islands.

As pleasant as this setting is, I feel uncomfortable. I can't shake the sense that I'm being watched. But that's crazy. I look around, then check my watch. It's quarter past. What's keeping Josh?

I wait another five minutes. What if he doesn't show? Maybe he's forgotten about our plans, or simply changed his mind. Maybe something came up and he forgot to cancel. Maybe this outing wasn't important to him. What started as a tiny tremor gains momentum, my doubts gaining strength until I'm shaking with self-righteous fury. Who does Josh think he is? Why would he go out of his way to invite me only to bail? It makes no sense, and yet I can't dismiss the idea or the ensuing tsunami of self-blame. Mr. Garlowski and his *carpe diems* be damned. I should have listened to Alana Mapplebee.

As if on cue, a cloud has slunk overhead. Without the sun, I'm chilly. My legs have cramped up from sitting cross-legged. Perhaps it's the cold, or this position, or the act of waiting, but one moment, I'm on Josh's dock, and the next, I'm pulled back in time. I was waiting for Josh that time too, a note clutched in my hand. It was too dark to read it, but I knew what it said: *I'm sorry. I made a mistake. I don't want Tonya. I want you. Please meet me at midnight in the Nature Hut.*

I fumbled my way past tables and shelves, hoping I wouldn't touch anything too gross, feeling the dust coat my fingertips. In the back corner, I crouched down and hugged my knees to wait, my breathing loud in that cramped space. While it wasn't that cold, I imagined puffs of water vapor coming out of my mouth. After some minutes of sitting still I could make out shapes and shadows in the dark: the pale glimmer of old animal bones and skulls, the grinning teeth of the taxidermied wolf and the equally mangy lynx, displays made by campers who were now middle-aged, monuments of chipped paint and moldering papier-mâché, everything dusty and decrepit. Even by day the Nature Hut was a creepy place. At night, it would have made a great setting for a horror movie. Just the smell freaked me out, mildew and dusty fur and rot, mixed with wood chips, roach spray, and mothballs. It made my nose itch and my throat dry. It made me long for my bunk and my warm sleeping bag, with my best friend sleeping down below.

My ears strained but heard nothing but my own scraping breaths. How long had I been waiting? I had no watch. I shifted and tried to wiggle my cold toes, stuffed, in the dark, into freezing wet shoes. Where was he?

People think black is black, but it's not. There are endless shades of black. Charcoal. Raven. Dog's nose. Shiny and matte. Deep and shallow blacks. I stared around the small room, killing time, but my eyes always went back to the door, willing it to crack open. It remained shut.

A noise, somewhere outside, the sharp snap of a twig, then another. I held my breath and hugged my knees tighter, torn between elation and fear. Finally! He was coming! Except what if it wasn't him?

Curled up, with my back against that rough wooden wall, I made myself even smaller and more inconspicuous. Bit my lip. Another sound, closer now, followed by more shuffling and scuffling—the unmistakable sounds of footsteps on the trail. Someone was walking this way, quickly and softly. My heart surged. It had to be him. He was almost here!

That noise? Had I imagined the soft tremor of the door, the handle just starting to turn? I must have because the door stayed tight shut, no light around the edges, no eager whisper of my name. I tried to slow my breathing, to be even quieter than I was already, to force my ears to be even sharper.

The floor was cold and hard. My butt hurt, and my knees felt welded in place. It was painful to stretch out my legs. I held onto a table and stood, as stiff and rickety as my Grannie Mei Li, in the hospital, a few days before she'd died. I forced myself to straighten up, forced myself to face the cold hard truth: I'd been waiting a long time. Too long. It was very late. My eyes felt gritty.

He wasn't coming.

A slow tentative shuffle to the door, my heart as heavy as my footsteps. Why did he write that note but not come? Had he been caught? Surely, if he could have, he'd have come to me.

A slick of silver lead my hand to the doorknob, which felt even colder than my creaky fingers. Cold and smooth. It started to turn but stopped. I tried again. And again. It was no use. The door was locked. It couldn't be!

I rattled the knob, desperate to escape, no longer caring about the noise, or who might come to investigate. I pushed the door. I rammed it with my shoulder until the pain made me stop. The door barely shook. I clawed at the wood with my fingernails.

Already in tears, I sank to my knees. Behind me, the hut grew smaller and darker. The walls were pressing closer. I could hear the dead things waking up. The wolf yawning and the lynx stretching. The snap of teeth. The skulls and bones starting to rattle.

But no, it was me shaking. No air! I was trapped.

The squawk of a gull brings me back. The bird hovers over-head, one keen black eye upon me. Overhead, it's still light. I'm sur-rounded by air and water, space. The breeze is fresh and salty. I look out to sea, inhaling gratefully, then gaze back at Josh's boat and yard. The lawn stretches up and away, perfect, but with no sign of life. I shake out my legs and stand up, try to shake off the memory of that night in the Nature Hut. I rub my cold hands together. I don't want to sit around waiting for Josh any more.

I walk stiffly toward the beach. I'd waited for thirty minutes. That's long enough. More than enough.

I'm near the end of the dock when I hear something behind me.

It's not a voice but a groan. I turn and listen and it comes again, from the direction of the boat. Is it the buoys grinding against the dock, or some piece of onboard equipment? Or is it an animal? There were paw prints on the deck. I wonder if Claude's making that sound. Maybe he's trapped on the boat, sick or injured. I turn back to investigate.

I set my pastry box on top of the cooler and climb aboard, then stop. I feel like I'm being watched. But that's ridiculous. Or is Josh watching me from the house, having decided he'd rather not see me today? It's a crazy idea but I can't help considering it. If it's true, what's wrong with the guy? I'm freshly furious.

"Josh?" I call, more for something to say than because I expect to find him onboard. Sure enough, the back deck lies empty, although someone was out here recently: a half-full glass of ice water is sitting on a table. I wish Quinn were here. I'm sure she could calculate how long it'd take ice to melt at any given temperature.

The doors to the salon are closed but have large glass panels, so of course, I peer inside. The interior looks impressive, with pale wood floors and light-colored furnishings offset by some tawny, textured pillows. Despite holding a cream leather sofa, a coffee table, a massive flat-screen TV, and two armchairs, the room looks spacious. I wonder if Louise Dobson decorated this room.

My nose is still pressed to the window when I hear a scuffling sound overhead. The hairs on my arms stiffen. I imagine Claude trying to drag himself across the floor. While I'm tempted to leave, I should check. Plus I'm curious. I've never been on a fancy yacht like this before.

A white staircase leads to the bridge, my unease increasing with each step. Where's Josh?

When I reach the bridge, I'm struck by how bright it is, everything from the deck to the table and chairs painted stark, gleaming white. It's sunny and I'm forced to squint. Then I see Claude sitting under a table. He's panting, his pink tongue hanging out. He hasn't been groomed since Tonya died and is looking bedraggled.

"Claude?" I ask, and the dog squirms, as though he's been ordered to stay put. Faced with this large, trembling poodle, I'm confused. Is he scared of me? Something's not right. Is he hurt, after all?

The dog's eyes move and I turn to follow his gaze, my confusion replaced by horror. Out of the corner of my eye I see Josh, one arm raised and a baseball hat low over his face. I try to duck. Something smashes into my skull.

I hear a loud crack and taste blood. I collapse. Pain and shock take my breath away. For a moment, I lie stunned. Behind me, something moves. I start crawling.

Through a haze of pain I see Claude watching me, the dog's eyes holding my tiny twin reflections, plus that of a man in a red hat with a rifle. I hear Josh take a step closer, and feel a rush of air. The dog whimpers. I roll under a table.

The second blow lands above my left ear, the force propelling me across the deck. I collide with a chair, which falls over. Behind shut eyes, I have a vision of Tonya's battered body. He's going to kill me! How could I have been so wrong? I was attracted to a killer!

My last thought, before blacking out, is of Quinn's baby. Pain fills my head like lightning, and yet I see it so clearly: screaming, wrinkled, and red, with Bruce's chin and Quinn's high forehead. The light fades and the image distorts. It takes all my strength to see—it's a girl! Darkness overtakes me.

As I slip under, I can feel my heart breaking. If I die, Quinn will name her Toby.

I'm not dead yet, although I know Josh plans to kill me. I'm on the boat, tied up, and my head hurts terribly. Josh hurt me. I feel sick with pain and betrayal.

I can hear the sound of the motor and waves slapping against the bow, and feel the boat moving beneath me. Finally, despite the pain, I manage to crack open one eye. The sun is much lower in the sky. What time is it? I must have been unconscious for hours. I try to wriggle my fingers and toes, which feel frozen. I wonder what Quinn will think when I fail to show up at her baby shower. She'll be furious, at first. She'll think I skipped her special day to spend time with Josh. She'll feel betrayed. She'll question why she picked someone so flaky to be her kid's godmother. When will she realize something's wrong? Is she already looking for me?

A slight tilt of my head reveals the chrome base of three stools. A pair of large Pumas-clad feet hangs from one. Looking up, I see Josh's back. He's wearing his red raincoat and is steering the boat with one hand, the rifle across his knees. To his right lies Tonya's dog, sleeping.

While it hurts to move, I force myself to peer around, which is when I realize: someone is lying beside me, clad in an old camel jacket with a smear of blood on the back. His face is turned away, but I recognize his wavy blond hair. It's Josh's brother, Mike. Is he breathing?

Faced with Mike's inert form, I feel even more hopeless. Did Josh attack him before or after he hit me? My head throbs. Am I just collateral damage, caught up in the Bartons' family feud? I recall Quinn's theory that Josh killed Tonya and was waiting for the right time to take revenge on Mike. If only I'd listened.

Like me, Mike is bound at the ankles and wrists, his hands tied tightly behind him. When the wind ruffles his hair I see blood on his scalp. He might be dead, or fatally injured. I slide closer and nudge him with my knees, steeling myself for his body to be limp. Instead, he rolls over.

There's a gash over his left eye, the blood dried to resemble a gruesome eye patch. I catch my breath. I was wrong. It's not Mike but Josh. In my dazed state, this is hard to grasp. Despite my grim situation, I feel a wave of relief. Thank God! It wasn't Josh who attacked me. I mixed them up, again.

For a brief instant, Josh looks happy to see me. He opens his mouth, as if to speak. I flick my eyes toward the wheel and he freezes. Staring at his brother's back, fear and anger fill his blue eyes.

Mike. I got it all wrong. He killed Tonya and plans to kill Josh. I should have known. No doubt he's after Josh's fortune.

Josh grimaces in pain. His head wound looks serious. I bet we both have concussions. Maybe that's why Mike didn't gag us. He figured we wouldn't regain consciousness. Plus, who cares if we yell? I move my head slowly in all directions but see only sky. We're alone in the middle of the ocean.

Overhead, a seagull squawks. Neither of us dares to move or speak, since one glance from Mike would be the end of us. It's too risky to whisper. Trussed up like pot roasts, it'd be so easy for him to dump us. It's hard not to feel hopeless.

The bindings on my wrists are painfully tight. I look around for something sharp but don't see anything. "Knife," mouths Josh, lowering his eyes toward his jeans' hip pocket. Moving slowly, I roll away, my back now toward him. Keeping one eye on Mike, I wriggle down until my hands are level with Josh's belt buckle.

My fingers are numb with cold and poor circulation. When I feel the bulge of Josh's button-fly, I fight down a hysterical laugh. This is not the way I'd hoped to get my hands into his pants.

I've worked a finger into Josh's pocket when Mike stretches. I freeze. He tosses an empty beer can overboard. Claude has woken up, his big black eyes upon me. I will the dog not to react. It's hard not to think of Claude as an enemy. Did he watch Tonya die? A wave of nausea overtakes me.

When Mike slips off the bar stool I squeeze my eyes shut, hoping he won't come closer. Where are we? Has he decided to dump us? The water off Vancouver Island is very deep. If he weights our bodies, we might never be found and he'll get away with three murders.

Josh and I lie as still as possible. When I dare open my eyes I see Mike rummaging around in a drinks cooler. He extracts another can of Molson and cracks it open. I hope he's had a lot to drink so his reflexes will be slower. He straightens up, then starts to turn our way. I bite my lip in terror. This is it. We're done for.

Mike must see something up ahead because he stops and shades his eyes, then strides back to the wheel. The boat turns gently to port and slows. My heart continues to race. Are we stopping here?

It's a relief when we speed up again. At least for now, Mike's attention is fixed on the horizon.

My fingers shake harder than ever as I resume my efforts to extract Josh's pocketknife. Since I can't see what I'm doing, and am working backward, it's hard to coordinate my stiff fingers. Eventually, I manage to grasp the knife, only to lose it again. After a few more failed attempts, I gently tug it free from Josh's pocket.

Opening it is even harder. Josh too rolls away from me, our bound hands touching behind us. Through trial and error, we work out a system: I hold the knife while he tries to pry it open. I've never been so focused in my life, or so desperate. Each time the knife slips, my panic grows. The sound of it bumping against the deck seems like a drumbeat. At any moment I expect Mike to spring from his chair and swing the rifle at us.

My arms and shoulders ache from the strain, and my fingers burn. Despite the agony, I keep trying. I think of my mother, and how devastated she'd be if I died. I can't leave her alone—not now, when she needs me. And I want to meet Quinn's baby.

Knowing Josh is here also helps. He's counting on me.

Somehow, the knife unfolds. I lie still as Josh starts to saw at the bonds. Also working blind and backward, he keeps nicking my wrists. I grit my teeth to stop myself from screaming.

When the last chord snaps, I feel euphoric. But we're not free yet. I wriggle my fingers and make fists. Then I slowly roll to face Josh and start hacking at his bonds. For the first time since I came to, I have hope. We might make it.

After Josh's wrists are free I wriggle down to start on his ankles. Josh keeps an eye on his brother. The closer we get to being untied, the more desperate I feel. We're so close. Please, please, don't let Mike turn around and see us.

I've been so focused that I failed to notice the fading light. The sun is lower and the sky full of dark clouds. The wind has risen too, the boat pitching and rolling.

Just as I manage to free Josh's ankles, Mike looks over his shoulder. He jumps to his feet and his hat flies off, his red raincoat flapping. His mouth tightens, except it's not Mike's mouth. I freeze in shock, unable to take this in. It's Mike's wife, Chantelle! Mike's not here. I just saw what I expected to see. But why would Chantelle want to hurt Josh? Or me, for that matter?

She raises her rifle. I scream: "Lookout, Josh!"

The rifle swings my way.

I roll left. My ears ring and pain sears my left shoulder. Another shot. A chair to my left explodes. Looking down, I see blood. My blood.

"No!" screams Josh. He leaps to his feet and springs toward Chantelle. Is that blood on her face? Or lipstick? The rifle bucks in her big white hands.

I scream and curl into a ball.

Instead of a shot I hear a loud grunt followed by a crash. Twisting around, I can see Chantelle and Josh rolling across the deck, fighting for the rifle. I am panting. Blood snakes hot down my arm. I clutch my shoulder and look for the knife. Where is it?

I see it about ten feet away. Compared to a rifle, a pocketknife isn't much help, but it's my best bet. I start to crawl, an ungainly wiggle since my feet are still tied and I can't put any weight on my left arm. Behind me, Josh and Chantelle are flailing on the metal deck. I pray that Josh is winning. He must be stronger, although he is injured. How badly, I don't dare think about.

The knife. I grasp it. My hands are sticky. It hurts to use my left hand, but I persevere, sawing through the ropes at my ankles.

Behind me, a loud thud is followed by a moan. Chantelle is on top of Josh, pressing the rifle butt to his throat. He twists and writhes under its weight. His eyes are like a panicked horse's, with too much white showing. The veins in Chantelle's thick neck stick out. I kick my legs free and stagger toward Josh. The deck is slick and I lurch like a drunk. My feet feel numb. It's raining, hard. When did it start? The cold drops sting my cheeks like tossed gravel.

Beneath wind-whipped, wet hair, Chantelle's mouth and nose are bleeding, horsy teeth bared in a wild grimace. Josh's face is dark pink, his eyes like a bubble-eyed goldfish's as he struggles to breathe.

His body convulses as he tries to push the rifle off his throat. I'm scared he'll pass out again.

"I should have done this years ago," snarls Chantelle, her face just inches above Josh's. "Always lording it over Mike! Your own brother!" She looks triumphant as she watches him struggle to breathe. "You bastard!"

I read somewhere that an overhand stab has less force behind it. I take a deep breath and swing the knife underhand.

I'm aiming for her chest but she moves. The knife strikes her right shoulder. She blinks in surprise and takes a hand off the rifle. Her fingers find the hole in her shoulder. Josh shoves the rifle off his throat and rolls out from under her. He pushes himself to his knees, panting. The color has started to drain from his face—blood red fading to bone white. He looks faint. He starts retching.

"You?" screeches Chantelle, her attention now fixed on me. She drags herself upright, looming over me. Even without the rifle, she is terrifying, red lipstick smeared across her chin and her eyes bulging. "You never could mind your own business!" Her voice rises to a howl. "Mike was counting on that partnership in the boat!" I back away but she sways closer. "You put Josh up to firing him, didn't you? What did you tell him, eh?"

The boat is lurching, sheets of rain and salt-spray washing over us. "The truth!" I yell. "That Mike was sleeping with Tonya!"

I figured Chantelle knew, but from the way her mouth falls open, like a lunchbox that's come unlatched, it's clear she didn't. Strands of wet hair writhe around her face. "Wha . . . No! You're lying!" She leaps at me.

I jump backward but slip. My hip hits the deck, hard. The pain knocks my breath away. The boat is really rocking now, the deck as slick as ice. I crab-crawl away from Chantelle.

I hear a high-pitched wail. What is that?

Chantelle is gaining on me. "You little bitch!" she screams. "Mike would never! Never!"

I'm on my butt, still backing away from her. "Isn't that why you killed her?" I ask. My back hits the side of the boat. I pull myself to my feet and clutch the boat's railing.

Chantelle stops moving and barks out a vicious laugh. "What? You're crazy! I didn't kill her!" She looks so surprised I think she might be telling the truth. Out of the corner of my eye I see a blue light. I realize it's gotten dark. And that strange wailing is louder now.

Chantelle must see the light too because she's staring off into space. Turning, I see a boat slide out of the gloom. A blue light spins on its mast, above a flapping Canada flag. My knees feel weak with relief. It's the coast guard.

Over the sound of the wind, I recognize Colin Destin's voice, amplified by a megaphone. "Stand back. We're boarding," he says.

"Help!" I yell. "Colin! Hurry!" The wind grabs my cries. I'm too exhausted to yell again. Icy rain fills my nose and mouth. Each time the boat dips, my grip on the rail weakens.

I'm so intent on the boat—and our imminent rescue—that I don't hear Chantelle's approach. She grabs me and lifts me as I cling to the railing. "Stay away!" she screeches. "Or I'll throw her in! Get away from me!"

A gust of wind pummels us. I'm scared we'll be swept overboard. I hear footsteps on the stairs. Below, the sea seethes, rising and falling.

"Get down! Get down!" yells a loud male voice. Volleys of hard, frigid raindrops blind us.

Chantelle is trying to climb over the railing and to drag me with her. I am fighting for my life, clinging to the rail, kicking at her. Time slows down. Rain stings my skin. The taste of blood fills my mouth. I can hear the coast guard vessel clanking against the *Great Escape*. I can smell beer on Chantelle's breath.

Three men in black are running our way. They drag Chantelle off me. She's kicking and screaming. Strong arms reach out to me. When I fall, someone catches me. It's Colin Destin.

"Chantelle," I mumble. My whole body feels limp.

"We know. Let's go," says Colin. He picks me up like I'm weightless and carries me down the spiral staircase.

"We need the paramedics, now!" says Colin, to someone behind me. "Can you get some towels?" He bears me into the fancy salon and lays me gently on the sofa.

Pressing a towel to my bloody shoulder, he holds my other hand. "You're going to be fine," he says. But there's a tremor in his voice.

I nod. His hand feels good—safe—but my mind is still whirring, full of images of my recent struggle. I know why Chantelle attacked Josh. Jealousy. Hatred. Greed. But is this the end of it? "Chantelle. Did . . . she kill Tonya?" I whisper.

Gazing down at me, Colin looks exasperated. "You've been shot," he says. "This can wait, Toby."

"Please," I say. I lick my lips. They feel numb. "Tell me."

He presses his lips together, then sighs. "Chantelle has an airtight alibi for the night Tonya died. She was a chaperone on her kid's school soccer trip to Kelowna." He squeezes my hand. "But seriously, Toby, just forget about this for now and—"

A paramedic rushes into the room, lugging a bag of equipment.

"Thank God!" says Colin. "She's lost a lot of blood! How's the other vic?" I know he means Josh. I hold my breath. Where is Josh?

"Critical. Looks like internal bleeding. Abdominal," says the medic. She's around my age, with short spiky red hair. She leans over me. "Hi. What's your name?" She's chewing gum. It smells like watermelon.

"Toby."

"Hi Toby. Can you make a fist?" I grimace as she inserts an IV line. Colin is still clutching my other hand. My eyelids feel weighted.

"Let's get her onto the boat," says the paramedic, and Colin nods. He scoops me up and carries me out of the salon. In his arms, I feel warm. Yet underneath that comfort, I'm terrified. Tonya's killer is still out there.

CHAPTER TWENTY-FOUR:

SHATTERED

The boat rolls beneath me. My whole body feels heavy. I try to focus on the medic's face leaning over me, the sound of her soothing words, the beeps of some machines off to one side. The sounds seem to be moving away from me. I can't stop my eyelids from sagging.

I'm on a stretcher, hooked up to an IV, in a small space, brightly lit. Josh is lying across a narrow aisle from me. But wait, now the small space has gone dark. I'm alone. I see myself pounding on a locked door, small and terrified. I am back at Camp Wikwakee, in the Nature Hut.

The smell. The old dead animals. The humiliation of knowing I'd been tricked. But by whom? It was all too much. I was sobbing hysterically.

I crawled to the one small window and tugged at the shutters, the hook rusted in place. My fingers were raw by the time I'd freed it, the shutters creaking open to permit some weak moonlight to filter through the dirty glass. But the sash wouldn't budge. It was painted shut. No amount of heaving could lift it.

A fumbling walk deeper into the room, where no moonlight fell, fingers brushing against old fur and dried leaves that crackled away to dust, damp newsprint, something squishy. I jerked my hand away, my heart in my throat. Another step forward and something scurried away. Mice? Rats? I spun around. Out of the corner of my eye I saw two small neon eyes, a devilish red-green glow. Something hissed. I screamed and lurched backward, my hip hitting a table before I collapsed to the hard floor, shaking.

I wanted to curl up in a ball, to quiver and cry, to call out for my mother. But there was no one here to help. I had to get out of here. My hip hurt but I forced myself up, took a few tiny steps, scared to touch anything. And then I found it—a rock, the size of a running shoe, good and heavy. I picked it up with both hands.

I crept back to the window and threw it as hard as I could, squeezed my eyes shut. The glass shattered.

I was crawling out when the flashlight beam struck, right in my face. "Who's there?" asked a loud angry man's voice. "Stop right there!"

I froze, blinded by the light—and panic. A piece of broken glass sliced my palm. "Ow," I said, gripping it, both hands already hot and sticky with blood.

The voice came again. "Hey! Girl! What are you doing here?"

There was no way to answer that.

Another voice now, smooth and assured. "Hey! Hey! I need you to take a deep slow breath. Yes." I blink. A middle-aged man in blue scrubs is leaning over me. There's a blue shower cap on his head. The room is very white and bright. I can see strange metallic machines. "Hey!" he says, when he sees my eyes are open. "That's good. What's your name?"

I think he's smiling behind his mask. "Toby," I mumble.

"Good, Toby, now take another deep breath for me."

I do as I'm told and the smile lines around his eyes deepen. He presses a stethoscope to my chest, listening intently.

He straightens up. "That's good, Toby. Very good." He sounds relieved. "You're in the OR," he says. "I'm going to operate on your gunshot wound. I'll administer a general anesthetic. Do you have any allergies, Toby?"

I manage to mumble no and he looks pleased, again. He seems easy to please, and I like him for that.

"When did you last eat?"

I have no idea. Then it comes to me. "Breakfast. This morning."

He nods. "Perfect. Now relax."

I want to ask his name except my lips aren't working the way they should. I feel a moment of frustration but realize it doesn't matter. I'm too warm and relaxed to care. I am sinking and floating away.

I'm cocooned in comfort.

Someone is touching me, lifting me. "She's going to Recovery," says a woman's voice. I'm too tired to figure out what she's talking about. It has nothing to do with me.

A jolt. I am on the move. Lights brighten and fade, brighten again. Rubber-soled shoes squeak softly below me. I can hear the sound of tires, rolling. A steel door swings open and shut. Another voice. Where is it coming from?

Someone is talking, very far away.

This new voice sounded furious.

"We know you were meeting someone in there!" said this angry new voice. "Who was it? Answer me!"

I blinked, but couldn't identify who was speaking. It was hard to see. After so long in the dark, the light was blinding in here.

"Were you meeting a boy?" It was Thelma, my old camp counsellor, her face scrunched up with fury. She leaned closer, menacing. Beneath a mop of frizzy orange hair she looked livid, her freckles merged into an angry red rash. She had a raincoat on over her cow-patterned pajamas, and Wellington boots on her feet.

"No!" My voice shook. I was in the camp's office, sitting on a metal folding chair. The camp's owners, Maureen and Dick Larange, were there, sunken-eyed and irate, along with Thelma and the camp nurse, a tall skinny woman who was wrapping gauze around my injured hand.

"Stop moving," she snapped.

I bit back a moan. "It hurts."

"You'd better tell us the boy's name," said Thelma through gritted teeth. "Or else!"

"I was alone! I swear!"

"Oh yeah. So why'd we find this?" She held it out on her palm, lips curled in disgust and chin raised in triumph. She thrust it under my nose, so close my vision blurred. Was that a candy? But no. My cheeks flushed. I'd seen one before, in Sex Ed. We'd had to unwrap one and roll it down onto a banana—an exercise of utter hilarity and embarrassment. My eyes watered.

"Well?" snapped Maureen Larange, taking over from Thelma. Her hands were on her massive hips, now wrapped in a nubby pink dressing gown. She loomed closer. She had a mustache. "What do you have to say for yourself, missy?"

Thelma slapped the wrapped condom down onto a large desk. "We're calling your mother," she said.

I roll onto my side. I feel cold all of a sudden and slightly nauseous. "She's coming to," says a soft female voice. Someone pulls a blanket higher up to my chin.

"I'm c . . . cold," I mumble.

The voice says, "Say that again."

"So cold."

"She's cold." She calls out, as if to someone else. "Hey Sally. Can you get her a blower? And an extra blanket?"

A soft hum starts up in my ears, and hot air blows against the small of my back. Another blanket is laid on top of me. The warmth feels wonderful. The nausea subsides and I relax. I feel cozy and safe. But then the nausea comes back. I screw my eyes shut but it's too bright and people keep passing by, making too much noise. I want to rest but someone's coughing. There are too many voices.

"What a slut! So who'd she do it with?"

"She didn't!"

"Seriously! Can you believe that skank?!"

High, excited girls' voices floated from around the corner. Squeals of fake shock and mockery.

I was sitting outside the camp's office, where I'd been kept all night, in disgrace. My eyes ached with fatigue and my hand throbbed. There was a massive bruise on my hip. The camp's owners were inside making arrangements for a car to take me home. They'd already called my mother.

Another whisper, followed by more titters. I recognized Chantelle's voice, loud and caustic: "I heard she was caught giving Danny Q a blow job." Danny Q weighed at least three hundred pounds and smelled like old socks and Doritos.

"Ewwww!" Squeals and derisive laughter. "No! Really? She didn't!"

I recognized Tonya's dismissive snort, her stage whisper. "Naw. But she was caught butt-naked, doing it with *both* Barton brothers."

A moment of silence as this sinks in. Some surprised snickers. "Well, that would be better than Danny G." Mumbles of assent.

"It was obvious she'd do *anything* for Josh!"

"Yeah, totally!" More laughter. "But his brother?"

"Oh my gawd! Wait! She like slept with both of them? At the same time?" Nervous titters. "But like, how?"

Tonya's low murmur.

"Seriously?"

"That's disgusting!"

"What a whore!"

And then, the chant started up, just Tonya's voice at first, soon joined by the others: *Me Chinese, me a slut. Me do sex in Nature Hut* . . . Over and over, until they were all laughing too hard to sing it anymore.

My cheeks were on fire and my eyes hot and heavy. I bowed my head and squeezed my hands into fists, even the one with the deep cut. It hurt but I was glad. At least I could focus on that.

I was not going to cry. I would not give Tonya that satisfaction.

CHAPTER TWENTY-FIVE:

IN RECOVERY

"Pssst, Toby."

My eyelids flutter open. Josh is lying on a white bed, maybe two meters away from me. A pale blue curtain separates us. Josh has dragged it open and is peering at me through the gap. He looks like an injured soldier, recently shipped out of some war zone, his right eye a squashed plum, with a big white bandage around his head. The white bandage and the dark bruises intensify the color of his left eye, which is now blinking at me. "You awake?" he whispers.

"Mmmm, yeah," I mumble, through heavy lips. My eyes feel heavy too. I try to turn my neck, but it hurts.

"We both had surgery," says Josh.

I take this in, and remember the boat. I see Chantelle swinging a rifle. This memory makes me flinch.

Josh licks his chapped lips. "You okay?" he asks.

I have stop to think about this. Physically, I feel fine. So long as I don't move, nothing hurts. Mentally, I'm not so sure. Each time a thought starts, it seems to fade away. "I . . . I'm tired," I say. "You?"

"Same. It's the anesthetic."

Again, I think about this. My thoughts are very slow. This must be how stupid people feel. Everything feels disconnected. Again, my thoughts turn back to camp. How vivid it all seems! My last morning at camp, sitting outside that decrepit camp office. It's like it all happened yesterday. Tonya's nasty chant starts up in my head. *Me Chinese, me a slut . . .* I dig my nails into my palms.

My throat is dry. I swallow. "Josh, d'you remember how I left camp?"

His answer comes slowly. "Yeah, what about it?"

"That last night, when we were all down on the dock playing Spin the Bottle, and you left with Tonya, what happened after that?"

His good eye blinks in slow motion. "Ummm, I don't remember . . ." I see him staring at the blue-painted ceiling with a blank look on his battered face. He can't even remember! I'm shocked to realize that this incident, which meant so much to me, left no traces for him. He turns back to me. "Wait, no. I do. I spun the bottle and it pointed at Tonya. We went down to the end of the dock and she kissed me. I remember a lot of guys were jealous 'cause you know, Tonya was really hot, and she wanted us to go someplace private so I left with her . . ." He's back to staring up at the ceiling. "We made out a little and I . . ." He frowns. "I told her I had to leave. I really liked you and . . ." He blinks. "I was a virgin and Tonya just seemed so . . ." His lips twitch into a half smile. "So experienced, like she expected us to, you know, have sex. It sort of freaked me out, so I just took off on her."

"And the note?"

He turns to look at me. "What note?"

"I found a note in my bunk, supposedly from you, asking me to meet you in the Nature Hut."

He frowns. His tongue flicks against his front teeth. "Wait, you thought I set you up?"

I want to close my eyes now. I feel spent. I imagine Tonya's face when he rejected her. Who better to vent her fury on? I always knew she'd locked me in. Now I know why she'd hated me so much. "Not really," I say. "But I wasn't . . ." I bite my lip. "I was never totally sure. I thought maybe you and Tonya did it together, like she put you up to it."

He's still holding the curtain, which falls from his hands. He retrieves it and pulls it back again. His pale face looks stricken. "No! I'd never."

"Okay."

"God, I'm sorry," he says.

"For what?"

"For leaving with her. And the next morning, when everyone was saying bad stuff about you." His Adam's apple bobs and his good eye slides away. "I never said goodbye."

I nod. Did he know what people were saying about me? And about him and Mike? About me and all those other boys? Had he denied it? Had he defended me? My head aches. "Did you believe any of it?"

"No."

My heart falls. He'd looked down, just before he'd said it. I shut my eyes. "I'm so tired, Josh."

"Yeah, same. I . . . Rest."

"You too." The curtain drops.

I feel a tear slide out of my eye and down my left cheek. Am I feeling disappointment or relief? Or is this just fatigue? I'm not even sure why I'm crying.

CHAPTER TWENTY-SIX:

CATFIGHT

I slept for thirteen hours straight—no mean feat in a hospital, where the wards are always noisy with beeping machines, snoring patients, and prowling nurses. It was past 2:00 p.m. when a nurse finally woke me to check my vitals. Now, still clad in a wrap-around hospital robe, I'm in a wheelchair, bound for Imaging, pushed by a skinny volunteer who's still in high school. With each step, the wheelchair creaks and the girl's rubber-soled sneakers squeak. The hallway is long, white and—apart from the creaks and squeaks—utterly silent. I feel like I'm floating down a long, bright white tunnel. It's so brightly lit I'm reminded of people's descriptions of near death experiences. My forehead pulses. Yesterday's boat trip feels like decades ago. All the painkillers have left me woozy.

We turn a corner. I hear tapping and scuffling sounds. Another corner reveals two women, still far away but coming closer. I squint through my headache. The women get bigger, both figures somehow familiar, one slender and long-haired, the other tall and dumpy, with a crew cut. And then, I recognize them: Alana Mapplebee and Louise Dobson. I'm surprised to see them together. How do they know each other? But then, this is Victoria. Forget six degrees of separation. It's more like point-six.

They look equally surprised to see me. Or maybe they're just stunned by my injuries.

Their steps slow. "Oh my God!" says Alana. "Toby?" She gapes at my black eye, split lip, and bandaged arm. "What happened?" Louise looks scared, like my injuries might be contagious.

I ask the young girl who's pushing me to stop. "Chantelle Orker," I say, through fat lips. "I mean Barton. Mike's wife, she attacked me."

Alana gasps. "You were there? On Josh's boat?" Despite my

condition, she looks jealous, her glossed lips forming a little pout. "We heard about Josh," she says, frowning. "Is he okay?"

I nod, having just quizzed the nurse who changed my IV bag. "He needed surgery on his spleen but will recover."

Louise pushes her white Lanvin glasses back up her wide nose. "Right. That's good news," she says, curtly. She's carrying a bouquet of calla lilies, which I think of as funeral flowers. "We're on our way up to see him." She taps a foot, clearly eager to get going.

"Well, I hope you feel better soon," says Alana, sliding her purse's gold chain back onto her thin shoulder. She twirls a perfectly curled strand of hair around one manicured finger. "We were *so* worried about Josh. Weren't we, Louise?" She looks sideways at Louise, then down the hall. Her eyes shine with excitement. I guess she's thrilled to have this excuse to see Josh again. No doubt she's hoping a brush with death has made him see the light and realize they're soulmates.

Looking down, I see that Alana is in turquoise high-heeled boots, while Louise is wearing those same nasty mustard vinyl loafers. I think of the stereotype of lesbian footwear. I hope they're at least comfortable.

"So how do you know each other?" I ask. It's hard to picture these two being friends. They're so different. There's a pause. Is it my imagination or do they both look strained?

"Oh, Louise has redecorated a bunch of rental properties I handle," says Alana.

Louise looks pointedly at her watch. "We'd better go," she says. "I have another meeting at four."

"Okay, well, get well soon," says Alana, again, obviously eager to get to Josh's room. She swings her quilted black purse onto her other arm.

"Thanks. Bye," I say.

As I watch them step out of my wheelchair's way, something niggles the back of my brain. "Wait!" I say. "Alana, your Chanel purse. Who'd you buy it from?"

Alana purses her shiny mouth, clearly confused. She turns to

Louise, whose face resembles an ice sculpture. "Oh, from Louise here. Why?"

Through narrowed eyes, Louise glares at me. I study her expensive eyeglasses. Why would a woman who spends that much on designer bags and glasses wear cheap shoes? All of a sudden, I get it.

"You were stealing stuff," I say. "From Tonya." I shake my head in amazement. "She was such a shopaholic, she didn't even notice." Like Josh said, she left the tags on a bunch of the crap she bought. Sunglasses. Pens. Purses. All those fancy brand names I've seen on Louise. I look back at her mustard loafers. "But her feet were smaller than yours."

The knuckles gripping Louise's calla lilies are almost as white as the flowers. "You don't know what you're talking about!" she snarls. "Tonya gave me that stuff! We were best friends!" Her voice breaks. "She loved me! She gave me lots of gifts!"

Looking at Louise's darting eyes, I know she's lying. "How'd she find out?" I ask.

I expect her to keep denying everything, but her face crumples. Tears gush from beneath her designer frames, forcing her to remove them. "She needed me!" she whines. "I was the only one who was there for her!" She points a finger to her chest, her nail bitten to the quick. "When she got those scary messages, I was the first person she called! Me!" Her small eyes glitter with crazed pride. "She needed me!"

I blink. Everything is coming into focus. Louise is fifty shades of crazy. "You're the stalker," I say. "Scaring Tonya and reassuring her made you feel needed. Then you kept doing it, to Josh and Alana and me."

Alana's mouth flies open. "What?" she squeals. "That was you? That dead crow? But why me? What did I ever do to you?"

Louise rounds on her, causing Alana to shrink back. Behind me, the high school candy striper's shoes squeak.

"You hurt her!" hisses Louise. "Sleeping with Josh when you knew he was married! She found out that night . . ." Louise's chin falls to her chest and her lips quiver. "She went to the marina to confront that cheating scumbag! She was so upset!" Her voice rises to a shrill whine. "I just wanted to comfort her!"

The self-pity in her voice horrifies me. "Comfort her?" I ask. "I bet you're the one who told her about Josh and Alana in the first place."

Two bright spots have appeared on Louise's cheeks, the rest of her face chalky. She lowers her head, like a bull preparing to charge. "How dare you judge me?" she hisses at me. "After what you did at camp!" She looms closer.

The poor high school volunteer wheels me sharply backward. "I'm calling security," says the girl, shakily, but stays put. Louise ignores her. She's wielding those lilies like a baton. Following my recent run-in with Chantelle and her rifle, the threat of getting whacked with a bouquet doesn't seem so bad. But given that I'm concussed, full of stitches, and wheelchair-bound, I don't want another fight. And if I want Louise to keep talking, I'd better change my tone. Louise feeds on sympathy.

"I'm sure you did comfort Tonya," I say, soothingly. "You were her best friend, right?" Louise nods vigorously. "Of course you were. So that last night, at the marina. Did she ask you for help?"

Louise's eyes seem to cloud over. She sways, like she's seeing that fateful night. Her eyes fill with tears again. When she answers, her voice is a strangled sob. "She was hysterical, so I raced over there," she says. "I was in such a rush I forgot to take off the Pucci scarf . . ." She swipes her hand under her nose, sorrow changing to rage. "She recognized it and tried to grab it off me. She accused me of taking it! After everything I did for her!" Louise shakes the lilies.

Because I'm sitting, her hands are at eye level. I see her white knuckles around the lilies' green stalks, and her rings, flashing. She's only wearing three silver rings today, one a plain band, one with a chunk of malachite (spiritual transformation), and one with a turquoise cabochon (protection). I lean back. It's crazy what you notice in times of stress. I grip the armrest of my wheelchair, scared she'll strike me.

From down the hall come male voices. Louise must hear them too because she swings around. There's a crazed look in her piggy eyes. She looks from me to Alana to the young candy striper, like she's deciding whom to attack first. She throws the lilies to the ground and charges straight at me.

I scream as she knocks over my wheelchair. As I start to tip, I manage to kick her in the knee, slowing her a little. She staggers but recovers, pushing Alana into a wall. The poor schoolgirl goes flying.

I put down my hand to break my fall and feel a sharp crack in my wrist. So much for my good arm. The rest of the fall happens in slow motion. Every bone in my body hurts. When the motion stops, I curl into a fetal position. I'm scared that Louise will hit me again, and I try to protect my head.

"Are you okay?" Someone grabs my shoulder.

"Ow!" I yell. I open my eyes to see Alana leaning over me. She looks like a doll defaced by someone's naughty little brother: her lipstick smeared, goggle-eyed, and her curls in wild disarray. Over Alana's shoulder, I can see Louise's retreating back. "Stop her!" I scream.

The poor high school girl staggers to her feet. "Help! Security!" she shrieks. When she sees the weird angle of my wrist her face blanches and her voice rises a few more octaves. "Help! We need a doctor!"

Far down the hall, I can still hear Louise's ugly loafers slapping against the tiles. I grit my teeth against the pain and shut my eyes. I've been attacked twice in two days. And I thought island life would be peaceful. "Alana," I say. "Do you have a phone?"

With shaking hands, she pulls a little pink phone from her purse. "I'm calling 911!" she says.

"No," I manage to whisper. "Call Colin Destin."

CHAPTER TWENTY-SEVEN:

FULL CIRCLE

My bedside table is full of bottles and jars of herbal remedies, all of them dark green or brown, frothy and smelly. Since I'm hooked up to machines, there's no escaping my mom's ministrations. "I caaaaaan't, Mom," I say, aware that I'm whining like a six-year-old.

"Come on, just one sip," says my mother. "It boosts immunity."

I squeeze my lips shut. This has been going on since the doctor let her in, after I was wheeled, yet again, out of Recovery. "Nooooo," I say.

"Pleeeeeease," begs my mother. Any minute now she'll start pretending the spoon is an airplane. "Just a little sip. Okay?"

I take a deep breath. "Fine." I lack the strength to keep arguing. My mom looks thrilled. She raises the spoon to my lips and I swallow and gag. It tastes like pond scum. I start to dry heave.

My mother beams. "Good girl," she says.

For a few minutes, she's satisfied. Then she starts rifling through her gigantic bag in search of fresh tortures. She sticks a shiny lump of hematite under my pillow. "To form new blood cells," she explains. I nod. Fine, so long as I don't have to drink it.

My eyelids sag. My mom bustles around the room, lighting aromatic candles. I know she means well but she's driving me crazy. "Mom," I say. "Can you sit down?"

She stops what she's doing and walks over to me. "Toby? Are you okay?" I can hear fear in her voice.

"Mom, I love you."

My mother blinks. From the hollows beneath her eyes, it's clear she didn't get much sleep. "I . . . I love you, too."

"I know it was hard on you," I say.

Her beautiful face creases as if in pain. "When Quinn called looking for you, I knew something was wrong. What with your terrible reading and all . . ."

I cut in. "No, I meant when I was a kid. When Dad left." I think of the morning I was driven back from camp, all alone in a Bluebird cab, in utter disgrace.

"Oh." She sinks into the chair by my bedside.

For a few moments we're silent. It's probably the first time in years I've seen my mom sitting still, doing nothing. Her hands are always busy: knitting or stirring or chopping or shuffling cards. Stringing beads onto wire. Kneading grainy bread. Petting her overfed cat. Except now they're in her lap and she's just staring into space. "It was all such a shock," she says. "It seems crazy . . . but I thought we had a good marriage. Well, a normal marriage . . ." Her voice falters. "And it happened at a hard age for you, fourteen." She sighs. "Fourteen is tough at the best of times."

I stay quiet, my thoughts on that morning, me alone in that expensive taxi I knew my parents would have to pay for, utterly shell-shocked.

We turned into the parking lot, my back rigid with fatigue and fury. The humiliation was bad, but the sense of injustice was much worse. It wasn't fair. Yes, I'd snuck out, but that was it. I hadn't done any of things they'd said I did.

At the far end of the parking lot I could see my mom's silver Audi. She was stepping out of it. Through sore dry eyes I took in her outfit. What was she wearing? Her standard twinset, slacks, and pearls had been replaced by a weird thrift-store dress. And what was up with that crazy hat? She looked tired and too thin in her loose Indian-print frock, like a bag lady.

I heaved my backpack onto one shoulder and staggered out of the taxi. Who cared what my mom was wearing, she was here—and she would comfort me. She was the one person on earth I could count on, no matter what. She'd understand the injustice I'd endured. She'd listen to the full story and be furious on my behalf. She'd be on the phone within minutes. She'd write scathing letters.

"Mom?" I stumbled off the bus.

I expected her to throw her arms around me, to ask me, gently, what happened, to tell me it was okay, I was home. None of it mattered anymore.

Instead, she just stood there with a blank shocked look on her pretty face. When she met my eyes I saw something I'd never seen before: doubt. My mom doubted me. That was worse than Josh's rejection, worse than being locked in that dank scary space, worse than being accused of stuff I could barely imagine and all the horrible names I'd been called. I dropped my bag and shoved my hands into my pockets. My stomach was a hard hot knot.

My mom shook herself, like someone roused from a bad dream. "I . . . are you okay?"

I couldn't even nod. Her arms went around me except it was too late. I'd seen that look in her eyes.

"Toby?"

I wrenched away from her. "What?" This one word was swung at her like a bat, heavy with hurt and betrayal.

My mom leaned back. Her mouth screwed up. "Daddy and I . . . we've separated." It was hard to see her eyes in the shade of that floppy hat. Her throat sounded raw. "He left already." I realized she was crying. "He's in Calgary."

I felt myself reeling. Blow upon blow. My dad left home without even saying goodbye. Was it because of me? What they said I did at camp? Did he not love me anymore?

My dad had always been a distant figure, more at work than at home. On the weekends he sailed and came home late, smelling of salt and beer. But still, he was part of my life. My dad. Dr. Parsons, the orthodontist. Half the kids at school had braces fitted by my dad. He was the reason we had a nice house, two new cars, the reason we could afford all my lessons, horse-riding and gymnastics and violin, and my brand-name clothes and toys. Daddy worked hard for us. He loved us. My mom said it all the time. How could he just be gone? To another city! He had to know I hadn't done anything wrong!

It must have been shock, but just for a moment, I saw us from above: a slight Asian woman and an even smaller girl, like carbon copies, both blank-eyed, their skinny shoulders hunched. Some moments stay with you and I knew this was one of them. I'd never seen my mom so sad, so scared and broken. Yet through the selfish prism of a fourteen-year-old, I had just one thought: Why was this happening to me? My life would never ever be the same again.

"Toby?"

I look up, startled. My mom's hands are still clasped in her lap. She hasn't moved. "I didn't see it coming," she says quietly. "Until your dad left. I found out three days before you got back from camp, about his . . . mistress." She shudders. "I went a little nuts, throwing out all of his stuff, and the things he'd bought for me." She gives a wry smile. "Remember that golfer Tiger Wood's wife, running down the street, bashing his car with a golf club? Well, that was me, pretty much. I burned his suits in the wood stove and smashed his sailing trophy with a hammer." She shifts in her chair. "I was that mad."

My mom rubs her eyes. She looks so drawn I want to reach out to her, but hesitate on account of my IV. She licks her lips, her voice softer now. "I was so wrapped up in my own sorrow I don't think I was there for you, for a while." She turns and looks into my eyes. "You were such a great kid," she says.

I smile. "And you were—you are—a great mom," I say. It's the truth. Even at her wackiest, I knew she'd do anything for me.

My mother smiles. She leans forward and strokes my cheek. "You were all I ever wanted," she says. "My perfect little girl." She studies my bruised and swollen face. I feel a great welling of love for her.

My mom is still gazing at me. I can see her mind ticking over. She raises her pinkie to her lips, looking pensive, then nods. "A paste of cabbage and comfrey leaves," she says. "That's what you need. It works wonders for bruising."

I groan but my mom is already on her feet. She reaches for her bag. "I'm off to the organic grocer," she says. She trots to the door. "I'll be back in no time."

I must have nodded off because I wake to see Quinn sitting at my bedside. "What's on your face?" she asks, when she sees that my eyes are open.

Since I can't actually touch my face, I have no idea. "Bandages?" I say.

"It looks like coleslaw."

I grit my teeth. My mom must have applied it when I was sleeping. "Comfrey and cabbage leaves," I say. "Get it off me!"

"With what?"

"I don't know. A wet wipe?"

"I don't have any."

"Well you'd better get some!" I snap. "Don't you have one of those massive diaper bags yet?"

Quinn stomps off to the toilet and returns with some wet paper towels. She daubs gingerly at my swollen face. I hold my breath. "Is it all off?"

"Mmmm, mostly."

She throws the paper towels into the trash and collapses back into the chair. Like my mom, she looks tired. "How are you feeling?"

"Great," I say, which we both know means like total shit. "How was your baby shower?"

"Great. Except there were a bunch of dumb games. Like everyone had to cut up bits of string they thought would fit around my belly and there were pieces you could have wrapped around a mammoth."

I look at her belly. Yes, there might be a mammoth in there.

"I was totally pissed when you didn't show," continues Quinn. She leans forward to sniff at a purple freesia. My other bedside table is full of flowers: sunflowers from Quinn and Bruce; freesias from Ali and Jackie; purple asters from my mom's garden; an elaborate mixed bouquet from Greene & Olliartee; pale pink roses from Colin; and tall cream ones from Josh. Quinn looks guilty. "I suspected you were so wrapped up in Josh that you'd lost track of time and forgotten."

I nod. I figured she'd assume that.

She rearranges the sunflowers. "I was serving the cake when Colin called. By then, I was kind of worried." Satisfied with the sunflowers, she turns to the pink roses. "So Colin went by Josh's place and saw a cooler and a box of pastries on the dock. That's when I knew something was up. There's no way you'd have left an entire box of zeppoles lying around!"

I examine the cast on my right wrist and the bandages on my left shoulder and upper arm. Considering I was shot and concussed, it could have been much worse. Josh was lucky too. His spleen was badly damaged, but the surgery went well. He'll likely be discharged tomorrow.

A nurse enters the room with my lunch tray and sets it across my bed. I study the offerings: chicken noodle soup, an anemic salad, a bread roll, a carton of apple juice, and some pale green pudding. None of it looks tempting. I have a sudden longing for my mom's place and a big helping of her chicken rice soup.

"Are you going to eat that?" asks Quinn, as she reaches for the pudding. I tell her to go ahead, but she's already peeled back the plastic wrap. After licking the bowl clean, she clutches her belly. "False alarm," she says, when she sees my face. "I'm having Braxton Hicks contractions. They're these fake, preparatory contractions that help your body get ready for the real thing." Yet again, I'm struck by the thought that human reproduction is nature's cruel joke, at least for women.

Quinn reaches for my bread roll, then gives me a sly look. "So did anything happen with you and Josh?"

"What, besides being knocked unconscious, tied up by a psychopath, and shot?" I ask. "It wasn't exactly the Love Boat."

"He saved your life," she says. "That's pretty romantic."

"I saved his too," I say. "And then Colin saved both of us." Maybe it's because I'm sore and exhausted, but I'm not sure how I feel about Josh. I've spent so long wondering whether he likes me or not, that I've lost track of why I like him. I'm always second-guessing myself around Josh. Do I really want to be with someone who makes me so insecure? It's exhausting.

At that moment someone knocks on the door, which is already open. I expect to see the nurse but it's Josh, in a wheelchair. "Hi," he says. "Are you up for another visitor?"

"Sure," I say, then wish I'd washed my face, brushed my hair, and applied some foundation. Although it'd take more than that to make me presentable. My face resembles a white plastic bag full of squashed vegetables. I hope Quinn got all the cabbage-comfrey paste off. Not that Josh looks his best. His right eye is still swollen shut, there's a long white bandage over his right brow, and his chin looks like it's been rubbed with a cheese grater. And that's just above the neck.

"How are you?" we both say, in stereo. An orderly pushes him further into the room.

"You first," says Josh, when he's parked next to my bed. After giving me a searching look, he bends forward and kisses my cheek. He smells of antiseptic.

"I'm tired but okay," I say. "Thanks for the flowers." It was really sweet of him to send flowers, especially since he's also hospitalized.

Josh fiddles with the belt of his robe. He seems ill-at-ease. Quinn looks like she plans to get up, and I shoot her a warning look. I don't want her to leave. I'm glad to see Josh, and relieved that he's fine, but don't feel up to an intense heart-to-heart. Not yet. Not today.

The orderly has just left when there's a fresh knock on the door. Again, I expect to see the nurse. Instead, Colin Destin peers around the door and smiles. Then he sees Quinn and Josh. "Hey, is this a bad time?" He's holding a bulk jar of jelly beans.

"Not if you're bringing candy," says Quinn.

"Come in," I say. I realize I'm glad to see him.

Colin opens the jar and passes the jelly beans around. Quinn grabs a handful, then feeds me a few. Josh declines but changes his mind. I see him wince when he tries to chew. After that he sucks on his jelly beans.

Colin pulls up a chair beside Quinn's. "I came yesterday but you were asleep."

I nod.

"Are you feeling better?"

"Much."

"Good." He leans forward, green eyes glowing with excitement. "We arrested Louise Dobson. You were right about the dog's collar. Her thumbprint was on it, in Tonya's blood. She confessed. She and Tonya got into a fight about a scarf and Louise bashed her. The next day, she planted the bloody flashlight in the boat's engine room."

I shudder.

Josh looks stricken. "A scarf?" He rakes his hands through his hair. "She killed Tonya for a scarf? I . . . but why?" he asks.

Looking at Josh's distraught face, I have a vision: Tonya and Louise on the dock, late at night, screaming at each other. I see their hands on the scarf, Tonya's long coral nails and Louise's short bitten ones, tugging backward and forward. The yellow diamond on Tonya's hand flashes. The scarf rips. Her face clenched in rage, Louise raises her large flashlight.

I squeeze my eyes shut and push my head back against my pillow.

"Toby?" Quinn sounds alarmed. "Are you okay? You're so pale!"

"Should we call the doctor?" asks Colin.

I recall my meeting with Louise in her office at Island Deco. The rings on her fingers. It was right before my eyes but I didn't see it. I'd bet my weight in healing crystals that her yellow pinkie ring wasn't a citrine. I force my eyes open.

"I'm fine." My voice is a thin rasp. "Colin," I say. "Did you find Tonya's missing engagement ring? With the yellow diamond?"

He shakes his head. "Not yet. Why?"

"Louise stole it."

Colin frowns. "We're searching her place now." He pulls his phone from his pocket and excuses himself. "I'll tell the guys to keep an eye out for it." He turns to Josh. "Remind me what it looked like?"

As Josh describes the ring, my head pounds. What just happened to me? That scene on the dock—it was so clear. My throat feels parched. I ask Quinn for some water. She holds the glass to my lips.

"You need to sleep," she says.

I'm exhausted but don't want my friends to leave. And I still have more questions. "How about Chantelle?" I whisper, when Colin returns from making his phone call. Just thinking about her causes my heart to speed up.

"She'll be charged with two counts of attempted murder," says Colin. "It's pretty clear cut. Years of resentment built up. Mike's the main beneficiary in Josh's will. She saw a good opportunity to get rich quick and took it." He offers me some more jelly beans. "She didn't know about your *brunch*." I know he meant "date." He frowns. "Wrong place, wrong time, Toby."

I glance sideways at Josh. "And Mike?" I ask quietly. "Did he know what Chantelle was up to?"

Both men shake their heads. "Nothing indicates that," says Colin. I'm relieved for Josh. Colin crosses his arms.

Josh selects a green jelly bean. "Mike came to see me yesterday. I'm still mad at him about Tonya, of course, but . . ." He studies some machines parked next to my bed. "He's my brother. He's going to start working for me again, running the charters."

Quinn shifts in her chair. I see she's sweating. It's hot in here. "Thank God it's over," she says.

Colin nods. "Yes. It's been a strange case," he admits. "All of you going to that crazy summer camp. Camp Wiki?" He squints. "What was it called?"

"Camp Dickwhacker," I say.

Josh laughs. "I'd forgotten about that." His eyes crinkling with mirth, he starts to sing the camp song: "At Camp Wikwakee there's no trouble or strife. Just one summer that will change your life."

Colin laughs. "It sounds like a cult!" he says.

Quinn, who's also been laughing, looks suddenly serious. "But it did change our lives," she says. "We all still know each other. And everything that happened now, with Tonya and Chantelle and Louise, it all started back then . . ." She rubs her belly, as if for luck. "Anyways, it's over. And you're both okay." When she looks at me, I see tears in her blue eyes. All those hormones, again. She swallows hard, then attempts a smile. "For a while there, when I didn't know if you were d . . . alive or not, I figured my kid might end up being called Toby."

I smile back at her. I'm tempted to tell her it's a girl. Don't ask me how I know, but I'm sure the vision I had before passing out on the *Great Escape* is correct. I stare at Quinn's belly. She's having a daughter.

Quinn squeezes my hand, hard. "Ow," she says. "I don't think those are Braxton Hicks, after all."

While Josh and Colin look confused, one glance at Quinn's face tells me she's serious. "It's time!" I say. "The baby's coming!"

"Seriously?" asks Colin. "Should we call Bruce? Should we call your doctor?"

"I don't know," says Quinn. She grabs Colin's arm and looks at his watch. "I'd better time the contractions."

For a few minutes nobody speaks. We're all watching the clock and watching Quinn. "They're getting stronger," she says. "I guess I should call my OB." She starts digging through her purse in search of her mobile phone.

"Well, at least there are plenty of doctors nearby," says Josh. He points toward Colin. "And a policeman."

Colin grins. "Policemen only deliver babies in movies," he says. "Should I tell Bruce to get over here? Are you delivering here or in another hospital?"

"Here," says Quinn. She lets out a loud gasp. "Whoa," she says. "Tell Bruce to hurry!"

CHAPTER TWENTY-EIGHT

SEEING THE FUTURE

Abby Rose looks just like I pictured her. She is red and wrinkled and has Bruce's square chin and Quinn's high forehead. She also has the prettiest hands and feet I've ever seen, and a cry so loud I could almost hear her from my room, one floor up from Maternity. Once she gets home, I pity Bruce and Quinn's neighbors.

I've got my wheelchair pushed close to Quinn's bed. Since we're both exhausted, we haven't spoken much. Plus we're too busy staring at the baby.

Abby is fast asleep on Quinn's chest. Bruce is out in the hall, phoning everyone he knows. He's even sweatier than Quinn.

"She's gorgeous," I say, finally, and Quinn nods.

"I can't believe she's mine. I was sure it was a boy."

I tell her about the premonition I had after being cracked on the head aboard the *Great Escape*. "Not that that means much," I say, quickly. "It's a fifty-fifty chance, after all."

"Right," says Quinn. "Or maybe you've inherited some of Ivy's gift."

I think of Louise and Tonya's fight on the dock, how clearly I saw it all. But that was intuition, and logic. Putting two and two together. Plus some imagination. I'm not psychic and neither is my mother.

My skepticism must show because Quinn smiles. "Oh come on," she says. "After that thing about Claude's collar you're *still* doubting Ivy's ability?" There's a juice box on the bedside table and she reaches for it. She drains the box. "Maybe you should consult your mom about what to do about Josh and Colin," she says.

"What about them?" I ask, genuinely mystified. Quinn is using one finger to stroke Abby's head. Her hair is almost translucent.

Quinn's finger stops moving. "Which one to choose," she says.

Her expression makes it clear she thinks I'm being obtuse. "If Ivy knows their birth times she can tell if you're compatible."

Normally, I'd tell Quinn she's nuts. The last thing I need is to get my mom involved in my love life. Not that I have one. It might get her hopes up. But since Quinn's just given birth, I bite my tongue. "I don't believe in that stuff," I say.

Quinn perks up. "So you've made a decision?" Abby stirs and I hold my breath. I don't want her to start screaming again.

"There's nothing to decide," I say. "You're acting as though they're both crazily in love with me and all I have to do is choose."

"Well they are," says Quinn. She shakes her head. "Come on, Toby. It's obvious."

I'm tired, and my head hurts. Nothing is obvious. "What makes you think that?"

"The way they look at you, for a start. When they see you, their eyes light up. Even when you look like you do now." She laughs. "And you're not looking your best."

"Gee, thanks, Quinn," I say.

"Ha!" she smiles. "Do you have feelings for either of them?" She stops stroking Abby's head. I can feel her blue eyes boring into me.

"I . . . I think they're both great guys," I say.

"Who are you, The Bachelorette?" asks Quinn. "I don't want some diplomatic bullshit. I'm your best friend. I know you've had this weird obsession with Josh for most of your life. Now that he's reciprocating do you still feel it? Or is there something between you and Colin?"

I rub my forehead. "I don't know," I say. "Aren't I allowed to not know? I haven't even gone on a real date with either of them! I'm just . . ." I study my ragged nails. "I almost died a few days ago! I'm tired, you know? And happy. I just don't want to think too much."

Abby's little legs kick. It's hard to believe we all start out that small. I watch her tiny toes curl and uncurl. Quinn strokes her back, soothing her. Watching Abby, I'm surprised to realize it's true: I am happy. Happy to be alive, first of all, and happy to be here with

Quinn and Abby, who's so beautiful I want to cry. And two great guys seem interested in me. How can I not be happy about all of this?

"So what's your plan?" asks Quinn.

I shrug. For the first time since I can remember, I don't have one. "To get to know Josh and Colin better," I say. "And to spend time with my mom. And to help you with Abby."

Her smile crowds all the tiredness out of her face. She has a brilliant smile. I find myself grinning back at her. "That sounds like a great plan," she says. "Do you want a juice box? Grab one off the nightstand."

Quinn inserts my straw. I tap my juice box against hers. "To Abby Rose," I say.

"To old friends and new beginnings."

Sitting with my best friend sipping warm apple juice through a straw, I feel like a kid on the first day of summer holidays. Good times lie ahead.

ACKNOWLEDGMENTS

This book wouldn't exist without the brilliant guidance of my friend and mentor Deborah Nolan and the wisdom and patience of my agent Amy Tipton. It'd be a rougher read without the talent of Dan Mayer, my editor at Seventh Street Books. Thanks are also due to Patrick "Eagle Eyes" Smith and Marianna Vertullo.

I'm grateful to my high school English Literature teacher Mrs. Lana Simpson, who taught me, via poetry, that anything you feel has been felt before and you're never alone in a story. Toby's world owes a lot to Christina and Judith Kay, my real-life (only better) Quinn and Jackie.

I'm a reader and writer thanks to my intrepid parents, Gisela and Gerry Ray, who found money for books and traveling even when our house had no furniture. Finally, thanks to my kids, who inspired me to create Toby Wong, and to my husband, Thien Nguyen, for his relentless support and optimism.

ABOUT THE AUTHOR

Elka Ray writes fun romantic mysteries and dark thrillers—a dichotomy that reveals her belief in Yin and Yang, or life's balance of opposites. A great lover of scientific facts, she may be found clutching crystals for good luck; reads highbrow journals and tabloid trash; and shuns rom-coms yet moved in with her now-husband on their first date.

Elka has two previous novels: *Hanoi Jane*, a light mystery, and a noir thriller, *Saigon Dark*.